ANDREW G.
NELSON

Little Boy Lost
An Alex Taylor Novel

ANDREW G. NELSON

&

NANCY A. NELSON

Little Boy Lost

Published by Huntzman Enterprises

First Edition: December 2015
Second Edition: April 2020

ISBN-10: 0-9961334-7-X
ISBN-13: 978-0-9961334-7-0

Printed in the United States of America
1 3 5 7 9 10 8 6 4 2

DEDICATION

To God: For providing the path and the means to follow it.

To my wife, and co-author, Nancy: Who provided the support and encouragement to take those very first steps. She has been my biggest fan, my sounding board, and my editor. With the publication of this book she joins me as co-author, because without her input and ideas this book would not exist.

Romans 8:28

Other Titles by Andrew G. Nelson

Little boys have such a wonderful gift.

They wander throughout the day, moving seamlessly from pirate, to space adventurer, to superhero; their adventures curtailed only for a brief moment by sleep.

They do not take time to analyze this gift, they just simply live it; allowing their minds and bodies to wander freely through the world they live. It is only when they become older, and succumb to the realities of adulthood, that the wandering boy becomes lost.

Little Boy Lost - *Anonymous*

CHAPTER ONE

Founder's Day was a much-anticipated event in Penobscot, New Hampshire.

All along Main Street, colorful banners marked the 199th anniversary of the annual event. They had shut the streets surrounding city hall, allowing residents to stroll around the square, unimpeded by traffic. Children's rides lined the north side of city hall and vendors had set-up tents, hawking everything from commemorative t-shirts to books, along with the typical toys and trinkets, common with events such as this. The festive sound of children's laughter and arcade rides had already taken hold of the town square this Friday afternoon.

Summer had grudgingly relinquished its grip on the small New England enclave. The cool autumn air had a crisp feel to it. The lush green canopy of the elm, oak, and walnut trees, which provided some respite from summer's sultry temps, were now gone. In its place, the leaves were now awash in bright splotches of orange, red, and yellow colors.

On a large platform, set-up on the back lawn of city hall, Penobscot's city manager, Sheldon Abbott, stood at a podium making the opening remarks for this year's event. Abbott was a congenial man who always seemed to dress rather *eccentrically*. Today's ensemble comprised a pastel blue seersucker suit, paired with a light pink shirt and dark blue tie with white polka dots.

His choice of attire was intentional. It caused people to underestimate him, which was an error many people learned to late. Sheldon Abbott had a keen intellect that had allowed him to navigate his way through the political maze, ending up in the top spot. Through cunning, cajoling, coercion, and sometimes strong-arm tactics worthy of a big city politician, he kept it.

Today was one of those days when he had to put on a smile and go out to *perform* for the electorate; not that he ever needed an excuse to *talk*.

"It is my sincere honor and privilege to serve as your city manager," Abbott said. "It is especially significant for me, as we come together to celebrate the 199th Anniversary of our founding. I recognize that, while I represent the entirety of city government here in Penobscot, none of this would be possible without the dedicated effort of a great many city employees. Their hard work and effort, which goes into putting on this event, makes me extremely proud. I hope that you will all stand with me and salute those who have tirelessly worked to make this event a reality, even as they are busy preparing for next year's bi-centennial of our city."

A group of about two dozen people stood in front of the stage, listening to him speak, and clapped respectfully. Behind Abbott, the other members of the city council sat, eagerly awaiting the opportunity for them to rejoin their family and friends in the festivities.

"And so, with no further ado," Abbott continued. "I would like to take this opportunity to kick-off the Founder's Day weekend. Thank you all and have a wonderful time."

Abbott brought the small wooden gavel down on the podium's top and, from across the square, a ceremonial canon was fired; officially marking the start of the weekend's festivities.

Across the street from city hall, the Founder's Day committee had set-up a food booth in the large pavilion which was part of the Bradley R. Johnson Sports Complex. Johnson was a local sports phenom back in the 60s. He had passed up on a college baseball scholarship to enlist in the U.S. Navy.

Johnson's father, William, had served aboard the U.S.S. Washington (BB-56), during World War II, and had been awarded the Bronze Star and Purple Heart medals. Like his father before him, the younger Johnson felt that military service was something every able-bodied young man should do. He'd been assigned to the Mobile Riverine Force, the so-called *Brown Water Navy*, and was killed while saving the life of a fellow sailor during the *Tet Offensive* at *Cần Thơ*. It was just two weeks prior to him being shipped back to the United States.

There was a large granite memorial at the entrance to the park which honored his military service. Encased in the center of the memorial was the Silver Star medal that had been posthumously awarded to him.

The sports complex featured a baseball diamond, basketball court, children's playground, and a covered pavilion used to host holiday events, such as Founder's Day.

The opening day special was the fried halibut fish dinner served up by the Ladies Auxiliary of the American Legion. It was usually a sellout, so people arrived early, because you were guaranteed to wait in line.

It was the line Karla Marie Grayson stood in as she patiently waited her turn to pay for dinner. A cold breeze had kicked up and was blowing through the pavilion. She adjusted the knit cap she was wearing, pulling it down over her long brown hair.

The Founder's Day weekend provided an annual respite from her daily maternal duties, and she took full advantage of it, including the opportunity to get out of the kitchen. It was even more significant to her, since it occurred during the school year.

Grayson was the sixth grade English teacher at the Penobscot Elementary School. This weekend provided her a much needed break from her scholastic obligations, and her parental one in overseeing her own child's homework assignments. Most of the time, the constant juggling of her personal and professional lives made her feel old, much older than her thirty-three years of age. Motherhood was a tough enough job to begin with, but a single mom who also worked full-time as a teacher, was something different.

For now, she was ready and willing to surrender to a weekend filled with fattening foods, sugar rushes, and questionably *safe* carnival rides.

"Mom!" a shrill voice called out, just as Karla stepped up to the counter.

She looked down to see her eight-year-old son, Cory, staring up at her.

He had a mop of sandy blonde hair and bright blue eyes, which sparkled when he was excited. He was wearing denim jeans and a red flannel jacket, which gave him the look of a pint-sized construction worker. The only thing missing was the tool belt and a hard hat. As she gazed down at him, she couldn't help but see his father.

It was a look that still haunted her.

"Yes," she asked, chasing away the memories.

"Can I run over to Billy's house and see if he can go on the rides with me?"

"Don't you want to eat first?"

"I'm not hungry," he replied.

"I don't want to hear anything about how you are *starving* later," Karla replied.

"Is that a yes?" he asked.

"Yes," she replied, "but come right back!"

Her last words hung in the air, seemingly unheard, as she watched him sprint out of the pavilion, toward his friend's house.

"Kids," she said in a tone of exasperation.

"Isn't that the truth, sweetheart," a woman's voice replied.

"What was that, Mrs. Richards?" Karla asked, turning her attention back to the matronly woman who sat at the small card table, collecting money for the dinners.

Mona Richards was the head of the Founder's Day committee. In fact, no one could remember a time when she wasn't in charge. In the past she would ride around in a little golf cart, barking out orders, and ensuring that the event was run with military-like efficiency. However, over the last few years, age had finally caught up with her. Now she was relegated to overseeing things via walkie-talkie and working the cash box.

"They're all the same," Richards replied. "I remember when mine were little. They'd play from sunrise to sunset and never miss a beat."

"I wish I had his energy," Karla replied. "I just don't want to be fixing dinner at 10:00 p.m."

"Buy two," the woman replied. "If he doesn't eat it now, you can save the other for later, just in case. You can always re-heat the fish in the microwave."

"That's a good idea," Karla said with a smile. "I'll take two."

She removed the money from her purse and handed it to the woman.

"How old is he now?" Richards asked.

"Eight going on *eighty*," she said with a laugh. "I swear that there are moments when I see his father in him. I'm not sure if that is a good thing or bad."

"It'll wear off," Richards replied. "Eventually."

"It never did with his father."

"He had *other* issues, dear," Richards replied. "The whole family did."

"Why didn't anyone warn me back then?"

"Would you have listened?" Richards asked with a smile. "As I recall, you were very much in *love*."

"Love…," Karla said thoughtfully. "*Dumb* is more like it."

"Weren't we all?"

"Well, let's just hope I make it long enough to see it wear off," she said with a laugh.

"You just need to find yourself a *good* man. Someone, who will be a positive influence in the boy's life."

"I wish I had the time for that," Grayson replied, "but I'm doing my best to work on it."

"How's school going?" the woman asked.

"Oh, pretty good. Things have settled into a routine."

"Well that's good."

"We have our first parent / teacher meeting at the end of the month. That should prove interesting."

"Better you than me, dear."

"Thanks," Karla said, collecting her change and tickets. "Do you ever miss it?"

"I miss the monkeys, not the circus," Richards said with a smile.

"That's a saying I can appreciate. I guess I will see you tomorrow."

"I'll be here," Richards replied.

Grayson moved down the counter, handing the two tickets to another woman, working the serving station. As she watched, the woman filled two Styrofoam boxes with several pieces of fried halibut, along with french fries, salad, and a dinner roll. When she'd finished, she handed the boxes, along with two red plastic drink cups, to Grayson, who turned and made her way over to the drink table to get some sweet tea.

Dinners like this were a staple of rural communities. Whether it was fried halibut, chicken, or pulled-pork dinners at night; or maybe a pancake breakfast on Sunday morning, it was a time for folks to come together and connect. The men would sit around and talk about politics, sports, or hunting, while the women would sit around and share the latest gossip.

Grayson gathered up the food trays and drinks, before making her way into the crowded pavilion, disappearing among the mass of diners already enjoying their supper.

CHAPTER TWO

Officer Chris 'Hutch' Hutchinson sat at the small wooden picnic table, at the Penobscot Shooting Range, and stared down the spotting scope. As he watched, the ten ring in the center of the target, one hundred yards downrange, was methodically obliterated.

"Clear," Chief Alex Taylor called out as she dropped the magazine from her AR-15 patrol rifle.

"Damn, Chief," Hutch said. "Where the heck did you learn how to shoot like that?"

Alex cycled the rifle, visually checking the weapon to ensure that it was empty, and then laid it on top of the case.

"Practice, Hutch," Alex replied as she stood up. "All it takes is countless hours of practice."

"I wish I could shoot that good."

"You will, trust me," she said. "This isn't rocket science, Hutch. It's just a matter of putting in the time and effort."

"Well, now that I am *officially* done with the major repairs on my house, maybe I will have more time for that."

"Yeah, speaking of which," Alex said. "I got your *invitation* to the painting party."

"You are coming, aren't you?" Hutch asked.

"Yeah, I'm coming," she replied. "It's not like I have a life or anything."

"Well, everyone else seems to have one," Hutch replied. "So far it's just you, Abby, and my sister. Everyone else has an excuse."

"I'll see what I can do to drum up some extra hands," she said. "I don't see why we should be the only ones having all that *fun*."

"Thanks, Chief."

"So, are you ready to shoot?" Alex asked.

"As ready as I'll ever be," Hutch replied as he got up from the bench and began walking down range with Alex.

They'd only gotten a dozen yards when they heard the radio transmission come over the speaker in the patrol car.

"M-11-1, on the air?"

Both of them turned to look back in the car's direction.

"I guess they could have waited till we got all the way down to the twenty-five yard line," she replied sarcastically. "Go get yourself set-up and I'll see what they want."

"Yes, ma'am," he replied and continued heading down range.

Alex walked toward the unmarked car and reached through the open window to grab the radio mic from its holder.

"M-11-1 to base, go ahead with your message."

"M-11-1, we've got a report of a missing eight-year-old child over at the sports complex. M-11-7 is on the scene and requesting you to respond."

"10-4, base," Alex replied. "Show myself and M-11-3 responding."

Alex turned back and whistled for Hutch. When he turned around, she waved at him to come back to her. She then gathered up her rifle, putting it back in its case, and secured it in the trunk of her patrol car.

"What's going on, Chief?" he asked, when he rejoined her.

"Steve Harper is requesting us over at the park," she replied. "There's a missing kid."

"Already?" Hutch asked. "The weekend just got started."

"Hopefully we can find the little urchin quickly and return him home, before all the fun stuff begins tonight at the beer tent."

"You had to remind me, didn't you?"

"C'mon, Junior," Alex said. "It's time for us to earn our paychecks."

"If you say so, boss," Hutch replied as he got into his patrol car.

Fifteen minutes later, the two vehicles pulled up behind Steve Harper's car outside the sports complex. As Alex got out, she saw him over by the pavilion, talking to a woman, who kept scanning the surrounding area.

"Over here, Chief," Harper called out.

"Who's the woman?" Alex whispered as they walked over to where the two were standing.

"Karla Grayson," Hutch replied. "She's a teacher over at the elementary school."

"Any history I should know about?"

"Nothing special," Hutch replied. "Nice enough woman. She went through a divorce a half-dozen years back. The guy she was married to, Ricky Childers, is a local dickhead to be honest."

"What do you have, Steve?" Alex asked as she approached them.

"This is Ms. Karla Grayson, Chief," Harper replied. "She's reporting that her son, Cory Childers, is missing."

"Do we have a description?"

"Yes, ma'am," Harper replied. "He's a male, Caucasian, eight-years-old, with blonde hair, blue eyes, wearing denim jeans, a green tee shirt, and a red flannel jacket."

"When did you last see him, Ms. Grayson?" Alex asked.

"Here at the pavilion," Karla replied. "He asked to go over to his friend's house to see if he could come to the fair."

"Have we checked over there yet?" Alex asked.

"When he didn't come right back, I called over there," Grayson replied. "Sheila Turner, Billy's mother, said that Cory had stopped by, but that Billy wasn't feeling good. She said that Cory left and she saw him walking back this way."

"Where does Billy live?" Alex asked.

Grayson pivoted and pointed to her right, "About two blocks over, just off of Fisher Street."

"You know the house number?" Alex asked.

"I don't remember," the woman replied. "It's the third one off the corner, it has light blue siding."

"I know which one it is," Hutch replied.

"Ok, Steve, put out a description," Alex said. "Alert the committee people to keep an eye out. I want you to stay here with Ms. Grayson, in case her son comes back to the pavilion. I'll have Abby send you some help. Tell them to search the entire area, starting inside the pavilion and working their way out, into the surrounding streets. Hutch and I will head over to the Turner's house. Once we're done we'll meet you back over here."

"Yes, Chief," Harper replied.

"Don't worry, Ms. Grayson, we'll find him," Alex said.

"Thank you, Chief Taylor," the woman replied with a weak smile that barely held back the tears welling up in her eyes.

Alex turned and walked back to where the cars were parked with Hutch following her. As they approached her unmarked car she stopped to open the trunk, removing her duty jacket and putting it on. As the sun set, the temperature had taken a sharp decline.

"Couldn't they have scheduled Founder's Day for some time when it was warmer" she asked sarcastically. "Like July?"

"What, you mean like an *almost* Founder's Day weekend?" Hutch asked.

"Yeah, that would work," she said as she headed over toward the passenger side of Hutch's marked patrol car. "You drive."

"To be honest, the town was originally founded in August, but the locals didn't like the idea of sharing the holiday with all the tourists," Hutch explained. "So they moved it to October after everyone left."

"Well that makes perfect fucking sense," Alex said.

"Welcome to Penobscot," Hutch replied as he unlocked the door.

A few moments later Hutch pulled the car up in front of the Turner house. They got out of the car and walked up the steps to the front porch. Alex pressed the doorbell and they waited for a response.

When the door opened, a woman, whom Alex guessed was in her early thirties, stood in the entryway.

"Hi, can I help you?" she said.

"Are you Mrs. Turner?" Alex asked.

"Yes, is there something wrong?"

"I'm Chief Taylor, this is Officer Hutchinson. We're looking for Cory Childers, his mother reported him missing."

"Oh my God," the woman replied. "Karla still hasn't found him? He was just here a little while ago."

"No, ma'am," Alex said. "That's why we are here, Mrs. Turner. Do you mind if we come in?"

"Honey, who's there?" a man's voice called out from inside the house.

"It's the police," she replied as she opened the door. "Yes, please come in."

Alex and Hutch walked into the living room, just as a man emerged from the back of the house.

"What's going on?" he asked.

"I'm Chief Taylor, and you are?"

"Grant Turner," the man replied. "Is everything all right?"

"We're investigating a report of a missing child, Cory Childers," Alex replied.

"Karla's son?" the man asked, looking at his wife.

"He was just here a little while ago," Sheila replied. "He wanted Billy to go over to the fair with him, but Billy came home from school with a slight fever and I didn't think it was a good idea."

"Did you see where he went?" Alex asked.

"I watched him walk down the steps and head toward the pavilion," the woman replied. "You don't think anything happened to him, do you?"

"We can't rule anything out," Alex said. "Did you happen to notice anything, Mr. Turner?"

"No, actually I just got home from work a few minutes ago," the man replied.

"How long have Cory and Billy been friends?" Alex asked.

"For the last few years," Sheila replied. "They met in first grade."

"Do you know Ms. Grayson?"

"Karla? Yes, she's a wonderful teacher. Our oldest daughter had her last year. We've gotten to know her socially, ever since Billy and Cory became friends."

"Well, this was the last place he was seen, so would you mind if we looked around?" Alex asked.

"No, not at all," Grant Turner replied. "Anything we can do to help."

"Hutch, you look around the outside of the house, I'll look inside."

"Yes, Chief," Hutch replied and headed toward the front door.

"Could one of you show me around?" Alex asked.

"Yes, please come with me," Sheila said.

She led Alex through the house, starting on the top floor, where the bedrooms were, and working their way down to the basement. It wasn't an overly large house and the search, methodical as it was, took only about fifteen minutes.

"Thank you for your time," Alex said. "If you can think of anything, please call us."

"We certainly will," Sheila said. "Please tell Karla that we will be praying for her."

"I will," Alex replied as she opened the front door. "Have a good night."

She stepped out onto the front porch and withdrew a pack of cigarettes from the jacket pocket. She lit one up, just as Hutch came around the side of the house.

"I thought you were quitting?" he asked.

Alex took a drag, then formed her lips into a circle and exhaled, blowing a perfect smoke ring into the cool night air.

"I'm cutting back, *mother*," she replied. "Did you find anything?"

"Nothing," he replied. "The exterior is buttoned up tight and there is no way an eight-year-old is going to scale the house to get inside. What about you?"

"Same," Alex said. "Little Billy is upstairs in his bed, and nothing seems amiss. Sheila could stand to dust a little more often, but other than that, nothing was setting off my *spidey sense*."

"So where do we go now?"

"Let's take a ride back to the park," Alex replied, taking a drag on the cigarette. "See if they have turned up anything else."

14

By the time they arrived back, word had spread throughout the fair about the missing child. Sheldon Abbott spotted Alex getting out of the car and made a bee-line over to her.

"Is it true, Alex?" he asked. "Do we have a missing child?"

"Yes we do," Alex replied.

"What are you going to do about it?" Abbott asked, a hint of panic in his voice.

Alex knew that it had nothing to do with the missing child. Not that the man was heartless, it was just that Sheldon Abbott, and by extension his career, came first. Missing children were bad news for small cities, such as Penobscot. It wouldn't take long for the local media to show up and begin to dig. Eventually they would find something to fixate on. The longer this went on, the more likely that the cable news would latch onto the story. Then nothing would be safe, including the city manager.

"We're already searching for him, Sheldon," she replied.

"Isn't there anything more you can do?" he asked.

Alex turned to look at the man.

"Sheldon, this isn't my first missing person report," she replied.

"I know, but it's Founder's Day," he said whispered conspiratorially. "We don't want people thinking it's *not safe*."

"I'm sure he will turn up soon," Alex replied. "As soon as I know something more, you will be the first to know."

"Ok, thank you," he replied. "I'll let the other board members know."

"Good idea," she said, watching as he scurried away.

He was an odd little man; flamboyant in his mannerisms and dress, but in the short amount of time that she had been chief, Alex had seen another side. Sheldon Abbott was many things, but stupid was not one of them. It was all a shrewd act, designed to conceal a sharp intellect and a number of sins. She knew the day would come when the two of them would battle, and she was grateful for the file she had at home that detailed a few of those sins.

Until then, Alex followed the adage; *one should keep your friends close, but keep your enemies closer.*

"That man makes my skin crawl," Hutch said, his voice filled with disdain, as Abbott walked away.

"Good," Alex said. "That's your brains way of letting your body know to be careful. Try to raise Steve on the radio and see if he has an update for us."

Hutch reached up and keyed the radio mic attached to his left epaulet.

"M-11-3 to M-11-7, on the air?"

"M-11-7, on the air, go with your message."

"Do you have an update on the search?" Hutch asked.

"Negative at this time," Harper replied. "We're just finishing up the interior search of the grounds."

Hutch looked over at Alex.

"Have him bring Karla Grayson over here," Alex said.

"M-11-7, can you bring the complainant over to our location?"

"10-4, we're on our way."

A few minutes later Harper emerged from the pavilion with Karla Grayson in tow.

"Did you find him?" Grayson asked, her voice breaking as the words came out.

"Not yet, ma'am," Alex replied. "Beside Billy's house, can you think of anywhere else he may have gone?"

"No, we live outside of town. Billy is the only one that Cory is allowed to play with."

"I will need you to come to the police station with me and answer a few questions. The officers will continue to search and we will keep you updated, I promise."

"Okay," she replied.

"Hutch, you're in charge," Alex said. "Gather everyone up. I want you to send some officers out to search the streets and backyards from here to the Turner's. Have them go door to door, see if anyone saw anything. Start making some noise, see who comes out. Maybe we'll get lucky. Interview those who are eating here and see if they remember anything. Talk to the staff and try to get the names of anyone who left. Also issue an Amber Alert."

"Yes, ma'am," Hutch replied.

"When I get back to the office, I'll check and see if the state police can spare some people to help."

"Okay," Hutch said. "Let me know if you turn up anything useful from the interview."

"I will," Alex said. "Call me if you need anything."

CHAPTER THREE

Alex led Karla Grayson into the Penobscot Police Department, which was on the first floor of city hall.

"Abby, this is Karla Grayson. Her son Cory is our missing child from the fair," Alex said as they entered the main office area. "I need you to set her up in the interview room so she can give us her statement. Then get on the phone and start calling in the late tour guys. When you're done, see if you can get any of the reserves who aren't already working. I want as many bodies as we can muster out searching for him."

"Sure thing, Chief," Abby said as she got up from her desk.

"Ms. Grayson, Officer Simpson will help you out with the paperwork," Alex said to the woman. "I have to make some phone calls, but as soon as I am done I'll come back and interview you."

"Thank you, Chief Taylor."

"Would you like some coffee, ma'am?" Abby asked.

"That would be great," Karla replied.

"Please follow me, Ms. Grayson," Abby said.

As the two women walked away, Alex turned and headed to her office. She closed the door and hung her jacket up, then sat down at the desk.

Alex fished the pack of cigarettes from her pocket and lit one up before reaching over to pick-up the phone. She dialed the number from memory, listening to it ring.

"Major Crimes, Blackshear," the man said tersely when he answered.

"Friday night, after hours, no wonder you sound grumpy," Alex said.

"Damn governor's office called the colonel, wanting year to date crime numbers and investigative status updates by Monday morning," he said. "Apparently they are getting grief from some tree-huggers down in Concord. Those nitwits went home for the weekend and I'm chained to my fucking desk."

"Nice," Alex said, taking a drag on the cigarette. "Wish I could help, but I've got my own shit storm I'm dealing with."

"I didn't think this was a social call," Blackshear replied. "What do you have going?"

"I have a missing eight-year-old," Alex said. "Walked over to his friend's house and then vanished."

"Jesus Christ," Blackshear said with a sigh.

"I'm sure He knows where the boy is," Alex replied, "but I'm going to need a bit more help to find him. I was wondering if you have any contacts over at Troop F, I'm not getting the warm and fuzzies on this one."

"Yeah, my old partner is the commanding officer up there. I'll call him on his cell and have him reach out to you."

"I appreciate that, Tom. Give him my cell number, It will be the easiest way to get in touch with me right now."

"You guys don't have a canine unit do you?" Blackshear asked.

"No," Alex said. "I've been trying to get funding for one, but the city council keeps dicking me around. I hope this doesn't turn into one of those 'I told you so' moments."

"Politicians," Blackshear said in a disgusted tone. "I'll call Field Operations and see if they can get a canine tracker to head your way."

"Thanks," Alex replied. "I owe you."

"A bottle of Jameson will be fine," he said. "Besides, you never have to worry about getting the wrong size."

"I'll deliver it personally when I get out from under this quagmire," she said. "Good luck on your number crunching."

"Sounds good, I'll talk to you later, Alex."

Alex hung up the phone just as Abby knocked on the door. She motioned for her to come in.

"I've got Ms. Grayson settled in the interview room," Abby said as she entered the office carrying a mug and set it on the desk. "I figured you could use a cup of coffee."

"Thanks, Abs," Alex said. "How are we doing with the call-out?"

"Late tour guys are on their way in and I notified the reserve sergeant that we need his people," she said. "He will notify everyone that isn't already working."

"Great," Alex replied as she took a sip of coffee and leaned back in her chair.

"What do you think about this one, boss?"

"Kid vanishes within two blocks of the park," Alex said softly. "I hope I'm wrong, but I've got a gut feeling that he was snatched."

"Have you ever handled something like this before?" Abby asked.

Alex nodded her head.

"How'd it work out?"

"Sometimes okay," Alex replied. "Sometimes, not okay."

"When you say not okay, you don't mean…."

"It's a tough world, Abby. Bad things happen to good people, even if they are kids."

"This is the part of the job I hate," Abby replied.

"Good," Alex said. "I'd be worried if it didn't bother you."

"What do you need me to do?"

"I can see that you're champing at the bit," Alex said. "Go suit up and help search. I have to interview Grayson, so there is no need for both of us to be here."

"Are you sure?"

"Yeah, I'm a multi-tasker," Alex replied. "If I can smoke and drink at the same time, I can certainly handle an interview and any phone calls that come in."

"Thanks, boss," Abby said and quickly headed out of the office.

Alex took a sip of her coffee and set it back down on the desk just as the cellphone rang.

"Penobscot Police, Chief Taylor."

"Chief, this is Mike Walsh. I'm the C.O. of Troop F. Tom Blackshear asked me to call you."

"Mike, Alex Taylor, thanks for getting back to me so quickly."

"No problem," the man said. "Tom said you had a missing juvenile."

"Yeah, an eight-year-old boy, he went missing from the Founder's Day fair that we have going on. I was hoping you might have some personnel to spare."

"I've got two units on the road up in your neck of the woods right now. I'll have them head your way."

"Thank you; I really appreciate that, Mike."

"No problem," Walsh replied. "Tom mentioned that he was going to have a canine unit respond."

"Yes, he was making some calls to see if they had anyone available to come up."

"Ok, well I'm down in Concord at a training seminar this weekend. Did my number come up on your phone?"

"Yes it did," Alex replied.

"That's my cell. If you need anything else, let me know. God forbid we have to continue the search into the weekend, but if so, I'll get you more personnel."

"I can't tell you how much I appreciate that, Mike."

"Don't worry, glad I can help. Call me if you need anything."

"Thanks," Alex said. "I will."

Alex took a final drag on the cigarette and crushed it out. She then got up, grabbing the coffee mug, and made her way out into the main room. She refilled her mug before heading into the interview room.

"How are you doing Ms. Grayson?" Alex asked as she peered into the room.

"I think I'm done," she replied. "I can't think of anything else to add."

Alex picked up the statement sheet from the desk and began to read it.

"Okay, well why don't you come with me," Alex said. "I just have a few other questions I'd like to ask."

Alex led Grayson back to her office and motioned for her to sit down in the chair across from the desk.

"Do you smoke?" Grayson asked.

"Yes, why?"

"Would you mind?" the woman asked as she removed a pack of cigarettes from her purse.

Alex smiled and slid the ash tray across the desk toward the woman.

Grayson lit the cigarette and took a drag.

"We are becoming an increasingly unpopular group," Alex said as she lit one of her own.

"You're telling me, try being a teacher who smokes," the woman replied. "I can't smoke anywhere near the school and when the other teachers found out they looked at me like I was evil. Did you ever get that feeling?"

"I'm from Brooklyn," Alex replied. "Most people will tell you *I am* evil. Smoking is often the least of my vices."

"I've tried to quit," Grayson said. "I stopped for a few years, but then with the divorce…. Well, it hasn't been the most *stress-free* time in my life."

"I understand," Alex said. "We all have our reasons."

"Have you ever been married, Chief Taylor?"

"No, and please, call me Alex."

"Let me tell you, it's difficult."

"I take it things didn't go so well?" Alex asked.

Karla laughed.

"Where do I even begin?" she asked sarcastically.

"At the beginning," Alex replied.

"Do we have that long?"

"As long as you need," Alex said.

Karla gazed out the window and took a drag on her cigarette, exhaling slowly, as the memories of her life silently replayed in her mind.

"You know, it seems like a lifetime ago since I first met Ricky," she said. "I was fresh out of college and I'd just come back to Penobscot to teach. The principal is an old family friend and he'd offered me a job when I graduated. I was single then and trying to get re-acclimated with small town life. One of my old high school girlfriends thought she'd do me a *favor* and introduced me to her boyfriend's best friend. I should have known better. Almost from the beginning the bells and whistles went off. On our first date he picked me up and took me to the bowling alley for one dollar draft beers and *neon* pins."

"I've been on worse dates," Alex said with a laugh.

"Don't get me wrong, Ricky was a nice enough guy," Karla replied. "It's just that we were complete opposites. I had dreams, desires, and ambitions. Ricky, well, Ricky had the weekend. I don't think he was capable of thinking beyond a day at a time."

"So how did you two end up getting married?" Alex asked. "It doesn't seem like you had any of the same interests."

"How do most opposites end up that way? We had one wild weekend too many and then, nine months later, Cory was born."

"Ouch," Alex replied. "I guess you two had at least *one* shared interest."

"Well, Ricky had a few skills, and that was one of them," Karla said. "The problem was that he was never serious about anything. As long as he had a few bucks in his pocket for beer, bait, or bullets, he was happy. That just wasn't me. I wanted more out of life than racing around the mud flats in his pickup and then getting drunk on the tailgate."

"So what happened?"

"In the beginning we tried to make it work. I had some pipe dream that fatherhood would settle him down, but it didn't. If anything, it just drove him deeper into his work. He's an electrician, but when the company he worked for went out of business, he started taking union jobs. Suddenly he's working jobs down south, or even out of state, for weeks on end."

"That had to be rough," Alex said, taking a drag on her cigarette and crushing it out in the ashtray.

"It was," Karla replied. "I was trying to juggle my new career with one hand, while I had a baby anchored to my hip with the other. One night, after I had put Cory down for bed, I sat on the porch having a cigarette and realized that I was doing it all alone. Somewhere along the way, I realized this was my life, a single parent, and I had become great at it. I wondered what purpose there was in being married any longer. I got pissed-off and took a ride over to the bar to confront him and saw a bleach-blonde bimbo riding his lap."

"That must have gone over well," Alex said.

"Actually, I turned and walked out," Karla replied. "I never said a word. The next day he left for a job down by Nashua. Two weeks later, when he came home looking for a piece of ass, he got served divorce papers instead."

"How'd he take that?"

"Oh, he went ballistic, screaming and hollering like a cat on a hot tin roof. At first he begged me to take him back, said that he would change and make things better. When I didn't, he threatened to make my life a living hell. That's when I knew I was done, when neither the pleading, nor the threats, had elicited any emotional response."

"What happened after the divorce?" Alex asked.

"I'd already moved out before he'd come home," Karla replied. "When I got pregnant I had moved into his place. He had a house, here in town, that he rented, but it didn't feel like home to me. So I moved back to my parent's place with Cory. They had an old farm, just north of town. Dad had passed away a year earlier, so my mother enjoyed having us around. She'd watch Cory during the day for me while I worked. That lightened my load financially. Then two years ago mom died, so it has just been the two of us out there now."

"Didn't you get any help from Ricky? Any child support?"

Karla let out a laugh and lit another cigarette. She absent-mindedly ran her fingers through her long, auburn hair.

"Ricky didn't seem to understand the complexities of the court order. He paid when he wanted and then would *forget* for months at a time."

"Did you take him to court?"

"A few times, but he would feign ignorance or come in with a sad tale of how bad times were and how he had been struggling to find work."

"I take it you didn't believe him," Alex said.

"Before the divorce I would hear Ricky and his friends laughing about how they would screw the system, taking side gigs for cash. I knew he was working, but I couldn't prove it. I didn't have the cash to waste on a private investigator to chase him around New England and he knew that. After a while I quit bothering. I'd call him and break his balls. I'd guilt him into sending some money, telling him how I never asked for spousal maintenance and the least he could do was provide for his kid. That would work for a time, but then he'd go back to *forgetting*. It's a vicious cycle with him and the courts could not care less."

"When was the last time you saw him?"

"Probably a week, maybe ten days ago," Karla replied. "One of my 'cash calls,' as he refers to them. He complained about not having any work and how I was just a 'mean, spiteful bitch,' whose only interest was in 'robbing him blind.'"

"He sounds like a real gem," Alex said.

"When he's not drinking, he can be quite charming. The only problem is that he tends to drink a lot."

"How much interaction does he have with Cory?" Alex asked.

"Now, hardly none," she replied. "In the beginning, he would come around a lot. He began putting in an effort at being a dad. Then, when he realized that it wasn't having an impact on me, he quit. I think he just wanted to get me back and when that didn't work, he went back to being *selfish Ricky*."

Just then there was a knock on the door. Alex looked up to see Abby standing outside and motioned her to come in.

"Hey, Chief, sorry to bother you," Abby said. "Can I talk to you for a minute?"

"Sure, Abs," Alex said as she stood up. "I'll be just a minute. Can I get you another cup of coffee?"

"Yes, please," she replied. "Black is fine."

"Ok, I'll be right back."

Alex walked out, closing the office door behind her, and approached Abby.

"What do you have, Abs?" she said as the two of them walked over to the coffee pot.

"Hutch told me to tell you that the search didn't turn up anything, boss," Simpson said. "They are interviewing the residents along the route, and they are still speaking to people over at the pavilion, but so far no one has seen the boy."

"Fuck me," Alex said as she poured two cups of coffee.

"State police just showed up, they are going to help with the interviews. They said a canine unit should be here in about fifteen minutes."

"Ok, hang out here for a bit," Alex said. "I'm just about done here and I'll need you to babysit her while I go back over to the park."

"Yes, ma'am," Abby replied.

Alex returned to the office, handing Grayson the cup of coffee and sat back down at her desk.

"They haven't found him yet, have they?" Karla asked.

"No, they haven't," Alex replied. "Karla, I have to ask, do you think your ex could be involved with Cory's disappearance?"

"Ricky?" Karla asked, a shocked look gripping her face. "You think Ricky took Cory?"

"I didn't say that," Alex replied, "but I can't rule anything out at this point. Judging from what you have told me, it sounds like he still has a bit of an axe to grind."

"I mean Ricky can be a major league asshole, but he has done nothing to hurt Cory."

"I'm not saying that he would hurt Cory, but it could be his way of hurting you."

Grayson clutched the coffee cup in her hand as she stared out the window, letting Alex's words sink in. A cold chill enveloped her, and she took comfort in the small bit of warmth that the coffee mug provided to her.

"Where does Ricky live?" Alex asked, interrupting the woman's thoughts.

"Huh?" Grayson said as she turned to look at Alex, her face masked by confusion. "Ricky? I guess he is still here in town."

"Where? I need an address."

"408 West North," Grayson replied. "It's just a few blocks from here."

"Do you have a number for him?"

"Yes, I have a cellphone number for him. He doesn't have a house phone."

Alex slid a notepad across the desk toward Karla.

"Could you please write it down for me," Alex said. "Also write down his address, date of birth, and what kind of car he drives."

Karla wrote the information on the pad and passed it back to Alex. Alex got up from the desk and put on her jacket, slipping the notebook in her pocket. She walked over to the door and opened it.

"Abby, can you stay with Ms. Grayson for a little while," Alex said.

"Yes, Chief," Abby replied as she walked into Alex's office.

"We have a state police canine unit coming up to help in the search, Karla. When they arrive, Officer Simpson will take you over to them. Do you have anything of Cory's that would help them? Perhaps an article of clothing he recently wore?"

"I think I have a jacket of his in the car," Grayson replied. "Will that help?"

"Yes it will," Alex replied. "In the meantime, I will see if I can locate Ms. Grayson's ex. Call me if you need me, Abs"

"Will do, Chief," Abby said.

Alex walked out of city hall and made her way around the back of the building to where her unmarked Dodge Charger was parked. She got in and powered up the computer, running Ricky Childers' name through the state database, as she drove over to the address Grayson had given her. When she pulled up, the house was dark.

Alex checked the computer terminal. Childers had a handful of misdemeanor charges, mostly for disorderly conduct, and a D.U.I. from August 2011. The only vehicle registered to him was a 2004 Dodge Dakota pick-up truck.

She got out of the car and walked up to the darkened porch. Alex pulled a flashlight out of her pocket and peered into the window. The interior was sparsely furnished. She could make out a small recliner and a television set, in what appeared to be the living room, and a small dinette just beyond that. Alex tried the door knob, but it was locked. She pressed the doorbell, hearing it ring loudly inside the house.

Alex stepped off the porch, staring up at the second floor, looking for any sign that someone was inside. After waiting a few moments, she made her way to the side of the house. Alex kneeled down to look through the basement window, her flashlight lighting up the barren interior. She could easily make out a furnace and hot water heater, sitting in the middle of the room, but there did not appear to be anything else, aside from a few partially opened boxes scattered about the concrete floor.

Standing up, she continued toward the rear of the house where an old garage sat. Alex peered through a side window, but the garage was as empty as the rest of the house. She then made her way back to her car.

"Can I help you, officer?"

Alex turned around, in the direction the voice had come, and saw an elderly man standing across the street. She closed the car's door and walked over to the man.

"Good evening," she said. "I'm Chief Taylor."

"Tony," the man replied. "Tony Burton, are you looking for someone?"

"Nice to meet you, Tony," Alex replied. "I was wondering, is there any chance that you might have seen Ricky Childers today?"

"Yes, I did," the man replied. "Is there a problem?"

"Not sure," Alex said. "We are investigating a missing person. Do you remember what time you saw Mr. Childers?"

"Hmmmm," the man said with a frown. "Must have been two or three hours ago. I was cleaning out the gutters and heard an awful ruckus. I looked over and saw him throwing stuff into the back of his truck."

"What kind of stuff?" Alex asked.

"Just some bags," the man replied. "I didn't get a good look because I was up on the ladder. Then I heard him pull out of the driveway and race up the street. I planned on talking to him when I saw him again; he was going pretty fast down our road, especially in a neighborhood where so many children play outside."

"Which way did he go?" Alex asked.

"North," the man replied, his arm extending out in that direction.

"Is there anything else that you can remember? Did you see anyone in the vehicle with him?"

"No, like I said, I only glanced over for a moment," Burton replied. "About that same time my wife called me for dinner."

"Okay, well thank you, sir," Alex said. "I appreciate you taking the time to talk to me. If you do remember anything, or you see Ricky come back, can you call me?"

"No problem. I'm always happy to help."

"You have a great evening."

"Thank you, you too, officer."

Alex turned and headed back to the car. She got in, closing the door, and pulled out her cellphone and the notepad. She dialed the number Karla Grayson had given her. Almost immediately she heard an electronic *warble* tone.

'We're sorry, the number you have dialed has been disconnected.'

"*Sonofabitch*," Alex said, ending the call.

She reached over and picked up the radio mic.

"M-11-1 to County Dispatch, are you on the air?"

"County Dispatch, on the air, M-11-1," a female voice said over the radio. "Go with your message."

"Dispatch, I need you to put a BOLO out on a Richard M. Childers, male, Caucasian, date-of-birth November 17th, 1982. He was last seen driving a blue, 2004 Dodge Dakota, heading north from the city of Penobscot. Subject is wanted for questioning in the disappearance of a minor child, Cory Childers. Possible parental abduction, approach with caution, unknown at this time if any weapons are involved. Please add this information onto the previous Amber Alert issued for the missing child."

"M-11-1, copy broadcast. All units, all units, Penobscot Police Department is looking for Richard M. Childers, male, Caucasian, date-of-birth November 17th, 1982. Subject was last seen driving a blue, 2004 Dodge Dakota, heading north from the city of Penobscot. Subject is wanted for questioning in connection with a possible parental abduction regarding the disappearance of Cory Childers. Unknown if the subject is in possession of any weapons so approach with caution."

"M-11-1 to County Dispatch, can you also notify the FBI Child Abduction Rapid Deployment Team and request that they respond?"

"10-4, M-11-1," the dispatcher replied. "10-4. I'm notifying FBI Portsmouth and requesting the response of the CARD team."

Alex put the car in drive and headed back toward the pavilion. They were all in for a very long night.

CHAPTER FOUR

"Are you fucking serious?" Alex screamed into the phone.

"Please, Chief Taylor, there is no need for that kind of language," FBI Special Agent Reginald Peterson replied.

Alex could hear the pretentious tone of the man's voice coming through the phone as if he was standing in the room. Which, given the nature of their current conversation, would not have bode well for the man's physical well-being. It would not have been the first time that Alex went over a desk at someone.

"Surely you can appreciate the fact that the Bureau has only a finite amount of resources at its disposal. We must remain vigilant to address needs as they may arise."

"Agent Peterson, what does the acronym CARD stand for?"

Alex could hear the man sigh on the other end.

"CARD is the Bureau's Child Abduction Rapid Deployment team, Chief," he replied.

"That's pretty funny, Agent Peterson, because I just so happen to have a child whom I believe has been abducted. You would think the *Bureau* would be eager to do what it advertises."

"I understand that, Chief," Peterson replied. "It's just that in this particular instance the Bureau cannot assign a team to assist you."

Alex reached into her pocket and removed the pack of cigarettes. She tapped one out angrily and lit it, taking a long drag.

"And why exactly is the Bureau unable to send me a team, in *this particular instance*?"

"It's because the abduction does not fit within the parameters of the CARD team's mission."

"For fucks sake, Peterson," Alex exploded. "I have a missing eight-year-old child, and you're going to tell me that the FBI has fucking *parameters* as to when they can respond? What kind of horseshit is this? What do I have to do? Ask *mother may I*?"

"It's just that we don't respond to abductions involving parents."

"What a fucking joke," Alex said, the anger in her voice growing clearer with each second.

"However, I've been instructed to let you know that the Bureau is very interested in this case being resolved. So they have assigned me to act as a liaison with you and to monitor the situation. If there is anything you need, please let me know."

"You know there is something I would like to know," Alex said. "What is the status of the CARD team right now? Are they investigating anything at this moment?"

There was a long pause on the phone.

"Are you there, Peterson?"

"Yes, Chief Taylor, I'm here," the man replied hesitantly. "I don't know the exact status of the regional unit."

"Really? That's amazing. You mean to tell me you don't know if they are in the field on in the office?"

"I don't believe that they are in the field, at this very moment," the man replied.

"Great,' Alex said sarcastically. "So I have a missing child who gets kicked to the curb by the *infamous* FBI, because he doesn't fit the right *parameters*, while the team sits on their collective asses waiting for something that ticks the proper boxes."

"I'm sorry, Chief Taylor," Peterson replied. "It's above my pay grade."

"That's funny, Agent Peterson," Alex said. "Everyone always says 'it's above my pay grade,' when they don't have a real answer. How about we just cut through the bullshit and call it for what it is? The truth is, the government doesn't really give a shit, unless you're well-connected and you happen to know the person who has the *pay grade* to make the decision."

"Like I said, Chief Taylor, I will monitor the situation. Please let me know if you need anything."

"Here's a word of advice, Special Agent Peterson. I strongly suggest you turn on your television and monitor the situation from Portsmouth, because if you step foot in Penobscot, I'll have you arrested for interfering in an investigation. And, just so we're clear, that is within my pay grade, *capiche*?"

"Loud and clear, Chief Taylor."

"Asshole," Alex said as she slammed the phone down on the receiver and crushed the cigarette out in the ashtray.

Alex stared out the window. It was raining outside, a cold, bone-chilling rain, but it was no match for the white-hot rage that she fought to control within her.

Cory Childers had been missing for nearly twenty hours and the investigation had come to a grinding halt. Now she was being told that her best chance at getting additional resources had just hit a brick wall because the potential abductor was the boy's father and not a non-family member.

So far, the search had failed to turn up any tangible leads and the initial interviews had been a bust. Most people were more interested in their food, than they were of what was going on around them. Those who had looked up from their plates vaguely recalled seeing the teacher and maybe her son, but they weren't positive.

At first, things were looking up when the state police canine had picked up a scent. The track went from the pavilion to the Turner's residence, but they lost it on a side street, a block away. It was of little consolation to Alex that the area where they had lost the scent was toward Ricky Childers' house.

Alex didn't want to get *tunnel vision*, focusing on Ricky, instead of the facts, but the only thing they were certain of was that Cory Childers had vanished and his father was nowhere to be found. Twenty hours into the investigation and they were no closer to breaking the case than they were when Grayson first reported her son missing.

Alex got up from the desk and headed out into the main room to get another cup of coffee.

"How'd it go, Chief?" Abby asked.

"You know what FBI stands for, Abs?" Alex asked.

"Federal Bureau of Investigation?" Abby replied hesitantly.

"No, *Famous, But Incompetent*," Alex said.

"That's funny, boss."

"The fuckers love a press conference, but ask them to do a little work and suddenly they have *parameters*."

"I take it they aren't coming to help."

"Apparently they only respond to *non-family* abductions," Alex replied. "You know, I remember we had a bank robbery in Brooklyn one time and those pricks had the audacity to ask if it was an *FDIC* insured bank. More fucking parameters I guess."

"What can I do to help?" Abby asked.

"Nothing, Abs," Alex replied. "I'm just venting. I get so annoyed at suits that seem to be more interested in appearing in front of the cameras, than getting their hands dirty. What pisses me off more than anything is that I can guarantee you if someone down in New Castle, or on the governor's staff, had their kid abducted by another parent, the parameters would be *modified*."

"Then it's a good thing that Penobscot has you."

"Thanks, Abs," Alex said with a smile. "Coffee?"

"Sure, it's too early for anything stronger."

"I thought that myself. It's a helluva way to start a Saturday morning. Speaking of which, where's Hutch?"

"He and Steve were going out to canvas this morning," Abby replied. "Trying to interview anyone they had missed."

"That's a good idea," Alex said. "Maybe we will get lucky."

"So now what do we do?" Simpson asked.

"Well, we're fast approaching the twenty-four-hour mark," Alex replied. "That isn't good. There is just too much distance you can cover in that period of time."

Alex sat down at one of the desks and lit up a cigarette. Abby reached down, opening one of the desk drawers and pulled out an ashtray.

"Thanks," Alex said. "I feel like I'm back to chain-smoking these things."

"Under the circumstances, I think you get a pass," Abby said. "So what's your gut feeling about this?"

"I honestly don't know. I'm having a hard time with this one. All I know is that we need to find the father and fast."

"Where do you think he is?"

"That's the million dollar question," Alex said. "I think I need to go back to square one."

"Karla Grayson?"

"Yeah, at the moment, she's the best source of information on Ricky Childers."

"What if she has nothing else?"

"Then we are stuck," Alex replied.

"Do you think we will find him?" Abby asked.

Alex took a drag on the cigarette and twirled the burning ember around the edge of the ashtray, dislodging the ash, as she contemplated the question. She didn't have a straightforward answer.

"Every forty seconds there is a child reported missing or abducted in the United States," Alex finally replied. "Most of them involve a family member or an acquaintance and not every abduction ends well."

"You mean they aren't found?" Abby asked.

"The first three hours are the most critical. About seventy-five percent of abducted children, who end up being killed, are usually killed within this period of time."

"Let's hope he is in the minority."

"Well, we won't find him sitting here and talking about it," Alex replied as she stood up and crushed the cigarette out in the ashtray. "I better head over to Grayson's and see if she can think of anything else that might help."

Alex grabbed her jacket and headed toward the door. She paused for a moment and looked back. "Hey, Abs, do me a favor. As much as I like the father on this, I don't want to put blinders on either. Get in contact with the school's principal and pull the records for the kids in Cory's class. I want you to do a background check on the parent's, starting with Sheila and Grant Turner. Let me know if anything pops."

"Yes, ma'am," Abby said.

"Thank you," Alex said as she headed out the door.

There was a pause in the rain, but the dark, foreboding sky made it feel much colder than it was. Alex adjusted the collar on her jacket as she made her way over to the Charger. She drove along the square and followed the route that Cory Childers would have taken to the Turner's house. It seemed like such a short distance, yet experience had taught her that tragedy could happen in the most innocuous of places and in the blink of an eye.

It was a ten-minute ride out to Karla Grayson's home, which sat on the western edge of town. The house was styled after an old red barn, with wood clapboard siding and a white porch. It contrasted nicely with the autumn colors of the surrounding trees and looked as if it belonged in one of those *Americana* coffee table books.

Alex made her way along the long gravel driveway, pulling up next to Grayson's black Jeep Grand Cherokee. Parked beside Grayson's car was a red Ford Focus. Alex reached into her pocket and removed the notepad. She jotted down the license plate number and put it back in her pocket.

She got out of the car and made her way up the stairs to the front porch. As she approached the screen door, she could hear muffled voices coming from somewhere inside the house. She waited a moment, hoping to make out the conversation, then gave up and rang the doorbell. A moment later, Grayson appeared.

"Have you found him, Chief Taylor?" the woman asked anxiously as she approached the door.

Alex could tell by the redness in her eyes that she had recently been crying. There was also weariness in her appearance that belied the fact that she had not been getting much sleep.

"No, I'm afraid not," Alex replied. "I hoped that I might ask you a few more questions."

"Please, come in," Grayson said dejectedly as she opened the door.

"I hope that I'm not interrupting anything."

"No, not at all," Grayson said. "A friend from school heard about Cory and stopped by for support."

Karla led Alex through the main part of the house and back into the kitchen where a man sat at the small kitchen table.

"Chief Taylor, this is John Connolly," Grayson said.

The man got up from the table and extended his hand toward Alex. She gave the man a once over as she shook his hand, noting the way his hand hung limp, like a dead fish.

The man was probably in his mid-30's, with sandy blonde hair and a fair complexion. He was wearing a salmon colored dress shirt and jeans that had an ironed crease in them.

"Nice to meet you, Chief," the man said in a rather demure voice. "Karla was just saying how well your department has been treating her since all this happened."

"We are doing the best we can, under the circumstances," Alex replied.

"Please have a seat, Chief," Karla said. "Can I get you some coffee?"

"Yes, thank you," Alex replied. "So, Mr. Connelly, Karla says you know each other from school, are you a teacher also?"

"Yes, I am," Connolly replied, "and please, call me John. I teach fourth grade."

"So Cory wasn't one of your students, John?" Alex asked.

"No, Cory had just started third grade, but I'm looking forward to having him next year."

Karla smiled warmly at John as she set the coffee mug down on the table in front of Alex.

"John, would you like a refill?" she asked.

"No, I really should be going," the man replied. "I'm sure that you two have a lot to discuss and I don't want to interrupt."

"Well, thanks for checking up on me," Karla replied. "Let me walk you to the door. I'll only be a minute, Chief."

"Take your time," Alex said as she took a sip of coffee.

A few moments later Grayson returned and took the seat across from Alex.

"Since word got out about Cory, everybody from work has been calling or stopping by," Karla said. "They have been so supportive."

"I'm sure that has to help," Alex said. "I'm sorry to have disturbed your visit."

"Well, I didn't think you stopped by for a social call. Is there any news?"

"Unfortunately, no," Alex replied. "We have an alert out for your ex and we hope that something will surface soon. In the meantime, I wanted to ask you a few more questions."

"By all means," Karla said as she removed a cigarette from the pack on the table and lit it. "Ask me anything you need to."

"You mentioned that Ricky had taken union jobs that required him to travel, do you remember where?"

"I can do you one better," the woman said getting up from her chair. "I used to keep a record of his jobs for taxes, so I have the dates and locations in a book."

Karla left the room and returned a minute later with a black and white composition notebook.

"Tools of the trade," she said with a laugh as she laid the book down on the table and thumbed through the pages.

"I understand," Alex said as she removed her notepad from her jacket pocket. "The way I go through these things I always thought I should buy stock in the company."

Karla reached a page and turned the book around to face Alex.

"This is where the traveling began," she explained. "At first it was local stuff, all in New Hampshire, but as each job finished they expanded, including a bunch of out-of-state jobs."

Alex began copying the dates and locations into the notepad.

"Does Ricky have any family in the area?" Alex asked.

"In Penobscot?" Karla asked. "No, not really. That was one thing Ricky seemed to enjoy, having my family around in the beginning."

"What about his?" Alex asked. "Did he ever speak about them?"

"Both of his parents are dead," Karla said. "He mentioned having an uncle once, but they weren't close. At least I never knew of them having any interaction while we were together. He has more friends than anything else."

"What about banking, credit cards?"

"I doubt he has a credit card. I heard he filed for a bankruptcy not that long ago. When he pays his child support, the checks are all from the same bank, the Penobscot Savings and Loan."

"What about any property?"

"Ricky?" Karla said sarcastically. "Ricky had a hard enough time keeping money in his pocket through the weekend, let alone owning any property."

"You mentioned bait and bullets before; did he hunt or fish in any specific areas?"

"He fished out on the lake, like everyone else. He has a buddy who owns some land, just north of town. That's where they would hunt."

"Would you have a name?" Alex asked.

"Elwood Jones," Karla replied, "but everyone calls him Bubba. He works over at Reilly Marine Diesel, or at least he did. I haven't spoken to him in a while."

"I'll look into it. Is there anything else that you can think of? Any place that he might have gone?"

Karla took a drag on her cigarette as she mulled the question over. Alex could see something was bothering her.

"Anything, even if you think it's inconsequential."

"The last I heard, Ricky was seeing a *dancer* named Destiny. I believe she works at the Pussy Cat Club in Alton."

"Sounds serious," Alex said.

"Yeah," Karla scoffed, "if you like your women to have fake boobs and hang upside down from a pole."

"She's probably just paying off her *student loans*," Alex replied.

"I don't think they have degree programs in stripping," Karla said sarcastically.

"Hey, I'm from New York City, they have degree programs for *anything* down there."

"I'll stick with teaching," Grayson replied.

"All right, so there is nothing else you can think of?" Alex asked.

"No, not really," Karla said. "Do you think it was Ricky, Chief Taylor?"

"Most child abductions involve a family member," Alex said. "With any luck he'll surface in a day or so and this will all come to an end."

"Do you believe that?"

Alex looked at the woman. The stress of the last day was taking its toll and it showed on her face. Alex struggled to find the right words, which would bring her comfort at this moment, but the reality of the situation was different.

Alex had spent too many years in law enforcement, watching as the bad guys literally got away with murder because of a technicality. She knew in her heart that bad things happened to good people, and just because you *wanted* a happy outcome, didn't mean that it would happen.

One of the worst cases she had handled was a missing nine-year-old girl in Brooklyn. It had started out as a quiet Sunday morning in January. All the trouble makers from the previous late tour were sleeping; pushed off the streets by a brutal cold front that had crept in and held the city in a stranglehold. Alex was enjoying a break in the never-ending stream of radio runs that were a hallmark of police life in Brooklyn North. Her partner had just come out of a local bodega with coffee when the radio came alive.

"Seven-Three Adam on the air?"

"Fuck me," Alex said as her partner closed the door. She reached over and grabbed the portable radio from its perch up on the dashboard.

"Three Adam, on the air."

"Adam, no Housing units available," the dispatcher replied. "We have a report of a 10-68, see complainant about a possible missing nine-year-old female, confines of the Tilden Houses. Complainant will be on the corner of Livonia and Rock."

"Adam, 10-4," Alex said and tossed the radio back up on the dash.

"Three Sergeant, did you copy Adam's job?" the dispatcher asked.

"Three Sergeant, copy," a man's voice said over the radio. "Show me responding to that location."

"I didn't want to stay warm anyway," Alex's partner, Joe Turner, said as he popped the top on the Styrofoam cup and took a sip.

"Fucking Housing is a myth," Alex said, more than a bit annoyed. "They're like *unicorns*. You hear people talk about them, but you never see one."

"They're probably having a sit down breakfast in the records room," Turner replied.

"Yeah, and all I get is a shitty cup of coffee and a cigarette."

"The NYPD, it's not just a job, it's an adventure," Turner said with a big smile as he pulled the patrol car from the curb and headed toward the call.

They had spent the next six hours, with the help of the Brooklyn North Task Force, combing through the Samuel J. Tilden Housing Authority complex looking for the missing girl. It was an officer from the Task Force who had found her brutally beaten body in the basement of one of the buildings.

Alex stood outside, smoking a cigarette as the young girl's body was removed from the building by the Medical Examiner's Office. She glanced up at the windows, overlooking the courtyard, and her gaze was met by those looking down. There was nothing in their eyes. No empathy, no pain, no anger at what had happened. As heartless as it might have seemed, it was just another day on the mean streets of Brooklyn North.

This wasn't the first body of an innocent child that would be removed in a body bag and it wouldn't be the last. The residents had come to accept it and just stared out the window as if it were a television drama unfolding before them. Life was tough here; it was tougher still if you let it get to you. Folks here just learned to harden their hearts. It was just a cruel reality and the only way you survived there was by accepting that fact.

That was Brooklyn, not Penobscot, she reminded herself.

Alex shook the memory from her mind and looked at the woman sitting across from her. "Yes, Karla, I believe it. If I didn't, I couldn't do this job."

"Thank you," the woman replied. "I don't know if I could last another minute without hope."

Their conversation was interrupted by the doorbell and a voice calling out from the porch.

"Karla, are you in there?"

"Yes," Grayson replied. "Come on back."

A moment later an elderly woman entered the kitchen carrying a bag of food. It didn't matter the occasion, wedding, funeral, sickness, they always brought food. It was a small town's way of saying, '*we are here for you.*'

"Chief Taylor, this is my Aunt Elsie."

"Pleased to meet you, ma'am," Alex said as she stood up.

"I'm not her aunt," the woman replied, "but Karla's mother and I were like sisters."

"Well, that's all that counts, isn't it?" Alex asked.

"I just wish more of the young kids today had the same respect for their elders."

"It is becoming quite rare," Alex replied. "I won't keep you anymore, Ms. Grayson."

"Thank you for stopping by," Karla said. "If I can think of anything else, I will let you know."

"I'll show myself out," Alex said.

As she got to the kitchen doorway, she paused, then turned and looked back at Grayson.

"There is one thing you can do, Karla," Alex said. "When you get a chance, can you find out the name of Ricky's uncle and any other friends that you can think of?"

"Sure," she replied. "I'll work on that tonight."

"Great," Alex said. "When you're done, just call the station and they will pass along the information to me."

"Okay, I'll get that done quickly."

Alex made her way out to the car and leaned up against the front-end. She removed the pack of cigarettes from her pocket and lit one up. Her eyes glanced up at the empty windows of the old farmhouse. There were no expressionless gawkers looking back at her.

Maybe that is a good omen, she thought as she took a drag on the cigarette. *Maybe this time it will end differently.*

CHAPTER FIVE

Alex sat in her living room, staring out the large bay window that overlooked Lake Moriah. On the other side of the lake, the sloping mountainside was awash in rich autumn colors.

As she sipped the glass of wine, she closed her eyes and listened to the crackling sounds of the fireplace. For the briefest of moments her mind slipped far away from here, but the minute she opened them back up reality came crashing down.

Spread out on the coffee table were the contents of the case file on Cory Childers. Despite hours spent reviewing the paperwork, she couldn't find any additional clues that would help find the missing child.

Alex had tracked down Ricky's friend, Bubba, but that interview failed to shine any light on the man's current whereabouts. It turned out that the two men's relationship had hit a sour note. Bubba had told her that over the summer, Ricky had asked him to do some engine work on a boat he had picked-up for a good price. The theory was, they would do some quick repairs and turn it around for a profit. Theoretically, it was a solid idea, at least it was until Ricky pocketed the profit, leaving Bubba with the tab for the parts he'd used to fix the motor.

Needless to say, Bubba was more than willing to provide any information he could to help Alex locate his *old friend*. The only problem was the information he had was weeks old. It seemed word had gotten around that Bubba was not entirely happy with Ricky and he was steering a wide berth around the man. Alex understood why, as she watched the man effortlessly lift an outboard motor onto a workbench as if it was a child's toy.

Next she had tried the number for the union that Ricky was a member of, but the guy who handled work assignments was conveniently out of town. Despite several attempts, they seemed unable to locate the man, but they promised to get back to her as soon as they could. Alex wasn't about to hold her breath. Right or wrong, Ricky was a union brother and they weren't about to help her locate him.

Even the background checks she'd asked Abby do, on the other parents, met with negative results. Except for a handful of traffic citations, one DUI, and a shoplifting arrest, there was nothing that would point a finger in a new direction.

She picked up the small school photo that Karla Grayson had given her and stared at the young, wide-eyed boy. He was smiling and had that look of innocence that only a young child could truly know. To him, the only monsters in the world were the ones under his bed or in the closet.

"Where are you, Cory?" she whispered as she laid the photo down on the coffee table.

Alex leaned back against the couch and propped her feet up on the coffee table as she finished her drink. There wasn't much more they could do. They'd searched the entire town and interviewed all of the area residents, but turned up nothing for their efforts. In addition, none of the attendees at the dinner recalled seeing the young boy after he had left the pavilion. It really was as if he had vanished into thin air.

"C'mon, God, something's got to give."

She got up and walked back to the kitchen to refill her glass. Next she grabbed the pack of cigarettes from the coffee table, before heading out onto the front porch. It was your typical, chilly fall day, but the sun was shining brightly, so the cold didn't feel as bad. The front yard was filled with a sea of fallen red, orange, and yellow leaves. She set the wine glass down on the porch railing and lit a cigarette.

It was so quiet here in Penobscot, so pristine. It seemed like a lifetime ago since she had been in New York, but in reality it had only been a little more than a year.

Alex remembered the phone call she had received from her old partner, James Maguire. It had been several months after her career with the NYPD had come to an abrupt end, the result of a losing battle with the bottle that had claimed what should have been a stellar career. The call came at her lowest point, sitting in the dark, windowless basement apartment in North Bellmore, Long Island, surrounded by a collection of empty whiskey bottles and overflowing ashtrays.

At first, the prospect of interviewing for the job of police chief seemed *beneath* her. She'd been a highly decorated member of the NYPD and she was being told to take a job somewhere in the sticks, far removed from the only world she ever known. If the call had come from anyone else, she would have hung up and opened another bottle, but he was different.

Maguire had been the only man Alex had ever really loved, but her battle with the bottle had let that ship sail, while she was passed out at the dock. She knew that if there would ever be an opportunity for her to get her shit together, and perhaps earn a second chance at love, then she would have to abandon the habits that had gotten her to that place to begin with.

Now, as she watched the wind send a new shower of leaves fluttering through the air, she knew it had been the right decision. She had carved out a new life for herself here, but the second chance at love still eluded her. It didn't help that the object of her *unrequited love* had not only found himself a rich girlfriend, but, in a cruel twist of fate, that same girlfriend now called Alex her *friend*.

"You gave up drinking way too soon," she said, hoisting her glass toward the sky, in a mock toast.

Just then, the shrill ring of the house phone drew her back to reality. She turned and made her way inside, grabbing the phone from its cradle on the wall.

"Hello," Alex said.

"Chief, are you all right?" asked Hutch.

"I'm fine, junior," she replied, "but it's nice of you to ask."

"I've been trying to call your cell, but it kept going to voice mail."

"No, I was just outside taking in this lovely autumn afternoon."

"Gotcha," Hutch replied. "Well, it just got lovelier. We got a call from the Vermont State Police. They got a hit on Childers' license plate."

"Seriously?" Alex asked. "When?"

"Early this morning," Hutch replied. "They got a call for a drunken dispute at a roadside motel, just outside Montpelier. As the troopers were clearing from the job, they spotted the truck. They have a car sitting on the location and are waiting for direction from us."

"Do you have a call back number?" Alex asked.

"Yeah," Hutch replied and read the number off for her. "Contact is a Sergeant Vanessa Miller."

"Thanks, Hutch," Alex said. "If I need you, are you going to be around?"

"Sure," he replied "I know how you love to ruin my weekends."

"I'll call you back," she said and hung up the phone.

Alex grabbed her cellphone, dialing the number that Hutch had given her and listened as it rang.

"Vermont State Police, Troop A, this is Sergeant Miller, how can I help you?"

"Sarge, this is Chief Taylor from the Penobscot Police Department in New Hampshire. I understand that you have a vehicle I'm looking for."

"Hey, Chief," the woman replied. "Yeah, I have a car sitting on it waiting for direction."

"Can you give me a brief about how you located it?" Alex asked.

"Yeah, we got a call for a dispute over at one of the local motels, off of Route 2," Miller said. "You know, the usual weekend drunken romance gone awry. Anyway, as they were getting ready to leave, they spotted the truck you're interested in. They checked with the motel manager and the name comes back to your wanted, Ricky Childers."

"Is the vehicle still there?" Alex asked.

"Yeah, I had the marked car take-off, and I have an unmarked monitoring it. I'm just waiting for you to tell me what to do."

"Can you have your people check out the room under some pretense of investigating a disturbance? Tell him some bullshit story like they are checking the rooms for bullet holes or something. I just want to know if there are any signs of a child in the room."

"Okay, Chief," the woman said. "Are you going to be at this number?"

"Yeah, Sarge, this is my private cell. I'll be waiting for your call."

"All right, I'll get back to you as soon as I know something more."

"Thanks," Alex said and ended the call.

She laid the cellphone on the coffee table and picked up the pack of cigarettes. She removed one and lit it, taking a drag.

Is this the break we've been looking for? she thought. *Will the next phone call bring news that they've found Cory?*

Alex sat down on the couch and stared up at the clock on the wall, watching as the minutes passed by agonizingly slow. It was nearly an hour before the cellphone rang.

"Hello," Alex said anxiously.

"Chief Taylor? This is Sergeant Miller."

"Yeah, Sarge, what do you have for me?"

"My guys interviewed the subject. He was cooperative, but there was no sign of a child in the room."

"Fuck," Alex exclaimed.

"What would you like us to do?" Miller asked.

"Is there any way you can keep an eye out on the car, Sarge?" Alex asked. "I'm going to head over there now to interview this guy. I know I am asking a lot, but it's the only lead I have on this abduction and I don't want to lose it."

"Sure, we can do that. I'll contact one of the sergeant's over at the Montpelier PD and we will coordinate the observation. I'll let you know if he moves."

"That would be great," Alex replied. "I'll call you when we get closer."

She ended the call and dialed Hutch's number.

"Hey, Chief," Hutch said when he answered the phone. "What's going on?"

"Remember when you said you knew how much I enjoyed ruining your weekends?"

"Seriously?" Hutch asked.

"Like a heart attack," Alex replied. "Gas up the car and come pick me up. We're going for a little ride."

"See you in about twenty minutes," Hutch said.

"Make it fifteen," she replied and hung up.

Alex made her way to the bedroom and changed out of her sweats. She put on a pair of jeans and a polo shirt with a gold badge embroidered over the left breast and the lettering *Chief – Penobscot Police Dept,* underneath it. She slid her belt through the loops on her jeans and affixed her holstered gun to her right side.

Alex was just finishing putting on her makeup when she heard a car coming up the gravel driveway. A moment later she heard the front door open.

"Chief?" Hutch called from the doorway.

"I'll be right out," Alex replied.

She capped the lipstick tube, tossing it in the vanity drawer, and made her way back outside.

"Do we know where we are going?" Alex asked.

"Vermont?" Hutch replied.

"That's close enough for government work," Alex said as she grabbed her jacket. "We'll figure out the details on the way."

CHAPTER SIX

Montpelier, Vermont had the distinction of being the smallest capital city in the United States. With a population of just over seventy-eight hundred people, it was actually much smaller than Penobscot.

It was just before two o'clock when Hutch pulled into the gas station parking lot, off of Route 2, where Sgt. Miller had said she would meet them.

"Hey," Alex said. "You want some coffee while we wait?"

"Sure," Hutch replied. "Can you see if they have any donuts?"

"I've gone and created a monster," Alex said as she got out of the car.

She made her way inside the gas station and located the coffee machine. When she emerged a few minutes later there was a green Chevy Tahoe, with a yellow stripe down the side, parked next to Hutch's patrol car.

He was standing outside the car, talking to a tall, female trooper with dark blonde hair pulled up into a tight bun. Alex made her way over and handed one of the cups to Hutch.

"Chief, this is Sergeant Miller," Hutch said, taking the cup.

"Hi, Vanessa, it's nice to meet you," Alex said, extending her hand to shake the woman's. "I'm Alex Taylor."

"The pleasure is mine, Chief," Miller said. "I was just telling Officer Hutchinson that the truck hasn't moved from the motel."

"Well, after a two-hour car drive with this guy," Alex said, hooking a thumb in Hutch's direction. "I'm just about ready to ruin someone else's weekend."

"Well, if you follow me, I'll take you over to the motel," Miller said.

"Lead the way, Sarge," Alex replied.

Alex and Hutch got back in the car and headed out of the parking, following the SUV.

"Stick your tongue back in your mouth, junior," Alex said as she took a sip of coffee.

"Huh?" Hutch replied. "What do you mean?"

"You know *exactly* what I mean," Alex replied as she removed the pack of cigarettes from her pocket and lit one.

"I think you're hallucinating, Chief," Hutch said.

"Which part, your tongue hanging out or you undressing her with your eyes?"

"Chief!"

"Not that I think there is anything wrong with that," Alex said, choosing to torment him a bit more. "She is kinda hot."

"I was simply having a professional conversation with her, that's all," Hutch said defensively.

"Hey, whatever helps get you through the night," she said sarcastically. "Once I take Childers in for questioning, you should have some free time to make your move."

"You're crazy," Hutch said.

"Uh huh," Alex said as she took a drag on the cigarette. "Just remember to get her cell number before we leave. I'm not good at playing match-maker."

"That's not funny," Hutch replied.

"I'm not joking," Alex said.

A few minutes later the two vehicles pulled off of Route 2 and into the parking lot of the Cherry Tree Hill Motel. They followed the Tahoe toward the rear of the location, pulling into the parking spot next to Ricky's truck.

Alex and Hutch followed Vanessa up the stairs to the second floor landing, followed by another uniformed trooper.

They made their way down to the room and Vanessa knocked on the door.

"Who is it?" a man's voice called out from inside the room.

"State Police," Miller answered.

The door opened slightly and a man peered out.

"Are you Ricky Childers?" Miller asked.

"Yeah, what's this all about?" he said. "I've spoken to you guys once already."

"These officers here would like to speak with you," Miller explained.

Alex stepped up to the door and took a long, hard look at the man.

If this was the guy Karla Grayson had married, life must have taken a brutal turn for the worse. He looked much older than his actual age, and the ratty mullet haircut he was sporting didn't do anything to help his appearance. The man was wearing an old faded white t-shirt, that barely concealed his beer belly, and a pair of boxer shorts. He rubbed his eyes as if he had just woken up.

"Mr. Childers, I'm Chief Taylor, from the Penobscot Police Department, this is Officer Hutchinson. We'd like to talk to you about your ex-wife."

"Is she dead?" the man asked. "Please tell me she's dead."

"No, she's not dead," Alex said angrily.

"Of course not," Childers replied gruffly. "You can't kill evil like that."

"Ricky, who is it?" a woman's voice called out from the back of the room. "If it's the cops again, you don't have to talk to them without a warrant."

He turned in the direction that the voice had come. "Can you just shut the hell up, Sapphire? It's none of your goddamn business."

56

Then he turned back to face Alex. "Sorry, she's the last person I need legal advice from. She slides down a pole for a living."

"Mr. Childers, I need you to come talk to me," Alex said. "It won't take long."

"Am I under arrest?" he asked.

"No," Alex said.

"Then why don't you and *Howdy-Doody* over there go fuck yourself," he replied and began to close the door.

Alex reached out and grabbed the door, forcing it backward.

"Listen, asshole," Alex said. "If you fuck with me again, I'll have you arrested for abduction and tossed into general population. You'll be lucky to be alive when, and if, your bimbo posts bail."

Something in the way she looked, told Childers that this wasn't a woman to screw around with.

"What the hell are you talking about?" he asked defensively. "I didn't abduct anyone."

"Then the interview will be *really* short," Alex replied. "We'll even give you a ride back here to *Shangri-La*"

"Ok, let me get dressed," the man said.

"Leave the door open," Alex said. "You've got one minute, or *Howdy-Doody* here will come in and give you a hand. Trust me, he's many things, but gentle isn't one of them."

Alex watched as Childers scrambled to get his clothes on. She was pretty sure it took a slight bit longer than sixty seconds, but it was fun watching him trip and fumble as he fought with his clothing.

"If I'm not back by dinner, Sapphire, call a lawyer," Childers said and stepped outside, closing the door behind him. "Let's make this quick, will ya? I've got places to be."

The man rode to the state police barracks in the back of the Tahoe as Alex and Hutch followed behind. A short time later they pulled into the parking lot of a squat, one story, tan brick building.

"Welcome to Middlesex Barracks, Chief," Miller said. "It's not pretty, but it's home."

"Trust me, I've worked in a lot worse," Alex said.

They walked into the barracks and Miller instructed the trooper with her to take Childers to one of the interview rooms.

"Coffee?" Miller asked.

"I'd love some," Alex replied. "I take it that this is a smoke free environment?"

"Yes, it is," Miller said. "If you follow this hallway, it will take you to the back door. That's where all the smokers congregate."

"Thanks," Alex replied and headed down the hall.

Once outside she lit up a cigarette and took in the scenery. The barracks was nestled in among the trees, and the air was crisp and clean. It was a far cry from her days in Brooklyn North. Suddenly the door behind her opened and Miller stepped outside holding two coffee cups, handing one to Alex.

"Thanks, Vanessa," Alex said.

"No problem, Chief," the woman replied.

"Please, call me Alex," she said. "I'm a long way from home. Besides, it wasn't so long ago that I wore stripes on my sleeves instead of stars."

"Hard to break old habits," Miller said.

"I know what you mean," Alex said.

"That's the funniest New Hampshire accent I ever heard."

"Yeah, I'm a transplant from New York City."

"Seriously?"

"Yep, born and raised, did sixteen years with NYPD."

"No shit?" Miller said. "What was that like?"

"Probably like here, just more of it."

"I doubt that," the woman said with a laugh. "You guys get many calls involving black bear or moose?"

"No, not really," Alex replied, "but we do have some enormous rats."

"Thanks, but I think I'll stick with the moose," Miller said. "I can't imagine what it's like to live in a big city like New York, let alone be a cop there."

"Everything is a lot faster," Alex said as she took a drag on her cigarette. "You don't get too many second chances to be wrong."

"I grew up watching NYPD shows on TV," Miller admitted. "It was one of the things that drove me into law enforcement."

"It's much more glamorous on TV," Alex said. "They have a much higher *conviction* rate than real life."

"Would you mind if I sat in on the interview with you?"

"No, not at all," Alex said. "It would probably make him more comfortable."

"Why do you say that?" Miller asked.

Alex took a final drag on the cigarette, crushing it out in a metal receptacle mounted on a wooden post. She glanced back over at Miller, giving her a head to toe *once over*. "Call it a woman's intuition."

"If you say so," Miller replied.

"Men love to be interrogated by women," Alex said. "It's either a character flaw or mommy issues. They think they are smarter, so they tend to talk a lot more. Bat your eyelashes, unbutton an extra button, and just listen. Most of the time they will dig the hole for you."

"I'll follow your lead," Miller said as the two women made their way back inside the barracks.

The interview room was small, with a metal table, secured to the concrete floor, and three chairs. Alex and Vanessa sat down across from Childers, while Hutch stood in the hallway and kept a watchful eye through the two-way mirror.

"So are you going to tell me what this is all about?" Childers asked.

"Well, Ricky," Alex said. "You've got some problems."

"Oh really," the man said defensively. "Why is that?"

"Because your son is missing and your ex-wife has painted you as the prime suspect in his disappearance."

"What do you mean Cory's missing?" Childers asked. "Are you sure? That's insane. Listen to me, that bitch is lying if she said I had anything to do with it."

"Well, that's why we are here," Alex said. "We want to give you the opportunity to share your side of the story, Ricky."

"What do you want to know?" the man asked.

"Tell me about you and Karla," she said.

"There's not much to tell," Childers replied. "We met after she came back from college. She was a lot of fun in the beginning, but after we got married, she became a pain in the ass. I guess we didn't share the same standard of living."

"How's that?" Alex asked.

"When we were going out she was a blast," Childers said. "A real party girl, if you know what I mean."

"Really," Alex replied. "Are you sure it wasn't just your winning personality that was bringing it out in her?"

"Well, I guess it could have been that," Childers said, completely missing the sarcasm in Alex's comment. "All I know is that once we got married, she started being a complete buzz kill."

"That didn't stop you from having a kid," Alex said.

"I thought she was on the pill. Her pregnancy was a complete shock to me."

"I bet it was," Alex said. "Then what happened?"

"She became an even bigger bitch," he said. "Nothing I ever did was right. I didn't work hard enough, I wasn't home enough, and I drank too much. All she ever did was break my balls."

"What did you do?" Alex asked.

"What would you have done?" the man asked rhetorically. "I started finding excuses to stay away. If we were doing a job out of town, I'd start staying away an extra day at a friend's place. It gave me a chance to unwind a bit before I had to go home and face the *wrath of Karla*."

"How the fuck did you manage to *unwind* with all that bullshit," Alex asked. "I can't imagine wanting to go home to someone who rode my ass like that."

Childers leaned back in the chair, relaxing a bit.

"It wasn't easy," he replied. "I couldn't hang out at a lot of my friend's homes anymore, because they didn't want her *drama* showing up on their doorstep."

"Man, that had to suck," Alex replied. "I mean, honestly, didn't she realize that bullshit would make you want to be home less?"

"You'd have thought," Ricky said. "We'd argue like cats and dogs. Then she would threaten to take Cory and leave me. I thought it was all just her usual crap, but then she actually did it."

"That had to piss you off."

"It did, at first," the man replied, "but then I got used to the quietness in the house. I'd actually forgotten what that sounded like. Suddenly my buddies were coming by and I realized that I might have lost a wife, but I gained my life back."

"What about Cory?"

"Oh, that was a different story," he said, getting visibly agitated. "That cunt used him like a pawn."

Suddenly, Childers remembered who he was speaking to.

"Oh, hey, I'm sorry, it's just that…"

"It's okay," Alex said. "I don't know about Sergeant Miller here, but I've known one or two of them in my time as well. So, how did she use Cory against you?"

"After the divorce she was all about the money," Ricky said. "They pegged me for child support based on when I was working full-time locally, but then the place I worked at closed down. So instead of having a steady income, now I was trying to find work, and most of what I found was just part-time."

"I take it she didn't quite understand your predicament."

"Understand? Hell, she couldn't give two shits less about my *predicament*. In fact, every time I was late with the *full amount* of her child support, she'd haul my ass back into court. I kept trying to explain that I was doing the best I could, but she didn't care. It was all about the money for Karla. I asked them to lower the child support, but they wouldn't budge. She said that I chose not to work full-time just to screw her."

"So what did you do?" Alex asked.

"I did the best I could," Ricky explained, "but I started having to do out-of-state gigs that the union found me. Then she had the nerve to bitch that I wasn't around enough for my son."

"You know I tried to call you on your cellphone when Cory went missing," Alex said.

"What number?"

Alex read off the number that Karla had given her.

"I haven't had that number in over a year," Childers replied. "I was paying so much to Karla that I couldn't afford the plan anymore. I had to get one of those pre-paid phones."

"Why didn't Karla have that number?" Alex asked.

"Are you nuts?" Childers said. "I was finally getting used to her *not* calling me every day, asking me where her money was."

"So why did you leave so suddenly on Friday?"

"Like I told you, times are tough. When I get a phone call from the union, I just ask when and where. They got me a two month job here in Montpelier working at a new *mega* hardware store chain, doing the electrical work for their grand opening. I just grab my gear and go."

"You had enough time to find Sapphire," Alex said.

"Sapphire, Diamond, Emerald,… Every town has a bar with a pole and a dozen women looking for a ticket out of there."

"So when was the last time you saw your son?" Alex asked.

"Probably a month or so ago," Childers said. "It was right before school started. I dropped off a check to Karla. She gets all *warm and fuzzy* when she gets money in her pocket, so she let me take him for a ride on the four-wheeler."

"And you haven't seen him since then?"

"No," the man replied.

"Any ideas on who might have taken him?"

Childers shook his head. "I honestly have no idea."

"Write down your phone number," Alex said, sliding a note pad over to the man.

"Why do you need that?"

"Since you will be working here for two months, if I need to speak with you I don't want to have to send Sergeant Miller over to your place of employment to haul your ass down to a pay phone. Unless you think your boss would be okay with that."

"Just don't waste my minutes on bullshit," the man said as he wrote the number down on the pad.

"Perish the thought," Alex replied as she took the pad back from him.

"So can I get a ride back to the motel?" Childers asked.

"I'll see what I can do," Miller said as she and Alex got up. "For now, you just wait here."

"Hey," Childers said as Alex walked out of the interview room. "I have a question."

"What is it, Ricky?"

"Since Cory is missing, do I still have to pay Karla child support?" Childers asked.

"You're a special kind of stupid, aren't you?" Alex replied, and then closed the door behind her.

"What do you want us to do with him?" Miller asked.

"What I want to do is illegal in just about every state," Alex said. "For the time being do you think you can keep an eye out on him and see what he does?"

"Oh yeah," Vanessa said. "This asshole just hit the top spot on my shit list."

Alex reached into her pocket and pulled out a business card, writing her cellphone number on the back.

"I owe you one," Alex said as she handed Miller the card. "Call me anytime, day or night, and I'll return the favor."

"I'll remember that," Miller said, pocketing the card.

CHAPTER SEVEN

"You okay, Boss?" Hutch asked as they crossed over the state line into New Hampshire.

"Yeah," Alex said as she stared out the window. "I'm okay."

"Are you sure?"

"Yeah, I am. It's just that no matter how often you handle cases like this, you never quite seem to be able to accept just how screwed up human beings can be."

"How so?"

"During the entire time interview, how many times did Ricky ask about his kid?"

"I don't think he did," Hutch replied.

"No, he didn't. That fucking idiot and his wife have spent so many years at each other's throats over money, that they have forgotten they have a kid together."

"You think he is involved?" Hutch asked.

"I don't know, Hutch," Alex replied, removing the pack of cigarettes from her pocket and lighting one up. "There's a lot of anger there. That causes otherwise normally intelligent people to do incredibly dumb things. That being said, in case you hadn't noticed, Ricky Childers is not what I would consider *normally intelligent*."

"Yeah, but do you think he kidnapped his own kid?" Hutch asked. "I mean that's messed up."

Alex took a drag on her cigarette and blew the smoke through the opening in the passenger window. "Hutch, I've seen parents do some pretty fucked up shit to their kids."

"Yeah, but who hurts their own kid?"

"Charles Evers came home one night and beat his wife into a coma. When we arrested him, he said that he had stopped by the landlord's apartment, but the landlord told him they had already paid the rent. He assumed his wife, Lorraine, had been fucking the landlord to pay the rent. Evers was a raging alcoholic who'd forgotten that he had paid the landlord the previous week. Anyway, after we locked him up and shipped her off to the hospital, we had Child Protective Services come out and pick-up their four children."

"That's fucked up," Hutch said.

"No, Hutch, that wasn't the fucked-up part," Alex said. "After Lorraine got out of the hospital, she contacted CPS to find out what was going on with the kids. When they told her that the four of them had been placed in foster care, she called the precinct in a panic."

"What was wrong?" Hutch asked.

Alex flicked the cigarette out the window, and quickly lit another one, taking a long drag as she relived the nightmare in her mind.

"It turns out that the Evers' had five children," she finally said. "Charles Evers thought the last kid wasn't his, so after he beat his wife senseless, he decided to do something about the baby. We found the remains in a backyard doghouse."

"Fuck," Hutch said, his hands gripping the steering wheel so tight his knuckles turned white.

"Life's cheap, Hutch," Alex said, her face a hard, cold, impenetrable mask. "The faster you accept that, the easier this job will be."

"So you think Ricky Childers might be involved?"

"I don't know," Alex said, "but until we do, I want you to turn that motherfucker's life upside down. By Monday morning I want to know everything about this piece of shit. Who he knows, where he has worked, how much he has earned down to the penny. I also want you to check his phone records, confirm that he got a call for a job."

"You know that it's Sunday night?" he said.

"Do you think Cory Childers knows that?"

"Sorry," Hutch replied. "I didn't mean it that way."

"I know, Hutch," Alex said as she leaned back in the seat and closed her eyes.

By the time they pulled into Penobscot it was nearly seven o'clock.

"You want to stop and get something to eat before I drop you off?" Hutch asked.

"No," Alex replied. "I don't think I can eat. I just want to go back home and have another go at the case folder. I keep feeling like I am missing something."

"Ok," Hutch said. "I'll drop you off and then head back over to the office to run checks."

"Don't stop with Ricky," Alex said. "Look into the whole damn dysfunctional family, warts and all. I want to put together a complete profile. Maybe there are others who have an axe to grind."

"You think something's up with Karla?" Hutch asked.

"They're both lying," Alex replied. "Which is not all that unusual for a divorced couple, but I'm just not sure why or who's lie is bigger."

When they pulled up at her house, Alex got out of the car.

"I'll call you if I find anything out," Hutch said.

"Ok, I'll see you in the morning," she said.

Alex walked into the dark house, flipping on the entryway light and hung up her coat. There was a chill in the house, so her first priority was to head over to the fireplace and get a fire going.

After she was done, she went to the kitchen and poured herself a much needed glass of wine. The long days had caught up with her, both mentally and physically, but she also knew that there would be more of them to come. Alex made her way into the living room and sat down on the couch. She took a sip, then set the glass on the table and lit another cigarette. She closed her eyes as she leaned back against the couch.

Alex knew that she needed to quit. It was bordering on chain-smoking now, but it was the only real satisfaction she had. The smoking allowed her to think, and right now she needed all the help that she could get.

She stared at the fire as it roared inside. She was transfixed by the flames as they danced across the logs. It was such a dichotomy, so beautiful and yet so deadly.

She finished her wine and took one final drag on the cigarette, before crushing it out in the ashtray. She got up and headed into the kitchen, setting her glass down on the counter before making her way back to the bathroom.

Alex turned on the shower, to let the water heat up, as she undressed. As steam filled the small room, she stepped into the shower, feeling the hot water cascading down over her head and body.

She stood in the shower for what felt like an eternity, letting the water wash away some of the stress that had been building up. It was her sanctuary, her escape, the only place she didn't have to be strong. Alex leaned her back against the tiled wall and let her body slide down until she was sitting on the floor. Then she began to cry, letting the façade of the *tough as nails* cop float down the drain.

A half hour later a shivering hand reached up, turning off the water and she got to her feet. Alex reached out to grab a towel from the rack and dried herself off. Then she headed into the closet where she slipped into a pair of dark blue sweatpants and a matching sweatshirt. On the way back to the kitchen, she stopped to grab a dry towel and wrapped her hair up in it.

Alex had just poured herself a glass of wine when the doorbell rang. She walked over to the end of the counter, removing the small handgun she kept in the kitchen drawer, and made her way to the front door. She peered through the peephole, seeing Doctor Peter Bates, family practitioner and Penobscot's medical examiner, standing on the other side.

"Oh, crap," she muttered as she reached up and removed the towel from her head. She dried her hair, as best she could, and hung it up on the hall tree.

For Alex, Peter had been one of the constant hints at normalcy in her life.

He, along with Mildred Parker, the former chief's wife, had become a good friend; one that didn't need anything from her professionally. That meant she could be as open as she wanted, and not fear that he was playing some type of angle. It also didn't hurt that he was easy on the eyes.

Bates was in his early thirties, with boyishly good looks, and bore a striking resemblance to a young James Dean. He had warm brown eyes and thick brown hair. She'd noticed that whenever he got nervous, he'd run his hand through it. He was just over six feet tall and prided himself on staying fit. Every so often, Alex would see him in the early morning hours running on the high school track.

She opened the door, keeping the small handgun hidden behind her back.

"If you were thinking about making a house call, I'd like to remind you I'm still very much *warm*," she said.

"That's not funny," Bates said. "I brought you food."

He held up a plastic bag and Alex could smell the familiar aroma of Chinese take-out. "Mrs. Lee said you like chicken lo-mein."

"Really?" Alex said as she opened the door wide to let him in. "And how exactly did you know I was home and that I hadn't already eaten?"

"I'd like to tell you," Bates replied as he sat the bag on the kitchen counter, "but I was sworn to secrecy."

"Really? And did this covert operative happen to resemble one of my *former* officers?"

"Don't go too hard on him, Alex," Peter replied. "He was worried about you."

Out of the corner of his eye, Bates caught Alex slipping the gun back inside the drawer.

"Were you expecting trouble?" he asked.

"How else do you think I've managed to remain *warm* all these years?"

"You need to start hanging around with a different class of people," he replied as he began removing the food containers from the bag.

"You're probably right about that," she said. "Want some wine?"

"I'd love some," Peter replied. "Hey, where are your forks?"

"Center drawer," Alex said as she removed another glass from the cabinet above the sink and poured him a glass.

"So how did your day go?" he asked.

"You want to talk shop?" Alex said with a laugh.

"I could tell you how my day went, but I wouldn't want to bore you."

"I don't know, Peter," Alex said. "Sometimes I wonder if boring wouldn't be a nice change of pace."

"Hutch said that you two had gone to Vermont on a case. Was it regarding Karla Grayson's son?"

"Yeah," Alex said as she picked up her wine glass and the food container, then made her way back to the couch.

"Not sure how you do it, Alex," he said, taking the seat next to. "I can't imagine doing your job every day, having to deal with so much pain and tragedy."

"You get immune to it after a while," she lied.

"If you say so," he said as the two of them ate.

"Thanks for dinner, Peter," Alex said. "I didn't mean to be so grumpy."

"Not at all," he replied. "I understand the stress you have. I don't have to deal with that. For me the clues are all in front of me, I just have to find them. You have to track them down, door-to-door, and I know that can be draining on a person; even someone as skilled at their job as you are."

Alex twirled her fork in the lo-mein and took a bite of the noodles, washing it down with a sip of wine. "Can you come to the next board meeting and be my representative? Tell those bastards I don't sit around on my ass all day wasting their money."

"What was it that Ron White used to say?" Peter asked. "'You can't fix stupid.'"

"No, but you can *kill* it," she replied, "so it doesn't breed."

"That seems drastic."

"That's only because most of your *clients* don't talk," Alex said. "Spend an hour with them telling you how you're not doing your job right, how you could do your job better, and why they should get someone to replace you."

"Is someone giving you a tough time on the missing boy?" Peter asked. "I mean for crying out loud, it's only been two days."

"No, not directly," she replied, "but you always hear the rumors, the snide comments. You can't help but get pissed."

"They're assholes, Alex. Worse than that, they are cowards who will never confront you, but will always let it be known *indirectly*, how you could do your job better."

"Thanks for the pep talk, Peter," Alex said. "The truth is, that bullshit is only getting to me because I feel like I have hit a brick wall with this case."

"You're doing the best you can, Alex. Not sure how you can do any more than that."

"Tell that to Cory Childers," she replied.

Alex took a sip of wine from her glass. It had been a long time since she wanted to get drunk, to just get to the point of being *comfortably numb*. She knew it was a bad sign, but it wasn't entirely unexpected. You never knew how you would respond to the stress of something major until it actually happened. Maybe it was more significant because a child was involved, or maybe she was just making excuses for the fact that she just wanted to get drunk.

"Are you okay," Peter asked.

"Huh? What?" Alex asked.

"I asked if you were okay."

"Sorry, I guess I zoned out. I can't seem to get my mind to shut off."

"You want more wine?" Peter asked.

"I'd love some," Alex replied, finishing what was left in her glass and handing it to him.

She grabbed the food container and began picking through it, selecting the chicken. The wine was making her light-headed and she knew she needed something to counter it. She hadn't had a decent meal lately and she was feeling the effects of it.

"Here you go," Peter said as he sat the glass back down in front of her.

"Thanks," Alex replied.

"So where do you go from here?" he asked, his hand pointing toward the papers lying on the floor.

"Fuck if I know," she replied. "Best lead I have is the father who's in Vermont and probably knocking the bottom out of a bar dancer as we speak."

"Gotta love a guy who is more concerned about getting his needs met then he is in finding his missing son."

"It sends up a red flag, doesn't it?"

"I guess I just don't get it," Peter said.

"What's not to get?" Alex asked. "To some people it's just sex. I used to work in a place where *booty calls* or *hook-up sex* was a dime a dozen. If the broad got knocked-up, that was her problem. Although, the reality was that she'd just get more public assistance. They called it getting a *pay raise* in the hood."

"I'm not so sure I like the world you used to play in," Peter said.

"I do have to say that it was never boring," Alex replied, taking a drink.

"Still, how do you live with that every day?"

"You learn to turn it off."

"Turn it off?" Peter said. "How the hell do you turn something like that off? I mean you just can't turn off life."

"I beg to differ, Doctor Bates," Alex said with a laugh.

Peter picked up his wine glass from the table and took a sip, staring at the flames crackling in the fireplace. He was a small-town physician who dealt with common colds, flu shots, and school vaccines. Occasionally he'd be called upon to stitch-up one of the high school football players or help at the local hospital.

Even his side gig as the town medical examiner was rather mundane. In fact, until Alex had shown up, the majority of his work had come courtesy of the local retirement home. Medically speaking, things were dull in Penobscot.

"I just don't understand that, Alex," he said.

"No one can, Peter. Not unless you've lived it."

Bates got up and walked over to the fireplace, kneeling down in front of it. He pulled away the screen and grabbed another log from the wood rack, setting it down on top of the others.

"It's like you're describing another world," he said, sitting back down on the couch.

"I am," Alex replied.

"I don't get it," Peter said. "How do two worlds so diametrically opposite from one another exist like this?"

"You don't get out much, do you?"

"I guess not," he replied, taking a sip of wine. "Maybe that's a good thing."

"It is," she replied. "The only problem I have is when people like you try to get involved in something you know nothing about."

"What do you mean?" he asked.

"Well, think of it this way," Alex said. "You're sitting at home, watching TV, and you see a news report about some poor unarmed person who was shot by the police. Right away, people jump to conclusions. They hear the media say *unarmed*, and they wonder how someone without a gun can be shot. The only problem is that they, like you, see things from a false perspective. They base it on what they *know* from the world they live in, not the world in which the incident occurred."

"I have a feeling you're going to tell me why they are different," Bates said.

"Let's say I pulled you over," Alex said. "What would you do?"

"I'd stop, and then I would get out my license and registration," he replied. "After that I would probably tell you how lucky I felt to get stopped by such an attractive looking officer."

Alex rolled her eyes as she took a sip of wine.

74

"Just for the record, that isn't a very effective opening line," she said, "but that illustrates my point. You're cooperative and doing everything that you are supposed to. You may not like the fact that you are being stopped, but you're not being combative."

Bates sipped his wine as he listened to Alex.

"In the world I worked in, that doesn't happen," Alex said. "You never knew when you walked up to the driver if you'd be staring down the barrel of a gun. In fact, most of the time they'd have open warrants, and they had no intention of *willingly* going back to jail courtesy of a female cop."

"Clearly that was their loss," Peter said with a laugh.

"You don't know what it's like to roll around the gutter with someone, at two o'clock in the morning, fighting over a gun," Alex said, her voice cold and monotone. "If you lose, they drape a flag over your coffin and the mayor says a prepared speech at your funeral. If you *win*, all the race baiters come crawling out of the woodwork and begin protesting your *brutality*. They pull out the sixth grade elementary school photo of the *victim*, and you hear story after story of how he was an *honor student* who wanted to rise above the life the system had given him. If you try to bring out the fact that he had a rap sheet, that went back years, including weapons and drug charges, you're instantly labeled a racist."

"I guess you're right," he said. "We live in a sheltered world here."

"That's not necessarily a bad thing," Alex replied. "It's just that when good people interject themselves in an issue, which they know very little about, it rarely ends well."

"You make it sound like an *us versus them* issue," Peter said.

"Think about it this way, Peter," she said. "There are only three types of people in the world: sheep, wolves, and the sheep dogs. The sheep are the good people. They are kind and caring. They have no real malice in their heart, no capacity for violence. If they hurt one another, it is generally the result of an accident. The sheep get up every day and live their lives in harmony with one another. They go off to work, or to school, and they just try to live peacefully. They genuinely want to believe that the world is a good place."

Alex reached out grabbing the pack of cigarettes off the table and lit one up.

"You said you were trying to quit," Peter said.

"I am," Alex said. "I said I was *trying* to quit, if I had quit I wouldn't be smoking."

"Point taken."

"As I was saying," Alex replied. "Then there are the wolves. Those are the ones that the sheep fear. They thrive by feeding on the weakest of the sheep. They are ruthless and take whatever they can get. The wolves have fangs and a propensity toward violence, which they will use whenever the opportunity presents itself. At the end of the day, the wolves do not concern themselves with the opinions of sheep."

"What about the sheep dogs?" Bates asked.

Alex smiled, swirling the wine around in her glass as she contemplated the answer to that question. She raised the glass to her lips and took a sip, setting the glass back down on the table.

"Sheep dogs are an oddity, Peter," Alex said. "I'm a sheep dog. We live in a gray area. The sheep don't trust us, because we remind them a lot of the wolves. We have the same fangs as the wolf and the same capacity for violence, but unlike the wolves, we have an inherent obligation to protect the sheep. Still, the sheep look down upon us, because we are a constant reminder that the wolves exist. They would prefer not to see us. That is until the day comes when the wolf appears. Then all the sheep huddle behind the lone sheep dog and pray that they can protect them."

"So what you're saying is that the sheep shouldn't question the means with which the sheep dogs deal with the wolves."

"More like those who would make war with their police should figure out how to make peace with criminals."

"Sounds ominous," Pete said.

"Does it?" Alex said, taking a drag on her cigarette before crushing it out in the ashtray. "I didn't mean it to be. I guess I'm just worn out."

"Come here," Peter said. "Let me hold you."

Alex grabbed her wine glass, taking a sip and set it on the table. She then leaned over, laying her head on Peter's shoulder and felt him wrap his arm around her shoulder. She closed her eyes, feeling the stress begin to melt away.

"Maybe you just need to take a vacation," Peter said. "Get away somewhere and let your hair down for a bit."

"Sounds like a wonderful idea," she said. "Seems like a lifetime since I've been to the beach."

"Not a bad destination when you're facing winter in northern New Hampshire," he said.

"With my luck, a meteor will strike and I'll have to cancel it," she replied.

"Well, so much for the power of positive thinking."

"I do seem to have a perpetual black cloud following me," Alex said with a laugh.

"I don't think you have a black cloud," Peter replied, "but try to avoid my house during thunderstorms, will you?"

Alex turned quickly, contorting her body till she was face to face with him.

"Oh really, Dr. Bates?" Alex said "And would you care to explain why?"

"No," Peter said, taking Alex's face in his hands and kissing her.

Seconds ticked away as their kiss grew from a spontaneous act to one being consumed by passion. Alex held his kiss, crawling up his body until she was straddling him. She wrapped her arms around his neck, submitting to her desires.

What the fuck am I doing? she thought.

She felt Peter's hands begin to caress her body. Alex broke the kiss and leaned back slightly, feeling his lips move down her jaw to her neck.

It has to be the wine, she reasoned to herself. *This is so not like me.*

Alex moaned as she felt one hand clasp the back of her head as the other moved down her back. Her body felt as if it was on fire and she allowed herself to get lost in the incredible rush of feelings.

Suddenly, she felt his hand slip beneath the edge of her sweatpants and felt the warmth of his hand on her skin. She reached back, slipping her own hand inside and sliding it down until it was on top of his.

Fuck!" Peter exclaimed, his eyes going wide, as pain radiated through his hand. "*Owh, Owh, Owh.*"

Alex slowly withdrew her hand, her thumb and index finger tightly clutching the webbing between Peter's thumb and index finger. A *compliance move* she had been taught many years ago at the police academy.

"Are you kidding me, Peter?" she said as she released her hold. "Did you really think that wine and Chinese take-out would get you to second base?"

"No, no, wait," Peter protested as he rubbed his throbbing hand. "It's not like that."

"Oh, so now I'm hallucinating," Alex said as she got up. "That really wasn't your hand on my ass?"

"Alex, I just got caught up," Peter tried to explain.

"Take it easy," she said, picking up the pack of cigarettes and lighting one. "I'm not angry."

Alex took a seat back on the couch and took a drink of wine.

"Is this the part where you say, 'it's not you, it's me?'" Peter asked.

She looked over at him; her eyebrows raised high in mock disbelief.

"Don't get carried away with yourself, slick," Alex said.

"Help me out here, Alex. I'm kind of getting mixed signals."

"It's nothing personal, Peter," Alex said, taking a drag on the cigarette. "Let's just say that I'm rusty in the *relationship* department."

"So, it's not that you *don't* like me?"

"Do you think I would have let you kiss me if I didn't like you?" Alex asked.

He lowered his head sheepishly and said, "No."

"What kind of girl do you think I am?" she asked.

Peter looked up at her. "A good girl?"

Alex laughed.

"You're almost right," she said. "I wouldn't have let you kiss me if I didn't like you, but I'm a *great* girl, not just good."

"So now what?" he asked. "Do we just forget that this happened?"

"No, Peter, we don't forget," Alex said. "You got to first base, be happy and we'll take it from there."

"As long as you're not angry," he said.

"Oh, trust me, you'd know if I was angry," Alex said. "Your bruised hand would be the last of your worries."

"You scare me sometimes, Alex," Peter said. "In a very odd, erotic sort of way."

"What can I say? I have a gift."

"Alex, I have to be honest, I am attracted to you."

"So your hand down my pants meant more than you just wanted to get lucky?"

"I got caught up in the moment," he said. "But yes, it meant more."

"I'm just giving you a hard time," Alex said.

"Thanks, I guess I deserve that."

"Listen, I like you too, Peter," she said, "but to be honest, I'm damaged goods. I have a bad track record when it comes to relationships and I don't want this to be yet another one of my screw-ups."

"It won't be," he replied.

"You sound so positive," Alex said.

"Perhaps I see something different in you."

"Maybe," she replied. "Or maybe you're just like every other horny guy who'd say anything to get a girl beneath the sheets."

"Alex, I'm thirty-six years old, I'm looking for more than a one-night stand."

"Good, so you'll understand when I say that I just want to take it slow," she said. "Is that okay?"

"That's perfect," he replied.

"So if I come back over there, you'll be okay with keeping your hands on the outside of my clothes?"

"At least for tonight," he said with a smile.

Alex crushed out the cigarette and got up. She walked back over to Peter, straddling his legs and reached her arms out, wrapping them around his neck. She stared into his eyes.

Something deep inside had awoken and she felt emotions swirling inside her that had remained dormant for so long. For a woman used to always being in control, the sudden rush of desire and sexual longing seemed to catch her by surprise. She bit her lip as she surrendered to the thoughts and images in her head.

"For tonight," she repeated, lowering her lips to his and kissing him.

CHAPTER EIGHT

"You okay, Boss?" Abby asked as she peered into Alex's office.

Alex was staring out the office window, her gaze fixated on the crystal clear blue sky.

"Huh?" she asked, swiveling in her chair to look over at the woman.

"Wow, you're zoned out today," Abby replied. "Does this case have you that perplexed?"

"Yes and no," Alex said. "That's still causing me sleepless nights, but it wasn't the case I was thinking about."

"Oh, really?" Abby replied. "What's his name?"

"Why do you think it's a man?"

"Call it woman's intuition."

"Close the door."

"Ooh, this sounds like it's going to be good," Abby said, shutting the door behind her and taking the seat across from the desk.

"Peter Bates stopped by my place last night," Alex said.

"Dr. Hunk? Are you serious?"

"Dr. *Hunk*?" Alex asked curiously.

"Well, it's not like Penobscot is crawling with good looking doctors," Abby said. "So when you say Dr. Hunk, everyone knows who you're talking about."

"I wonder what they call me?" Alex asked. "Chief *Bitch* has a nice ring to it, don't you think?"

"Nah, don't be so hard on yourself," Abby replied. "Besides, we're getting off track, what was Dr. Bates doing at your place?"

"He stopped by the house with Chinese food," Alex said. "He ran into Hutch at the restaurant, after we came back from Vermont. Next thing he showed up with take-out."

"And what happened?" Abby said, grabbing the cigarette pack from the desk and lighting one.

"I thought you quit?" Alex said with a stern look.

The two women regularly trained together at the gym and they rode each other unmercifully, constantly trying to push themselves further than the previous workout session. While they both worked out to stay in shape for the rigors of police work, Abby was also a semi-pro bodybuilder.

"That was only for the contest," Abby replied.

"I thought there was another contest coming up in January?"

"Shush, quit trying to change the subject," Abby said. "Get back to Dr. Hunk."

"Well, we ate, and had wine, and then we had more wine, and then,…"

"No, you didn't! Did you?" Abby asked, her eyes going wide in shock.

"No, we didn't," Alex retorted. "We were making out on the couch and then *someone's* hand decided it was time to head south for the winter."

"He didn't!" Abby exclaimed."

"Yep, he did, or at least he tried. It didn't last very long."

"What did you do?"

"Pressure point," Alex said as she grabbed the cigarette pack and lit one.

"Ouch. How'd the evening end up?"

"Actually, not too bad," she replied. "I just explained to him I liked him, but that I wanted to go slow. That I had too much baggage to go rushing into things."

"What did he say?" Abby asked.

"He was fine with it. After our brief chat, we went back to the previously interrupted make-out session, but with hands on the *outside*."

"Oh my God," Abby said, shaking her head. "You realize that if you two become an item, you'll piss off just about every woman in Penobscot."

"I can't think that far ahead," Alex said. "I'm still trying to figure out what I'm supposed to do. I can't remember the last time I even had a serious relationship."

"What's there to think about?" Abby asked. "Peter Bates is Penobscot's most eligible bachelor. He's drop dead gorgeous, he's a doctor, and he has the hots for you!"

"So what do I do?" Alex asked. "I'm beyond rusty with all this relationship bullshit."

"You play hard to get, boss," Abby said with a smile. "There's nothing else left for you to do. You're gonna have him eating out of your hand."

"I'm afraid that I may have scared him off."

"I doubt that," Abby said.

"Really?" Alex asked. "You don't think so? I mean, I didn't hold back. I tagged him good."

"Don't kid yourself. Men love a challenge. Give them something they want, they put it on a shelf and ignore it. Show them something they can't have and they become absolutely *possessed*. You went one better and chastised him. He'll be tripping over himself to make it up to you."

"I hope you're right," Alex replied. "If my luck with men holds true, I'll probably get served with a restraining order before lunch."

"Wanna bet?"

"No!"

"Why not?" Abby asked with a laugh. "Cause you know I'm right?"

"No, because you're gonna make me do something sadistically stupid, like those friggin' hundred rep sets."

"Please, girl. You know you love the *burn*."

"Yeah, I love the way it feels when I have to crawl to the bathroom in the morning to pee."

"Don't be such a boy," Abby said with a mischievous smile.

"Gym Nazi," Alex said.

"Don't hate the player, hate the game."

Alex looked up at the clock over the door. It was nearly three.

"Speaking of hating the game, I need to run over to the school and talk to Karla Grayson."

"Good luck with that," Abby said.

"Thanks," Alex said as she crushed out her cigarette and got up. "Call me if you need anything."

"Don't forget the gym tonight," Abby replied as she crushed out her own cigarette and followed her boss out the door.

"Oh, I almost forgot, I have to push it back to six thirty," Alex said. "I'm having dinner with Mildred Parker tonight."

"No problem," Abby said. "I'll do cardio at the beginning. This way I'll be nice and warmed up when you arrive."

"Awesome," Alex replied sarcastically, "another visit to the *House of Pain*."

Five minutes later, Alex pulled the unmarked car to the edge of the curb and put it in park. She'd had the misfortune of arriving just as the yellow buses had pulled into the school's long, u-shaped driveway, so she pulled her car over to the side of the road. As she waited for them to leave, she rolled down her window and lit a cigarette, watching as the kids streamed from the building.

"Like little rats abandoning a ship," she said with a chuckle as she watched them begin shouting and roughhousing.

The entire procession took about fifteen minutes before all the little urchins were finally loaded up and sent on their merry way. Slowly, a much wearier procession of teachers filed out of the building. They each headed over to their respective vehicles and quickly departed the parking lot. As Alex watched, Karla Grayson emerged and began heading toward her car. She was just about to drop the shifter into drive when she heard a voice call out the woman's name. She looked up to see John Connolly wave and walk over to where Karla was standing next to her vehicle.

Alex reclined the seat, making as low a profile as she could as she monitored the two of them. As she watched, they talked and Connolly pulled some papers out of his bag. He laid them on the hood of Grayson's car and Alex watched as the two continued their conversation, pointing back and forth to the documents. Within minutes, their vehicles were the only two left in the lot.

The two of them looked up furtively, glancing around the lot, and then back toward each other. Connolly gave Grayson a hug, one hand moving down her back and then he kissed her slowly on the lips.

"Hello," Alex said. "That's no *friend* kiss."

A moment later they separated, but held each other's gaze.

Guess I had you figured out all wrong, Mr. Connolly, she thought.

Karla got into her car and Connolly closed the door for her. She watched as Grayson's car pulled to the edge of the parking lot and then turned, heading north. Connolly waved, then walked over to his car and got in. Alex watched as he pulled out of the lot and headed west. Once he was out of sight, she put the car in drive and pulled away from the curb. She turned left at the corner and began following the vehicle.

She kept close enough to keep Connolly's car in sight, but far enough back so she did not tip him off that he was being followed. The black Charger was well suited for this, blending in nicely with the late afternoon fall shadows. If the man had checked his rearview mirror, he would have seen the *shadow* of a car and nothing more discernible.

The car pulled up to the Liberty Arms apartment complex on Franklin Street, in the southwest part of town. Alex watched as the man got out and headed over to an exterior staircase. He walked up to the second floor and entered one of the apartments. She reached into the glove compartment and removed a pair of small binoculars.

The old binoculars had served her well during her anti-crime days back in Brooklyn. She would sit up on the rooftops in the projects, watching drug deals going down and calling in the descriptions of the perps to the marked units waiting to grab them. Now she used them to scan the license plate of the Ford, which she wrote on the note pad sitting on the passenger seat.

What the fuck are you two up to? She wondered.

Alex pulled away from the curb and headed back north, making her way out to Karla Grayson's house. She was just pulling up the driveway as she watched the woman pull out of the barn on a dark green quad-runner.

"Hey, Chief," Grayson said as Alex pulled up beside her.

"Hi, Karla," Alex replied. "Nice quad."

"Yeah, it's an older one, but I'm more comfortable with it and it gets me where I need to go," she replied. "Besides, Cory rides the new one."

"I'm sorry, am I interrupting something?"

"No, I just like to take a ride in the evening. It kind of helps to clear my thoughts a bit. It lets me get the screaming kids out of my ears and replace it with the sounds of nature."

"Sounds wonderful to me," Alex replied. "How big of a place do you have?"

"Oh, it used to be much bigger when my dad farmed it," Karla said, "but there were no sons to take over the family business. Over the years, he sold off large sections. Right now it's down to about fifty acres, but most of that is all wooded. The property backs up to a section of the Birney River and I like riding down there. Sometimes we'll take the poles down and do a little fishing. Cory enjoys that."

"Lucky kid," Alex said. "I spent a few weekends down on the river myself, but I apparently repel trout."

"Honestly, you're better off on the Androscoggin," Grayson said. "That's where my dad used to take me. Cory isn't as picky."

"Thanks, I'll remember that," Alex said.

"I take it that this isn't a social call?" Grayson asked. "So, do you have any news?"

"Not sure," Alex said, putting the car into park. "I finally tracked down your ex."

"Really?" Grayson asked excitedly. "Where?"

"Vermont," Alex said. "He's working a commercial job up there."

"Was there any sign of Cory?" she asked.

"No, no sign of him," Alex replied. "I'm afraid he wasn't much help. He denied having anything to do with it. Said he left town Friday night when he got a sudden job offer. We're in the process of verifying that."

"So that's it?" Karla asked. "Nothing is going to happen to him?"

"We didn't have anything to hold him on so we had to let him go," Alex explained. "I have the locals watching him to see if he goes anywhere. If he does, they'll follow him and hopefully we can pick him up on something that will allow us to have some leverage to use against him."

"Well, if he is working, maybe now he'll have the money to make up the arrears."

"Yeah, well, I'm not sure if I would hold my breath on that one," Alex said. "It seemed like he might be making a large donation to the local booze and stripper's association."

"Christ, it never ends with that man," Grayson replied. "Did he even seem upset that his son was missing?"

"Well, I think we caught him a bit off guard, he looked like he was a little overwhelmed with everything."

"You don't need to make excuses for him," she replied. "There is a reason that I'm not married to him anymore."

"Not sure what to think," Alex said as she reached into her pocket and withdrew the pack of cigarettes. "I honestly couldn't get a read off of him."

"Ricky was always tough to read," Grayson replied. "It was infuriating when we would argue and I couldn't tell if he was pissed off or just bored."

"I'd imagine that would be annoying."

"There were times I'd have done anything just to get a reaction."

"I bet that took a lot to get over, in order to move back into the dating world, huh?" Alex asked as she took a drag on her cigarette.

"I'll let you know," Karla replied. "To be honest, I haven't found the courage yet to get my feet wet. I decided to stick to just teaching and raising Cory. I figured there would be time later for romance."

"Wow, you're better than me," Alex said. "I was the queen of the rebound relationships."

"Once bitten, twice shy, I guess."

"Completely understandable," Alex replied. "I blame it entirely on my mother. She tripped walking down the sidewalk and dropped me on my head as a child. I think it made me a bit slow to learn."

Grayson laughed. "Well, if it is any consolation, it probably beats going to bed alone every night."

"I don't know," Alex said. "I'm on a self-imposed sabbatical."

"Oh yeah?" Karla asked. "How's that working out for you?"

"I kind of enjoy having complete control over the remote and not having to worry about whether the seat is up or down," Alex replied.

"There is that," Karla said. "You know what always used to get to me? Having to be the one who decided what to make for dinner."

"Oh, hell yeah," Alex replied. "I mean, why is it always the woman's responsibility? I'd come home from work and he'd be sitting there with a beer in one hand, the remote in the other, and the first words out of his mouth was 'what's for dinner?' I'm lucky I'm not in prison."

"Please, Ricky did that to me all the time. The only thing worse was when he wouldn't come home, didn't call, and when he stumbled through the door, he'd want to know where his dinner was. That and whether I was *in the mood*."

"I understand why you're hesitant to get back in the game," Alex said. "I question whether or not I want to get back to dating as well."

"They make it hard," Karla said.

"You know what the funny thing is?" Alex asked. "I have a friend who is a lesbian. I thought that had to be the best of both worlds. Turns out, no, it's the same shit. Her significant other took on the role of the husband. Comes home, bitches about the same thing. You can't win."

"I think I'll maintain my autonomy for now."

"You and me both," Alex replied. "Hey, I've kept you long enough. Go enjoy your ride. If anything changes, I'll let you know."

"Thank you," Grayson replied as she put on her helmet and started the quad.

Alex watched as the woman drove off. She took a long drag of the cigarette and flicked it out the window.

"What are you hiding, Karla?" Alex said as the quad disappeared over a hill.

She dropped the car into drive and made a u-turn, heading back down the driveway. When she had pulled onto the main road, she reached over and picked up the cellphone.

"Hey, Chief," Hutch said when he answered.

"Put on your detective hat, junior," she said. "I need you to do me a favor."

"Okay, what do you need me to do?"

"Are you in the office?"

"Yeah."

"Okay, I want you to run a name for me, give me everything you can dig up," Alex said as she pulled the car over to the side of the road.

"You ready to copy?" she asked.

"Shoot."

She grabbed the notepad from the seat.

"Okay, the name is John Connolly, unknown date of birth, but I have a license plate number. It's a New Hampshire tag, tom-king-four-two-one. It should come back to a red Ford Focus. The registered address might be the apartment complex on Franklin."

"John Connolly, the teacher?"

"Yep," Alex replied.

"You think he is involved in all of this?"

"Not sure, but I think Karla Grayson is lying about her relationship with him," Alex said, "and that makes me curious."

"Okay, I'll get right on it," Hutch said.

"Hey, while you're at it, get me a printout of Ricky Childers support payments, will you?"

"Sure thing. Are you looking for anything in particular?"

"Curious to see how timely he is," Alex replied. "How are we doing on those re-interviews?"

"I got them done, nothing new. I went out to speak to Mrs. Richards today, but she's on vacation. She is supposed to be back at the end of the week. I'll follow-up with her then."

"Okay," Alex said. "Oh, and Hutch, the next time you have the urge to play matchmaker, you'll be walking a foot post down at the marina, in February. Do I make myself clear?"

"Crystal, ma'am."

"That's my boy," she said. "Hey, do me a favor and mark me off-duty."

"Sure thing," he replied. "I'll call you as soon as I know something."

"Thanks."

CHAPTER NINE

It was just after five o'clock when Alex pulled up in front of Mildred Parker's home. Mildred was the wife of the former chief of police, Charlie Parker, and they had met when Alex had taken the job.

Mildred was a lifelong resident of Penobscot. She was one of those people who knew everyone and everything that went on in the city. But she was also a very sweet woman who had graciously opened her home, and her dining room table, to Alex. Whenever Alex had a question about someone, or just needed to talk, her door was always open. She had become a surrogate mother to her, bringing some semblance of normalcy into Alex's life.

For her part, Alex made sure that the members of the department looked after Mildred. After all, she was family. She was part of the thin blue line, which bound a special group of people, not by blood, but by something much deeper. At times it was as dysfunctional as an Irish family, but when one of them was in danger; they would put aside all conflict as they looked to the threat. As the saying goes, *In this family, no one fights alone.*

Mildred may not have worn the uniform, but she had been an officer's spouse and that was just as tough. She didn't respond to the calls, but she had sat up at night waiting, wondering if her husband would come home. She might not have to deal with the stress of the job, but she dealt with the aftermath. Everything about being a cop was tough, but nothing about being a cop's spouse was easy.

Alex got out of the car and made her way up the walkway. The living room light was on and it cast a warm glow through the front picture window, lighting up the front porch. It was so inviting and Alex paused for a moment, taking in the entire scene.

She was a city kid, born and raised. The guys in the seven-three used to give her a hard time, claiming that she was from *East Cupcake*, the term used to identify those who lived out on

Eastern Long Island. But the town she had grown up in had a population of over three hundred thousand residents. It might have lacked some of the hardcore grit of New York City, but it was certainly not *Little House on the Prairie* either.

As Alex looked around at the tree-lined street, dotted with inviting homes, she smiled. There was something to be said about small town life.

She turned back toward the door and rang the doorbell, listening to the melodic chime ringing inside the house.

"Come in," Mildred's voice called out.

Alex opened the screen door and stepped inside. Immediately her senses were overwhelmed by the wonderful scent of home cooking.

"Hello," Alex called out.

She made her way into the living room, laying her jacket over the back of the couch.

"Good evening, my dear," Mildred said as she walked into the dining room, carrying a large glass bowl. "You have perfect timing."

"When it comes to food, yes I do," Alex said with a smile. "Can I help you with anything?"

"No," Mildred said, laying the bowl in the center of the table. "You just sit down and relax. Iced tea?"

"Yes, please," Alex replied.

Mildred returned to the kitchen and emerged a few moments later, carrying two large glass tumblers. She placed one glass down in front of Alex and then took the seat opposite from her.

"It looks superb," Alex said. "But you didn't have to go through all this trouble."

"Chicken and dumplings isn't any trouble," Mildred replied. "Especially for you, since I don't imagine you have been eating all that well lately."

"I can't argue with that," Alex said with a frown.

"Then let's pray for some better days, shall we?" Mildred asked.

"Yes, ma'am," Alex said, bowing her head.

"Dear Heavenly Father, we come to you this evening to give you thanks and praise for this meal," Mildred prayed. "We also ask that you bless our time together this evening and I once again beseech you to put a hedge of protection around Alex and all the members of the police department. They are your protectors, Father, and I ask that you keep them safe always. In Jesus' name, I pray. Amen"

"Amen," Alex repeated, looking up toward Mildred.

"So, how are things going?" Mildred asked as she removed the lid from the glass bowl.

"I've had better days," Alex replied.

"I take it that things aren't going well on your missing child case?" Mildred asked as she served dinner.

"No," Alex said dejectedly. "I'm hitting a wall with suspects."

"Charlie always said investigating cases was ninety percent hard work and ten percent luck, but that ten percent didn't come easy."

"I'd be happy with one percent luck right now," Alex replied.

"Do you have any suspects?"

"I have one," Alex said, "but it's not as strong as I would like."

"It's a good thing you work hard," Mildred said with a smile as she handed the plate to Alex. "Is your suspect family?"

"Yeah, Ricky Childers, Cory's dad," Alex replied and took a bite.

"Oh that boy has always been up to his neck in trouble."

"That's sort of the picture I got from his ex, Karla," Alex said. "Did you know him?"

"Oh yes, the Childers had quite the reputation in Penobscot," Mildred replied as she finished her plate and placed the cover back on the bowl. "Charlie had quite a few run-ins with them over the years. He locked both of them up several times."

"Anything serious?" Alex asked.

"Oh, the usual family arguments," Mildred said. "Ricky's parents, Mark and Joellen, had what I could only describe as a love / hate relationship."

"As in they loved to hate one another? Alex asked.

"Exactly," Mildred replied. "On top of that, they both had a big problem with the bottle."

"So they were domestic arrests?"

"Mostly," Mildred said, "but Mark had a tendency to end up at the bar and then he'd try to drive home. Charlie, and several of the other officers, arrested him for DUI."

"Sounds like they were a lovely family," Alex said as she took a sip of her iced tea.

"Let's just say that Ricky's home life wasn't what you would call *stable*," Mildred said. "Neither parent was particularly suited to raising a child, let alone three."

"I didn't know Ricky had any siblings," Alex said.

"Not unusual," Mildred said. "Ricky was the youngest; Joellen and Mark, had given up the other two for adoption before he was born. It seemed like they were quick to make them and just as quick to kick them to the curb."

"Amazing."

"In all honesty, I can't say that it was the wrong thing to do," Mildred replied. "Like I said, Mark was a raging alcoholic with an equally bad temper, and Joellen was prone to sleep around with whoever was more sober than Mark. Rumor going around was that they kept adopting out the kids, because they weren't sure they were Mark's."

"I've known a few folks like that in my day," Alex said.

"Well, it didn't sit too well with Joellen's parents. When they put Ricky up for adoption, that is when Joellen's dad, Roger Berman, blew a gasket. He took them to court and fought them for custody of Ricky."

"How'd that go over?" Alex asked.

"Like a lead balloon. It damn near divided the town. I knew Roger most of my life. I was childhood friends with his wife, Arlene, good Lord rest her soul. He was everything the Childers family wasn't; a respectable member of the community who ran an insurance company, here in town. He was also a deacon at the First Baptist Church and a former city board member. The Childers, well, let's just say that they were on the other side of the tracks; far, far away, on the other side. Their ilk started raising all sorts of ruckus in town. Someone even shot up the outside of Roger's house."

"You're talking Hatfield and McCoy feuding."

"Pretty much," Mildred said. "It always amazed me. They didn't want the kid, but they didn't want Joellen's parents to have him either."

"You wonder why he's so screwed up," Alex said.

"There was a rumor going around that Mark and Joellen were getting paid for the kids, and that was the reason they were fighting it. Supposedly they stood to lose money on the deal."

"Selling kids?"

"Private adoption," Mildred replied. "Allegedly they were being reimburse for the expenses related to the pregnancy, doctor's visits, etc.."

Alex shook her head in disgust. "That' some bullshit, but it explains why they didn't want to lose their money train."

As disgusting as it sounded, Alex knew it wasn't all that unusual. She had known a number of women in Brooklyn North who had turned pregnancies into a thriving business. Every time they got *knocked-up* it was like getting a cost-of-living pay raise for them. One girl that had five kids before she was twenty-two. She and her grandmother had a brilliant scam going, she'd have the kid and then the grandmother would contact children's services, claiming that the granddaughter was incapable of providing care. They gave the grandmother kinship foster care status and the state paid her to raise her grandbabies, to the tune of three-thousand dollars a month.

There was little oversight on these programs, because of the ever increasing demand and lack of investigators. Most applications were rubber stamped, especially if there was a lengthy family history. Occasionally some of the investigators got in on the act, getting a kick-back for fast tracking bogus applications. In the end, no one really cared, because it wasn't their money.

"So what happened?" Alex asked.

"Halfway through the court case, Mark got locked up on a DUI charge in Laconia. After they shipped Mark off to prison, it left Joellen without someone to pay the bills, so she hooked up with another guy and they left town in the dark of the night. Ultimately, Roger won the case and got custody of Ricky."

"What about Mark's parents? Didn't they have anything to do with Ricky?"

"Well, Mark was the way he was for a reason, dear," she replied. "The Childers' clan wasn't highly regarded for their parenting skills."

"Gotcha," Alex said. "So the maternal grandfather raised Ricky?"

"Oh God, did that man love that boy," she said.

"So what happened?" Alex asked.

"Genetics," Mildred said with a sigh. "By the time the teen years rolled around, Roger wasn't a youthful man. He couldn't keep up with Ricky and he just lost all control. Ricky started hanging out with some of the wrong kids and it went downhill from there. It killed Roger to think he had put so much effort into saving him, only to watch it all slip away."

"It's sad when you realize that, no matter how much effort you put into them, kids are their own persons and they have their own baggage."

"I think that was a very hard lesson for Roger to learn, watching Ricky just turn his back on him."

"So what happened with Ricky?"

"After he *barely* graduated high school, he left home," she said. "He and some of his friends got a place down by the south end of town."

Alex knew the area. It was one of those perennial places where the down on their luck types gravitated toward. During the summer months they would have to contend with an up-tick in drunk and disorderly calls. During the winter months it would switch to domestic calls, as the frigid weather kept everyone inside and on each other's nerves.

"It broke Roger's heart. He used to say he was just glad that his wife wasn't around to see it. He had always believed that Ricky would follow him into the insurance business, but the business died when he did."

"How long ago did he pass away?" Alex asked.

"It had to be right after Ricky and Karla got divorced," she said. "I think that was the final straw. I spoke to him when they had first gotten married, and he seemed genuinely happy. He believed that Karla would set Ricky on the straight and narrow. Then when they filed for divorce, he just gave up. I think the thought of losing his daughter, and then his grandson, just drained the will to live right out of him."

"Another kid ending up in another broken home," Alex replied.

"Basically."

"In retrospect, you'd have thought Ricky would have wanted better for his own kid."

"Deep down inside I think he did," Mildred replied, "but wanting something doesn't make it happen. Roger used to say how angry Ricky was about what happened to him and that he blamed Roger."

"How so?"

"He said that as Ricky got older, he believed that if Roger hadn't taken his parents to court to get custody that they would still be together."

"So he forgot the fact that they tried to put him up for adoption?"

"Selective memory, my dear," Mildred said. "Many kids have it these days."

"That's a helluva thing," Alex replied.

"Well, with both his parents gone, he created an alternative history, one where his parents loved him, but were hurting financial so they had to leave. Then he blamed Roger for not helping them out and breaking up their family."

"So the one sympathetic person in Ricky's life, who tried to do the right thing, gets blamed as the evil guy."

"That about sums it up," the Mildred replied.

"I'm so glad I don't have kids," Alex said.

"Oh, you're still young and I wouldn't rule them out altogether," Mildred said.

"If anyone's going to give me gray hair, it will be me and my poor life choices," Alex said with a laugh.

"As you get older, you call them *formative life experiences*. It sounds much better. Besides, I'm sure Dr. Bates has much better genes than Mark Childers."

Alex looked up to see a wry smile on Mildred Parker's face.

"There are no small town secrets, my dear."

"I'll try to remember that," Alex said. "Let me ask you a question. Just for argument's sake, does Ricky have any other family living in the area?"

"Not that I'm aware of," she said. "Neither of his parents ever returned to Penobscot."

"Karla said Ricky told her they were both dead."

"It's been a while since I heard about them, but I'm pretty sure they are both still alive," Mildred replied.

"What makes you say that?" Alex asked.

"Well, I remember Charlie having to go down south for a court case. Mark had an outstanding case in Penobscot for a hit-and-run vehicle accident, but he skipped town. He got himself arrested for DUI in Laconia where an elderly woman was badly injured in a traffic accident. They asked Charlie to come down and testify. The judge apparently threw the book at him, gave him ten years at the state prison in Concord. Last I heard, Mark found God in prison and was working at a ministry for recovering alcoholics in Plymouth."

"That's interesting," Alex said. "What about Ricky's mom?"

"Joellen had been living in either Littleton or Franconia, but that was a few years back. I guess he has two siblings living somewhere, but I don't even know who you could talk to find that information out."

"I'll look into it," Alex said. "I'm beginning to enjoy hitting my head against brick walls."

"Don't be so hard on yourself," Mildred said. "You're very smart and very tenacious. If anyone can figure this out, you can, Alex; with or without luck."

"Thanks for the vote of confidence," Alex said. "Oh, do you know if he had an uncle?"

"He did, Emmitt Childers," Mildred replied, "but he passed away about three years ago in a construction accident."

"Figures," Alex replied as she finished her meal and set her napkin on the table.

"Go have a cigarette while I get coffee and dessert ready."

"Are you sure I can't help?"

"No, I enjoy this, dear," Mildred said. "Besides, I gave you a lot to digest."

Alex got up from the table and walked over to the couch. She removed her cigarettes and lighter from the jacket pocket, along with her notepad, before heading outside.

The cool evening air felt good as she lit up a cigarette and sat down on one of the chairs. She opened the notepad and began writing what Parker had told her.

It seemed odd that Ricky had told Karla that his parents were dead, but maybe he was just too embarrassed. Creating a story was much easier than actually introducing your new wife to the crazy in-laws.

Either way, she'd make a point to track them down and see if they were still alive and kicking. Maybe a little heat would cause cracks to develop in the story.

Alex looked up as she heard the screen door open.

"I thought you'd like a cup of coffee with your cigarette," Mildred said as she handed Alex the mug.

"Thank you."

"I don't want to lecture you, dear, but you know that you should quit," Mildred said as she sat down in the other chair.

"I know," Alex replied, closing the notepad. "Trust me; it's on my to-do list."

"I smoked for thirty years, so I know how hard it can be."

"I didn't know that," Alex said.

"Oh yes, after dinner Charlie and I would both come out here with our coffee and relax. It was a nice way to unwind from the day."

"Why did you quit?"

"My sister developed breast cancer," Mildred said. "It was a wake-up call for me. I tried to get Charlie to quit, but he was always a stubborn mule."

Alex looked over at Parker, who was gazing out toward the street. She had a pained look on her face.

"Maybe if I tried harder, he might still be alive," she said.

"Don't do that, Mildred," Alex said. "Don't believe for one moment that you didn't do enough."

Mildred turned and looked at Alex.

"Did I?" the woman asked. "Or did I just shut my mouth and pretend to be the dutiful wife?"

"Charlie knew, just as I know, that these damn things are bad for your health and, just like me, he continued to do it."

"So does that mean you are going to ignore me too?" Mildred asked.

"You are one devious lady, Mildred Parker," Alex said with a smile.

"You think so?"

"Oh yes," Alex replied, a smirk growing on her face as she crushed the cigarette out in the ashtray. "That was nicely played."

"So you're going to quit?"

"Eventually," Alex said, getting up from the chair, "but not until after dessert."

"I guess it's a start," Mildred replied as the two women headed back inside.

CHAPTER TEN

"Rise and shine, Chief Taylor," Alex heard the voice say when she answered her cellphone.

"Fuck you, Rookie," she replied groggily, rolling over in bed to see what time it was. "Why are you calling me at five thirty in the fucking morning?"

"I'm on my way to 1PP and I was bored," Maguire said with a chuckle. "I figured you'd be sleeping in."

Alex sat up in bed, turning on the night light, and reached for the pack of cigarettes.

"You know how mean I am when I don't get my beauty rest," she said, lighting the cigarette.

"So that explains the problems we had all those years we were partners," he replied.

"Bite me," she said, taking a drag.

"You keep saying that and one day I will," Maguire said.

"Come on up, tough guy," Alex replied. "I'll make sure you get the best cell."

"You know there ain't no jail cell that can hold me, Alex," Maguire said.

"Hmmmm, we'll see," she replied. "So are you earning your pay yet, Commissioner?"

"I'm working up to it," Maguire laughed. "I don't want to solve all the problems in the city overnight. Otherwise I won't have a job."

"Spoken like a typical bureaucrat," she replied.

"How about you?" he asked.

"Oh no, I have to work for a living. No free passes up here in God's country."

"Please spare me. Is someone tipping over trashcans?"

"Actually, I have a missing eight-year-old kid, smartass," she replied. "Disappeared last Friday and hasn't been seen since."

"Sorry to hear that, Alex," Maguire said, the levity gone from his voice. "Any suspects?"

"No, not really," she replied, taking a drag on the cigarette. "Mother was having dinner at the fair and the kid asked to walk over to his friend's house. Made it there, but disappeared on the way back."

"Father?"

"Separated," she said, pulling her knees up to her chest and running her hand through her hair. "I tracked him down to some dive motel in Vermont; he's got a union job doing electrical work at a new mega store."

"You getting any vibes?"

"The father is kind of hinky; he likes his booze and bimbos more than he does making his monthly payments. The mother's got a boy-toy that she's trying to hide. So far nothing has popped on the *pedo* front," Alex replied. "I just can't seem to pin anything down. It's like the kid got sucked up by a UFO."

"Yeah, well I have yet to see a confirmed case of an ET doing a *snatch* and *grab*," Maguire said. "So unless you come up with some alien *goo* at the crime scene, focus on the mortal."

"This isn't my first rodeo, you know."

"Well, I thought the cold air and pine sap might have made you a bit fuzzy regarding the fundamental basics of police work," he said.

"Fundamental, my ass," Alex said. "You forget how I *carried* you when you were a *wet behind the ears* rookie."

"Hey, just because I had to slow myself down to let the rest of you keep up—"

"Yeah, yeah, whatever helps you sleep at night."

"So what are your plans?" he asked.

"I've got the locals in Vermont babysitting the father, so I think I will go fishing into the new boyfriend's past and see what pops up."

"Have you had any interaction with the guy yet?"

"Yeah, I had a brief conversation with him at mama's house. Neither let on they were anything more than colleagues. Then I saw them swapping spit outside the school where they work. Figured there is a reason they're trying to hide the relationship."

"She's a teacher, huh?" Maguire asked.

"Get your mind out of the gutter," Alex said.

"How'd you know it was in the gutter?"

"You're a man, you breathe air, where else would it be?"

"So, are you wearing a *uniform* yet, Alex?" Maguire asked teasingly.

"Guess you'll just have to come up and find out, won't you?"

"I think I'm due some vacation," Maguire replied.

"Yeah, I'm sure the city will be happy to see you leave," Alex said. "I mean it's not like they've experienced anything major, like terror attacks, with good old *black cloud* around. Oh, wait a minute, silly me, they have."

"That's cute," he replied.

"Besides," Alex said, taking a drag on her cigarette. "After you *disappeared* with me last time, do you think Melody will ever let you out of her sight again? She's probably terrified I'll corrupt her poor little James."

"Hey, I got a bad connection, Alex," Maguire said. "It's gonna sound like I hung up, but you just keep talking."

"Bye, James," Alex replied as she crushed the cigarette out in the ashtray. "Love ya."

"Me too, Alex, stay safe."

Alex laid the phone down on the night table.

"*Bye, James. Love ya,*" she repeated, her eyes wide in disbelief at what she had just said. "You fucking idiot, what the fuck were you thinking?"

Alex grabbed the pillow next to her on the bed, bringing it up to her face and screamed into it. She let the pillow drop into her lap and leaned back against the headboard, staring blankly at the ceiling. It was the closest she had ever come to saying how she truly felt about her old partner.

The brief conversation replayed itself over and over in her head. She didn't recall hearing any uncomfortable pause on his part. His response seemed perfectly in-sync with hers.

"*Me too,*" she said, repeating his words. "What does that mean?"

Alex looked over at the alarm clock. It was set to go off in fifteen minutes, so there was no point in her trying to go back to sleep. She swung her legs over the side of the bed and got up. She grabbed the robe from the end of the bed and slipped it on, before heading to the kitchen to turn on the coffee maker.

When the coffee was done brewing, she poured a mug, then grabbed a pack of cigarettes from the kitchen counter and headed out to the front porch.

Alex sat down in one of the Adirondack chairs and took a sip of coffee as she stared up into the black sky; the countless multitudes of stars sparking like diamonds above her. A wind kicked up and she heard the whistling sound it made as it rushed through the pine trees. She lit up her cigarette and inhaled deeply, enjoying the peacefulness of the moment.

It was sad to think many of those who lived up here had grown complacent to the beauty which surrounded them. This was something she never tired of. She remembered how, as a child, she would gaze up into the night sky. On a clear evening, she would try to count the stars above her. Never could she have imagined that she would ever see this many.

Being a city-girl, she had grown up to the ambient sounds of urban living, neighbor's voices, traffic, car horns, and sirens. Now, as she sat here, she heard nothing but nature in its most pristine form. She took a sip of coffee, letting the heat from the mug warm her hands.

Sunrise was still more than an hour away, but even now the shadows were withdrawing. Soon the first hints of daylight would break the horizon, filling the sky with pink and yellow strands, and the world would grudgingly come to life.

Will Cory Childers be watching the same sunrise? she wondered.

Alex took another drag on her cigarette. Something had to break in this case. She couldn't bear to think it would just go cold and be the end. Someone knew something, someone saw something, even if they didn't realize the relevance of what they knew or had seen. Now she just had to find them.

Every cop understood that you couldn't solve every case, but that knowledge didn't make it feel any better. The people expected you to be right all the time and why shouldn't they? They were raised watching television shows that portrayed the police as having cutting edge, state-of-the-art equipment, which allowed them to always catch the bad guy in sixty minutes or fewer.

The cold hard fact was that police work was difficult. The expectation that you could be one hundred percent right, every time, was unrealistic. Even within the department it was a numbers game, how many cases came in, how many arrests were made, what your closure rate was.

People considered professional athletes, who performed in the .500 and above range, as heroes and legends. The same could be said for the local weatherman who, more often than not, got it wrong. The vast majority of professions got a free pass at being imperfect, except when it came to the police. When they got it wrong, it was like a feeding frenzy.

Many a career had been tossed out on the trash heap, simply because of the one that got away. It usually had less to do with the officer's capabilities and more about the luck of the criminal. Unlike the police, they only had to be right once.

Alex took a drag on the cigarette. She'd already heard the grumblings after the Susan Waltham case. That she had solved the case didn't seem to matter as much as the fact that the killer had slipped away. No one seemed to care that the city fathers weren't lining up to pay her expenses to travel the country looking for the killer. She wasn't sure how people expected her to track someone down if she couldn't leave the city limits.

It also didn't help her cause that many of Penobscot's more influential residents were more than happy to let that case be put to bed. Sex scandals and small towns didn't mix very well.

Not that their opinions mattered to her. The only opinion that counted was the victims. At the end of the day, would they believe she had done everything she could for them? Unfortunately for her, in this particular case, the only way she would know the answer to that was to find Cory Childers.

Alex crushed the cigarette out and got up. She would not make any progress in this investigation sitting on her ass in the cold.

A half hour later, she walked into her office.

"Morning, Abs," she said as she hung her jacket up on the coat rack in her office and headed back out to the main room for coffee.

"Hey, Chief," Abby replied. "There's a note on your desk from a Sergeant Miller in Vermont. Just letting you know there's been no change. She left her number if you wanted to call."

"Okay, thanks. Has Hutch come on yet?"

"Yeah, he called in about five minutes ago. He's on his way."

"Okay," Alex said, pouring a cup of coffee, before heading back to her office.

She sat down and looked at the note, then reached over and picked up the phone. She dialed the number on the pad, listening to it ring.

"Vermont State Police, Troop A, Sergeant Miller. How can I help you?"

"Morning, Vanessa, this is Alex Taylor."

"Hey, Chief," Miller said. "Guess you got my note."

"Yeah, I hear my little social butterfly is still gracing your jurisdiction."

"Yep, just working over at that construction site and hitting the strip club after work."

"What a piece of shit," Alex said as she lit up her cigarette.

"No arguments here," Miller replied. "Not sure how someone can get drunk and toss dollar bills at washed up cheerleaders when their kid is missing."

"Job security, Vanessa," Alex said. "I keep telling myself its job security."

"What does that say about us?" the woman asked.

"Someone's got to stand in the breach," Alex replied, taking a drag on the cigarette.

"Do you ever get the feeling that no one cares whether or not we are there?"

"Yeah, I do," Alex said. "But then I remind myself again that we don't do this for someone else, we do it because that's who we are. If you want to be a hero, apply for the fire department test."

"I'll remember that," Miller said with a laugh. "I wanted to let you know that they're setting up a discrete surveillance on Childers later today. Some commercial vehicle they use with all the gadgets and gizmos. Maybe that will cause him to think we got bored and forgot about him."

"I hope so," Alex said. "I need to catch a break on this one."

"Well, I'll let you know if anything changes."

"Thanks, Vanessa. Stay safe."

"You too, Chief."

Alex hung up the phone and took a sip of coffee. She then began the tedious task of going through the previous days reports. There was nothing major in them, just two minor accidents and a report that someone had broken into the school over the weekend, helping themselves to a case of soda from a storage room.

She'd been trying to get the officers to revise their style of writing, focusing on just the facts, instead of the color commentary, but it could be an uphill battle at times. Fortunately for her, there was nothing wrong with the current batch of reports and she began signing off on them.

"Morning, boss," Hutch said from the doorway.

"Hey, Junior," she replied, laying the reports in her out-basket. "Grab a seat."

Hutch walked in, closing the door behind him, and sat down in the chair across from the desk.

"So, what do you have for me?" Alex said.

"It seems as if our John Connolly is a bit of a mystery man," he said, removing a note pad out of his pocket.

"You have my undivided attention," she replied.

"I came back yesterday and started running him through our databases, but there wasn't much to find. There was an earlier car, a blue 1996 Volvo, but the Ford Focus is the only car currently registered to him. You were right; it comes back to the address over on Franklin."

"No criminal history?"

"Nothing," he replied, "but something just didn't feel right. So I went back over the motor vehicle records and realized that the earliest entry was only in 2005. That would have brought him into his mid-twenties. Kids here get their licenses a lot earlier than that. So I ran his name through the search field for the local newspaper."

"I assume you found something?"

"You mean aside from the fact that the search returned over five hundred entries for John Connolly?"

"Are you serious?"

"Yeah, apparently Mr. Connolly is one very *active* teacher. Everything from PTA activities to getting the school involved in regional state scholastic competitions. Heck, he's even a local Cub Scout troop leader."

"Not exactly the poster child for a *Penobscot's Most Wanted* flyer, is he?"

"I don't know, it turns out that he isn't from here," Hutch replied. "Heck he's not even from New Hampshire originally."

"How did you find that out?" Alex asked.

"I found a small article from the summer of 2004 that announced the hiring of a new history teacher. Article said he was from North Carolina."

"You run him for out-of-state activity?"

"Yep, I sure did," Hutch replied. "Record showed the Volvo registered in North Carolina, some small town called Nags Head."

"Any criminal history?"

"No, the only thing was a speeding ticket issued in 2002 by the Jarvisburg Police Department."

"Fuck," Alex said, reaching for the cigarettes.

"I don't get it," Hutch said. "Isn't this a good thing? I mean, it sort of rules him out as a suspect."

"Yeah, but it leaves us nowhere closer to finding Cory," Alex said, lighting the cigarette. "I had been hoping that there would be something to press him on."

"Sorry, boss."

"Not your fault," Alex replied. "That was good work coming up with all that background information. Now go put it all into a concise report."

"Sure thing," Hutch said as he got up from the chair. "Oh, you asked about Childers' support payments."

"Yeah, what did you find out?"

"He spends most of his time in arrears and then makes a big payment. Right now he owes about three thousand dollars. It's like he's playing some sort of mind game with her. He strings her along, making her wait for it, but he never lets it get high enough that they'll bounce him in jail."

"If they only put their intellect to good use," she said.

"Like you always say, it's job security."

"You're learning, Hutch," Alex said. "Hey, do me a favor."

"Sure, what do you need?"

"Run down the names Mark and Joellen Childers for me. See if you can pull up a current residence for either of them. I don't think they are together anymore, but who knows."

"Ok, I'll let you know what pops," he replied, closing the door behind him.

Alex took a drag on the cigarette and laid it in the ashtray as she looked over some of her notes. She picked up the phone and dialed a number.

"Blackshear," she heard the man growl.

"Tom, it's Alex," she said.

"Hey, Alex, how are things going?"

"No runs, no hits, no errors," she said.

"Some days are like that," he replied. "What do you need?"

"I'm curious, if someone wanted to do a private adoption, how would that be handled in New Hampshire?"

"There's a bunch of different private and religious groups throughout the state that do them, but I believe they are all overseen by Health and Human Services," Blackshear replied. "You think your missing may have been sold?"

"Not sure, but from what I found out, the father had two siblings that were put up for private adoption," Alex said. "My take on it is that those adoptions might not have been completely *legal*, but I need to start somewhere."

"Well, I'd start with HHS," Blackshear said. "Call Sandy Oberti, she works in the commissioner's office. Tell her I said to call. HHS can be pissy at times, especially when it comes to releasing information, but she should be able to point you in the right direction."

"Thanks, Tom. I appreciate it."

"Anytime," he said. "Let me know if you need anything else."

"Will do," she replied and hung up the phone.

Just then, the cellphone on the desk buzzed.

Alex glanced down to see who was calling.

"Hey, Mel," she said as she answered the phone. "How are things in paradise?"

"Do you know how hard it is to get sheetrock dust out of a house?" Melody Anderson said, her voice filled with exasperation.

"I take it the nursery is still under construction?"

"No, it's been finished for a week," Melody replied. "It's the dust that doesn't want to leave."

"Good luck with that," Alex said.

"Thanks," she replied, "but that's not the reason I called."

"I kinda figured that," Alex said. "What's on your mind?"

"I was just checking to see if you were going to be able to make it down for the baby shower this weekend?"

Alex cringed inwardly. In all the commotion, she had completely forgotten about the baby shower they were having for Genevieve Gordon.

"Christ, Mel, I completely forgot," she said. "I have a missing kid and my mind is shot."

"There's no need to apologize," Melody said. "James and I spoke this morning and he told me about it. I figured you would be busy, so I thought I would call and check."

"I want to, but I'm just not sure where this case will take me," Alex replied.

"Well, I just want you to know that Gen and I will miss you not being here, but that boy needs you more than we do. Please don't worry if you can't make it."

"Thanks," Alex said. "How is Gen doing?"

"She's about ready to burst," Melody said with a laugh. "I think she's nearly as wide around as she is tall."

"Oh, God, I can't even imagine. She must be miserable."

"I told her she should consider herself lucky that it is October and not July."

"How'd that go over?" Alex asked.

"I believe she cursed me out in at least three languages," Melody replied. "Between you and me, I think it's just karma getting back at her for all the years she pigged out and never gained an ounce of weight."

"As much as I love Gen, I hate women like that," Alex said.

"You and me both," Melody replied. "I have to spend hours in the gym to stay in shape while Gen only has to wake up. I'm sure she'll lose it all quickly, but for now I am getting every laugh I can at her expense."

"How is Gregor handling it all?"

"Pretty well," Melody replied. "Better than I thought he would. I assumed his German *OCD* would clash with Gen's hormonal mood swings, but he has been dealing with it. I think there are days when he'd give anything to go back to the relative safety of chasing bad guys, but now he knows he is in the home stretch, so he is coping better."

"Wait till after the baby comes, then lets see how he handles that."

"True," Melody said. "Then again, we might all be moving out. You have enough room up there for us?"

"Tons," Alex said. "And the scenery is awesome."

"I'll keep that in mind."

"I will do my best to make it down there," Alex said.

"If you need a lift, I'll fly you down," Melody said. "Just say the word."

"I will, I just can't say right now."

"Don't worry, I need little in the way of notice," Melody replied.

"Well, give my love to Gen and Gregor, and tell them I hope to see them soon," Alex said.

"I will," Melody replied. "I know they have some news for Aunt Alex, but I'll let them tell you."

"Oh, that's so not fair," Alex said.

"Then do what you have to do to get down here," Melody said. "With Gen grounded, I need someone to party with."

"Ok, I'll let you know," Alex replied.

"That sounds good. I hope everything goes well with your missing kid."

"Thanks," Alex replied. "I'll talk to you soon."

"Bye, hon," Melody said.

Alex ended the call and laid the phone on the desk.

She felt a pang of guilt as she stared at the phone. Much to her surprise, she had grown fond of Melody Anderson over the last few months. Despite her original impression, she found her to be a genuinely nice person. It was something that took Alex a while to accept, but she did, albeit grudgingly.

From the beginning, Alex hadn't wanted to like the woman. Melody was the type of person who had always annoyed her. She was attractive, successful, and seemed to get whatever she set her mind on. More importantly, she had something Alex wanted.

On the several occasions she had gone back to New York she felt almost dirty, as she watched her and James together. What hurt more was that they looked genuinely happy together.

How much different would things have been if I'd told him how I felt all those years ago? she wondered.

She suddenly felt exhausted and rubbed her weary eyes.

Alex took a deep breath and chased away the thoughts. There was nothing she could do about the past right now. She needed her head back in the present, because she was the only hope that Cory Childers had at the moment.

She crushed the cigarette out in the ashtray and then lit a new one. Next she picked up the desk phone and hit one of the buttons.

"Yeah, boss?" Abby said on the other end.

"Abs, I need you to do me a favor. Track down a Sandy Oberti at HHS and tell her I need to talk to her about an adoption."

"No problem," Abby replied. "I'll put the call through when I get her on the line."

"Thank you," Alex said and hung the phone up.

She swiveled around in the chair and got up, opening the window behind her desk to let the cigarette smoke escape.

It was another beautiful fall day in Penobscot. The sky outside was a crystal clear blue and the air was crisp.

Alex took a drag and exhaled slowly, watching as the smoke lingered in the air before being caught by the draft and pulled out through the window. It was an interesting metaphor for this case. Every lead seemed to hang in the air, tantalizing her for a moment, until it was ripped away from her grasp.

She desperately needed a break.

CHAPTER ELEVEN

"Hey, Boss," Abby said as she peered into the office. "I got Sandy Oberti on line two for you."

Alex looked up and gave her a thumbs-up.

"Peter, can I call you back in a few," Alex said into the phone. "I have a business call."

She listened for a moment.

"Okay, I'll talk to you then," she said and hung up the phone.

"Great, Abs, put her through," Alex said.

"I told you so," Abby said, with a knowing smile, before walking back to her desk.

"Yeah, yeah, whatever," Alex called out with a laugh.

When the phone rang, she picked it up. "Chief Taylor."

"Hi, Chief, this is Sandy Oberti from HHS, what can I do for you?"

"Hi, Sandy, thanks for taking the time to talk to me and please, call me Alex."

"How can I help you, Alex?"

"Tom Blackshear gave me your name and said you might help point me in the right direction."

"I'll do my best," the woman said. "What's this regarding?"

"I have a missing child up here. During the investigation, I found out that my primary suspect, the boy's father, possibly has two older siblings who may have been adopted privately. I'm trying to confirm that."

"That's a tough one," the woman replied. "We have confidentiality issues to contend with."

"Yeah, trust me, I get that," Alex said. "I'm not asking you for anything tangible, just a yes or no if you even have a record of it. If you do, I'll petition the court for an order to release the records, I just don't want to waste my time if there is nothing there. I'm four days into this investigation and time is not on my side."

"I understand, do you have a name?" Oberti asked.

"Just the parent's," Alex replied. "The last name is Childers, mother is Joellen and father is Mark. Both were from Penobscot."

"Let me check the database," the woman replied.

Alex could hear the clicking sound of the computer keyboard as the woman conducted the search.

"You said Childers, correct?"

"Yes, C-H-I-L-D-E-R-S," Alex recited. "It would have been at least twenty-plus years ago."

"I don't see a record under that name," Oberti replied.

"Do all private adoptions come through your office?"

"Theoretically, yes," the woman said. "Realistically......, well let's just say that money does funny things to people."

"Don't I know that," Alex said.

"I'm the Assistant Director," Oberti said, "but I've only been here for two years. Let me talk to my people in the adoption section and see if I can find out anything else. If I do, I'll call you back."

"Thanks, Sandy, I appreciate the help."

"No problem," the woman replied. "Good luck with your missing."

"Thank you," Alex said and hung up the phone.

She grabbed her coffee cup and headed out of the office, toward the coffee pot.

"Anything good, Boss?" Abby asked.

"I wish," Alex said as she poured herself a cup. "If it wasn't for bad luck, I'd have none at all."

"Something's got to give," she replied. "Just hang in there."

"It's not me I'm worried about, Abs."

"I know, but you're doing everything you can."

Alex took a sip of coffee and set it down on the counter as she fished the cigarette pack out of her pocket.

"Another one?" Abby asked in a condescending tone.

"Yes, mother," Alex said as she lit the cigarette and inhaled deeply.

"You're incorrigible."

"It helps me think," Alex replied.

"Remind me how well that works for you, when you're gasping for air on the stair-climber machine."

"I hate that fucking thing," Alex said tersely.

"I'm still trying to figure out what piece of exercise equipment you do like," Abby said with a laugh.

"The sauna," Alex replied as she picked up her coffee cup and took a sip. "I'm okay with the sauna."

"Don't be late tonight," Abby said. "It's back and biceps night."

"Oh joy," Alex said. "I'll be there with bells on."

"The only bells you're gonna be playing with tonight are kettlebells."

Alex looked down at her watch.

"Excuse me, but as much as I would love to chat about things that will cause me extreme pain, I have to see a principal about some extracurricular hi-jinks," Alex said. "If you need me, call."

"You got it, Boss," Abby replied.

It was just before three o'clock when Alex approached the Penobscot Elementary School. Bicycles, belonging to the students inside, littered the front lawn of the building. She shook her head as she marveled at the sight, wondering how long it would have taken those same bikes to *disappear* back in Brownsville.

She had come to the school to speak with the principal, Dr. Terry Owen. It was a calculated move based on her observation the previous day, as to how quickly the students and staff both left the building. She wanted to know more about John Connolly, but didn't want Owen to have the opportunity to see or talk to him. So she waited till the school day was almost over, which minimized the odds of their paths crossing.

She made her way down the empty hallway, listening to her footsteps echo against the glazed brick walls. At the far end, Alex approached a door that had an old wooden sign above it, indicating that it was the principal's office. She opened the door and stepped inside a small reception room with a desk in the center.

A young lady sat at the desk holding a phone to her ear. She acknowledged Alex's presence, silently holding up one finger, as the voice on the other end of the phone continued talking.

"Ok, Mrs. Roberts," the woman said. "I'll make sure he knows you called."

The muffled voice continued speaking as the young woman looked at Alex and rolled her eyes. Alex smiled as she took a seat in one of the chairs and waited patiently.

"No, I agree with you, Mrs. Roberts, the children should not be crossing through your yard on the way home. I will make sure that Dr. Owen knows about the problem and he will address it."

Again, the voice continued talking as the woman discreetly covered the mouthpiece.

"I'm so sorry," she said. "She can't stop talking. This has been going on for a half hour. Can I help you?"

"Don't worry, I completely understand," Alex replied. "I'm Chief Taylor. I need to speak with Dr. Owen."

"Oh, okay, just one second," the woman said, removing her hand from the mouthpiece. "Mrs. Roberts, I need to put you on hold for just one moment. I'll be right back."

The woman hit the hold button on the phone console, then pressed another button and waited.

"Yes, Dr. Owen, I have Chief Taylor here to speak with you," she said, then listened to his reply.

"Okay, thank you," the woman said and ended the call. "Dr. Owen will see you, Chief. You can go right in."

"Thank you," Alex said as she got up from the chair and headed for the office door. "Good luck with Mrs. Roberts."

"Thanks, I'm going to need it."

Alex opened the door and walked inside, just as the man was coming around the desk to meet her.

"Ah, Chief Taylor, please come in."

Alex had met the man a handful of times over the last year, mostly at school social events and once at a school board meeting, where she had been a guest speaker. He was an older, slightly overweight man, in his early sixties, with dark blue eyes, gray hair, and a neatly trimmed beard that covered his round face. It amazed Alex that the man always seemed to be in a jovial mood and she couldn't help think he would make a great *Santa Claus*.

But today he looked every bit the part of a professional educator. He was wearing a brown tweed jacket over a white button-down shirt and a pair of khaki pants.

"What can I do for Penobscot's *finest*?" he asked, shaking her hand.

"Oh, I'm just following up on a few things regarding Karla Grayson's missing son. I was hoping you might have a moment for me."

"By all means," the man replied, motioning Alex over to a seating area in the office's corner. "This is such a terrible thing. I told Karla to take as much time off as she needed, but she refused. She said she couldn't bear the thought of being alone in that empty house while she waited."

"I can understand that," Alex said as she took a seat.

"Coffee?" the man asked as he sat down in the chair across from her.

"That would be great," she replied. "Black is fine."

Alex watched as the man picked up the carafe from the coffee table in front of him and poured two cups. He slid one mug over to Alex, who picked it up.

"Thank you," she said and took a sip.

"I don't know what I would do without my afternoon coffee," Owen said. "It gives me a much needed dose of energy at the end of the school day."

"I couldn't agree with you more," Alex said. "Speaking of Karla, how is she doing?"

"I think she is hiding her pain in her work," Owen said thoughtfully. "She has always been a very dedicated teacher and I believe she is finding some measure of comfort in doing the things she knows how to do."

"That's understandable," Alex said. "I don't know what I would do if I were in her shoes."

"No, it is an unimaginable horror," the man replied. "I am in awe of her steadfastness and indomitable spirit."

"I take it she is an excellent teacher?" Alex asked.

"She is one of the best," he replied, "and just an exceptionable woman. She has always been a true inspiration for her students and peers alike."

"How has her performance been the last few years?"

"You mean since her divorce?" he asked.

"Basically," Alex replied. "I imagine that going through a divorce and becoming a single mom has to be tough."

"I had thought as much myself," Owen replied, "In fact, I was monitoring her work, to ensure that her personal life didn't affect her classes, but I was astounded to find she handled it with unusual aplomb."

"How so?"

"Well, unless you knew that she had just gone through the divorce, you'd never have guessed it. She remained equally devoted to her job and child throughout the whole ordeal."

"That's interesting," Alex said.

"I've come to realize that Karla is one of those individuals that channels adversity and hardship. Where others might become bogged down and unable to function, Karla uses it to push through."

"So you're not worried about her mental state?" Alex asked.

"Not at all," Owen replied. "I had a long talk with her and I believe that she understands the seriousness of the situation, but also believes in the capabilities of you and your department to resolve this matter quickly."

Alex cringed inside. The compliment felt like a knife twisting inside her. She wondered how the two of them would feel if they knew she was here on a fishing expedition.

"That is very kind of you to say, Dr. Owen."

"Well, as much as we love the quaintness of our small town, I think I speak for the majority in saying that, under these circumstances, we are extremely happy to have a former big-city police officer handling this investigation."

There went another twist of the knife's blade.

"Did she ever have any problems with any of her student's parents, any conflicts?" Alex asked.

"No, none at all," Owen replied. "I have an annual teacher evaluation questionnaire that I send out to all the parents. It is something that I take seriously and, if I don't get one back, I make a point to do a phone follow-up. Karla consistently rates at the top of the faculty."

"Well, I appreciate the insight into her professional life," Alex said. "It helps give me a better understanding. We always worry about our victims and their ability to hold it together during the difficult periods of an investigation."

"I'm not sure what else I can tell you about Karla Grayson's work habits," Owen said. "Was there anything else that you needed to know?"

"Information mostly," she replied. "I'm just trying to get a better picture of the people who might have known Cory Childers."

"Is there anyone in particular you're interested in?"

"Well, most everyone is a local, except for one of your teachers, John Connolly. I was hoping you could tell me more about him."

"Ah, John, a wonderful man," Owen said with a smile. "What would you like to know?"

"How did he come to work here?" Alex asked.

"Oh, about midway through the 2003/04 school year, our fourth grade history teacher, Mrs. O'Brien, informed us she was pregnant and wouldn't be coming back for the next academic year. So we immediately began looking for a suitable replacement. We received a resume from John and interviewed him."

"Where is he from?" she asked, steering the conversation down the path she wanted to go.

"He's originally from North Carolina," Owen replied.

"Wow, that's quite a change of scenery," Alex said.

"Almost as big a change as someone coming from New York City," the man said with a twinkle in his eye.

"*Touché*," she replied. "Then again, I was from the city. When I think of North Carolina, I think of warm weather and ocean beaches. Not sure if you could pry me away from that."

"John used to joke he'd gone through one too many hurricane seasons and needed to put down roots in a place that didn't risk floating away," Owen replied. "I would often tease him that he just wanted to enjoy our splendid winters."

"I don't know about the *splendid* part," she said.

In the background she heard the school bell ring, marking the end of the school day. Almost immediately she could hear the sounds of children scampering down the hallway on the other side of the wall.

"The winters here will *grow* on you, my dear," the man said. "I'm just pleased as punch that we could hire him."

"Is he a good teacher?" Alex asked.

"I can honestly say that, in a career that has spanned some four decades, John Connolly is probably one of the finest educators I have ever had the pleasure of knowing."

"Wow, I'm impressed," she said. "Do you worry that you might lose someone like that? I mean, speaking from a management perspective, you always worry that the best and brightest will look to advance their careers."

"I'd be lying if I told you no," the man replied, taking a sip of coffee. "However, John seems to have acclimated well to being a *granite stater*. He's told me frequently that he has found his niche here in Penobscot"

"How do the kids like him?"

"They love him," Owen replied, "and so do the parents. He has been instrumental in elevating our after school curriculum. His second year here, he instituted a Scholastic Bowl program."

"*Scholastic Bowl*?" Alex asked curiously.

"Unfortunately, not every student that comes through our doors is an athlete," the man replied. "For them, this provides a venue for their own individual skills. Think of it as sort of a game of *Jeopardy* for kids. It pits schools against one another in a non-sporting type competition. Every team has someone knowledgeable in a particular academic area: math, science, English, history, and social studies."

"Sounds interesting," she said.

"The first year we had three schools involved. Last year we had twenty-one in our district."

"I can see why you're so impressed with him," Alex said.

"Well, he's also the co-chair of the PTA and is the local Cub Scout troop leader as well."

"Be careful," Alex said. "If he's that good I might try to hire him away from you."

"I'd be worried if I didn't know how much he loves the children," Owen replied. "I think he'll die in a classroom."

"Well, they say if you love your job, you'll never work a day in your life."

"That is very true."

Alex finished the coffee in her cup and set it on the table. "Well, you've certainly helped me to fill in some of the missing blanks, Dr. Owen. I appreciate you taking the time to talk to me."

"Not at all, Chief Taylor," the man replied. "How is the investigation going, if you don't mind me asking?"

"Slowly," she replied, "but each time we rule something out, we get one step closer to solving it."

"Well, please do not hesitate to call me if there is anything I can do to help."

"That is most gracious of you," Alex said as she stood up. "Of course, if there is anything you need from me, please do the same."

"I will, Chief Taylor," the man replied as he got up and accompanied Alex to the door. "You have a great evening."

"You too," she said as she made her way out into the now empty reception area, then turned back around to look at him. "Oh, wait; I have one other question. I'm sure you spoke to his previous employer. How did they take losing him?"

"Oh, they were very gracious when I called," Owen said. "I think they were a bit surprised to hear from us, given our distance from North Carolina. I spoke to the school superintendent down there and he gave John a glowing recommendation. He said they respected his decision."

"I guess that's all you can ask for," Alex said. "Maybe we all need a change of place from time to time."

"Not me, Chief," the man said with a smile. "I love Penobscot."

"So do I," she said with a wink. "See you around, Dr. Owen."

Alex made her way outside and immediately lit up a cigarette as she walked over to her car. Something about the story Terry Owen just shared wasn't sitting right with her.

She opened the car door, sat inside and started it up. She rolled down the window as she stared at the school. It was a small, squat building, but it served the needs of the community well; better than any inner city school she had ever known. There was no overcrowding here in Penobscot and it was unlikely that they had any real disciplinary problems either, as was so prevalent where she had come from.

Alex took a drag on her cigarette as she contemplated what Owen had said. It wasn't that she didn't believe the man, but the details of the story seemed to trouble her. A guy grows up in a major tourist destination, with a beautiful climate, sun, sand, and then chucks it all away for Penobscot?

Is it possible? she wondered.

Sure, anything was possible, she told herself. *Look at yourself; you're here, aren't you?*

129

Yes, it was true that she had landed here, but it hadn't been her choice. She'd been happy back in Brooklyn North, had loved her job, but she'd made some poor decisions, most of which revolved around a whiskey bottle. No, the proper question wasn't whether it was possible, but more like whether it was *probable*.

As nice as it was, Penobscot wasn't a destination you aspired to. As her old partner had said, it was purgatory with a pine tree scent. You came here to let the dust settle in the real world and prayed you'd get a second chance at redemption.

"So what is it you were running away from, John Connolly?" she asked aloud as she flicked her cigarette out the window.

Alex dropped the car into gear and pulled out of the parking lot.

Until now, the case had grown as cold as a winter's day in Penobscot after the sun went down. Maybe it was time for her to look for clues beyond the city limits.

CHAPTER TWELVE

Ricky Childers woke to the sound of his cellphone ringing on the nightstand next to the bed.

The motel room was still dark, and he glanced over at the clock to see what time it was.

"Three, fucking, thirty," he grumbled. "Somebody better be dead."

"Answer the damn phone already," the woman next to him said angrily.

"Shut the fuck up, Sapphire," Ricky replied as he reached over and picked up the phone.

"Yeah," the man said as he sat up, grabbing the pack of cigarettes from the nightstand and lighting one up.

He listened as a voice on the other end spoke.

"Are you're fucking kidding me," he said. "Right now?"

"Do they know what time it is," Sapphire asked, pulling the blanket over her head.

"What part of *shut the fuck up* didn't you understand?"

"Fuck you, Ricky," the woman replied.

"No, not you," Childers said to the person on the other end of the phone. "But you've got to give me a little more time than this. Your little *planning* screw-up doesn't mean it's an emergency to me."

A sudden burst of angry words poured out of the cellphone speaker as Ricky took a long drag off the cigarette.

"Listen, I don't need *you* to threaten me," Childers said. "I know my stake in all of this. Besides, I didn't say I would not do it; I'm just sick and tired of the last minute BS. I have a life."

Childers listened as the voice continued to speak.

"Yeah, I understand," he replied. "I'll gather up my stuff and head out soon. I'll call you when I'm on the road."

He hung up the phone and crushed out the cigarette.

"Who the fuck was that?" Sapphire asked.

"My boss," Ricky said as he got up from the bed. "There's a problem over in Burlington. They're shipping me out to fix it."

"Are you kidding me?"

"Do I sound like I'm kidding you?"

"What the fuck am I supposed to do?"

"Find another place to crash," he said as headed toward the shower.

"How long will you be gone?"

"What the fuck, do I look clairvoyant to you?" Childers asked. "I'll be gone as long as it takes. You have an outstanding *personality*, so I'm sure someone will be thrilled to open their door for you."

"If I have to find another place, you'll be looking for another *piece*," Sapphire yelled out.

Childers closed the bathroom door, and flipped on the light, as the woman continued yelling after him. He turned on the shower and the exhaust fan, partially drowning out the tantrum that raged on the other side of the door.

"Good, fucking, riddance," he mumbled.

He stared at himself in the mirror, taking in the disheveled image that looked back at him. He was too damn young to look this damn old. This *life* was catching up to him physically and having to play this fucking *game* wasn't helping. He just needed to cut his ties to it once and for all, but, for that to happen, he'd have to figure out a way to get *her* out of his life.

Ricky knew it didn't matter where he went, as long as *she* had her claws in him, he'd always be at her mercy; and he would always have to jump when the phone rang.

Outside, Sapphire was banging dresser drawers as she began packing.

"Women," he said as he stepped into the shower. "I should have just stuck with drinking and jerking off."

CHAPTER THIRTEEN

"Good morning," Abby said as Hutch strolled through the office door. "You're in early."

"Got to catch up on *paperwork*," he replied as he took his jacket off and hung it over the back of his desk chair. "The bane of police work."

"You're preaching to the choir," she said. "I thought computers were supposed to make our lives easier."

"That was the lie they told us so we would buy *more* computers," he said as he walked across the office to the coffeepot and poured himself a mug. "Want some?"

"No, I got my water," she replied.

"Don't you ever get tired of eating healthy?"

"Don't you ever get tired of me bench pressing more than you?" she teased.

"In my defense, you bench press more than *anyone* in the department."

"Don't be satisfied with maintaining the status quo, Hutch."

"For the record, I choose not to get *bigger* because I don't want to have to buy all new uniforms," he replied.

"Just because you keep repeating the lie, doesn't make it the truth," she said with a laugh. "You need any help on the reports?"

"Nah, I'm fine. I just got backlogged with the Childers' case and I kept putting it off."

"With everything going on, I never had time to ask how your range qualification went the other day," Abby asked.

"It went well," Hutch said as he looked up from the computer keyboard in front of him. "Although shooting with the chief can be a bit intimidating."

"I haven't shot with her yet, but I've heard she has skills."

"Good?" Hutch chuckled. "Abs, she's downright scary. I swear she could shoot the whiskers off of a black cat on a moonless night."

"Well, that's certainly *not* going to make me nervous when my time comes," she replied.

"You know, it's kind of strange to have to qualify," Hutch said, taking a drink from the coffee mug on the desk. "But I guess we should have been doing this all along."

"Yeah, I know. The boss said nothing to me directly, but I think you're right. Apparently there's a paper trail that says we were."

"I don't want to talk bad about old Chief Parker, but I feel that we weren't doing a lot of things we were supposed to."

"I have to hand it to her," Abby said. "If she found out that Parker wasn't doing things the right way, she never aired it out in public."

"I think it is nice how she has had everyone check up on Mrs. Parker," Hutch said. "I know the times I have sat down and talked with her seemed to mean a lot to her."

"Yeah, I took her shopping last week," Abby said. "She told me she was worried that she would be all alone. She'd spent so many years being a cop's wife, she knew nothing else but the police department."

"You know it's pretty funny looking back on things just before she got here," Hutch said. "Remember how everyone was so on edge about them bringing in a chief from outside the department."

"Don't forget about DJ, he got himself so worked up that he just up and quit."

"Yeah, that kind of blew my mind when he did that. Paul and I went out to talk to him, but he was adamant that he would not work for no one from outside the department, let alone from New York City."

"I never understood that," she said. "I mean at least give the person a chance, before you go and make a life-altering change."

"I agree," Hutch replied. "He said he didn't have enough time on the job to worry about it. Then again, I was never sure if DJ had what it took to be a cop anyway."

"You ever hear from him?" Abby asked.

"About three months ago he stopped by the house and told me he was working for a plumbing contractor down near Berlin. He was driving around in a new F150, so I guess he isn't hurting for cash."

"Oh well, to each his own, I guess. I just can't imagine throwing away a career over someone I hadn't even met."

"Who's throwing away a career?" Alex asked as she walked into the office.

"Not us, Chief," Hutch replied.

"Good, because I'm not quite done abusing the two of you yet," she replied.

Alex laid the box of Dunkin' Donuts *munchkins* on Hutch's desk.

"Cop food, yummy," Hutch said.

"Once you've achieved your *state of Zen*, come see me," she replied. "I need you to do something."

"Yes, ma'am," he replied, as he opened the box and carefully removed one of the small donuts. "Oh, by the way, I got that information you asked for on Ricky's parents."

"Anything interesting?" Alex asked.

"Mom is dead, but the father is still alive," Hutch replied, wiping traces of powdered sugar from his lips. "I left the info on your desk."

"Outstanding," Alex said, as she headed toward the office.

"Don't kill the messenger, boss," Abby said, "but you're not going to be happy when you go through the morning paperwork."

"Paperwork never makes me happy," Alex replied.

"This is more like a 'get on your broom and unleash the flying monkeys' kind of morning."

"Lovely," Alex mumbled, as she closed the door behind her.

She hung up her coat, removing the pack of cigarettes from her pocket, and opened the window.

The last thing I need is more bullshit, she thought, as she lit up her cigarette and sat down.

The stack of papers in her *in box* wasn't too daunting for a Wednesday morning, but she found herself going through them gingerly; like a bomb tech searching for an IED. It didn't take too long until she came to one that had a red *rejected* stamp emblazoned across the front of it.

"*Asshole*," she bellowed, as she grabbed the phone from the cradle.

In the main room, both Alex and Hutch looked up in the direction of the office.

"I warned her," Abby said. "You heard me tell her that she wasn't going to be happy."

"I heard you," Hutch replied, popping another donut into his mouth and went back to pecking away at the keyboard.

Alex listened as the phone rang, her impatience growing with each second. She was just about to hang up when, on the seventh ring, she heard the call go through.

"Sheldon Abbott's office, how can I help you?" the sugary-sweet voice of Candice Montgomery said when she answered the phone.

Candice, or Candi, as everyone called her, was the positively ebullient twenty-four-year-old daughter of Winston

Montgomery. She had attended the University of New Hampshire, where she received her bachelor's degree in political science. What actual work she had done to merit the degree was still up for debate, as most people agreed that she would be hard pressed to explain what a political science degree actually entailed. Candi, however, had other *attributes* going for her, which made her a natural for the role of Sheldon Abbott's secretary.

For starters, she was young, naïve, got her golden blonde tresses from the bottom of a bleach bottle, and had a habit of wearing rather tight fitting clothing, which greatly *enhanced* her ample curves. It also didn't hurt that her father was the head of the Penobscot Democratic Party and had been a major donor to Sheldon's re-election campaign.

"It's Chief Taylor," Alex said. "Let me speak to Sheldon."

"Let me see if he's in, Chief."

Alex took a drag on her cigarette as she watched the second hand on the old Seth Thomas office clock begin its march.

How hard could it be to look under your desk, bitch? Alex wondered, as the clock's hand hit the forty-five second mark.

A few moments later, she heard Candi's voice come back on the line.

"Mr. Abbott will be with you in one moment, Chief Taylor," she said.

Alex knew it was all a game. Sheldon was pretending to be something he wasn't, which was *busy*. He was nothing more than a small town city manager with unfulfilled greater aspirations. He just played these little mind games to make you believe he was much more significant than he actually was.

"Good morning, Alex," he said cheerfully, when he finally came on the line, a minute later. "What can I do for you?"

"Why did you reject my request?" she said tersely.

"I can't possibly understand why you would need a half dozen rifles," Abbott said. "For crying out loud, Alex, this is Penobscot, not Baghdad."

"Sheldon, have I ever asked you how many pencils you need?" Alex asked matter-of-factly.

"No, Alex, you haven't," he said, his tone a mixture of annoyance and grudging acceptance as to where this conversation was heading.

"Then why would you presume to question me about something you know absolutely nothing about?"

"And how do you suppose I will justify to the other board members the need to purchase these rifles, which, in all likelihood, you will never use?"

"First, you tell them we are getting them at a discount of fifty percent. These things don't *lose* their value. So, when the time comes to trade them in, we will probably make a substantial profit. Second, you ask them if, God forbid, something happened and one of my officers gets hurt because they are outgunned, how they plan on explaining that they went against me. Because I sure as shit will tell the press how the city council chose money over officer safety."

"Alex, there's no need to make threats," Abbott said.

"Threats? I didn't make any threats, Sheldon," Alex said. "I was simply stating what I would do if I found myself in that position."

"Yes, but between your ammo allotment and now this, we are talking about thousands of dollars."

"And just for the record, how much are you paying *Juggs* Montgomery a year to answer your phone?"

From across the room she heard her cellphone ringing from inside her coat pocket.

"Christ, Alex, don't call her that!" Abbott sputtered. "That's a rude and disparaging name for such an upstanding young woman. You of all people should understand that."

"Oh please, Sheldon, spare me the whole *war on women* monologue. I don't need any man to fight for me and don't forget, I shoot back. Besides, sweet little Candi couldn't find the word *disparaging* in the dictionary if you underlined it in red and removed the other twenty-five letters from the alphabet."

"I'll see what I can do, Alex," Sheldon said.

"I don't care what you *do*, Sheldon, but get me my guns," Alex said.

"You know, the first thing they will want to know is why, since you already have guns you carry, do you need bigger ones? Aren't they all guns?"

"I don't know, Sheldon, use your imagination. If they can't comprehend the need for having a suitable long-range weapon, then just tell them I'm like you, I like big, flashy things."

"That's not funny."

The cellphone in her jacket began buzzing again.

"If you don't think that's funny, see what happens when I don't get my guns," Alex replied. "I'll make it my personal mission to find *Juggs* a more rewarding job down in Concord. Then, you can start interviewing for a suitable replacement over at *Senior Village*. Because, in the end, aren't *all* secretaries really the same."

There was a momentary pause in the conversation, and Alex could almost see the pained look on Sheldon's face as he realized what he stood to lose. She knew she would get her guns, but it wasn't because Sheldon had to convince anyone on the board. Abbott ruled Penobscot, and the board was nothing more than a paper formality. No, her request would get its approval because he didn't want to take the chance that he would lose his eye-candy.

"Well, you do bring an experienced voice to the argument," Sheldon conceded. "I don't think anyone will be willing to deny you something you feel that you need."

Suddenly Alex's door opened and Abby stepped in.

"Boss, line two," she said, her voice filled with urgency. "It's Sergeant Miller from the state police."

"Sheldon, you're a peach, but I've got to go," she replied and disconnected the call, quickly hitting the button and changing lines.

"What's going on, Vanessa?"

"I tried calling your cell, Chief," the woman said.

"Sorry, it's in my coat," Alex explained.

"Well, it looks like your boy is skipping town," Miller replied. "My guys said he packed up his truck and headed out this morning in the opposite direction from the job site he was working on."

"What direction?"

"Northeast," she said. "He was heading toward the highway."

"What's up there?"

"Canada."

"Fuck," Alex exclaimed. "Do they think he's on to them?"

"I doubt it. The team watching him lost him at first, but a marked unit spotted him just as he got on the highway. They stayed with him until another unmarked picked him back up in a vehicle that hadn't been used before."

"How long did they lose him for?" Alex asked.

"Not long, maybe fifteen minutes or so."

Alex cringed.

Fifteen minutes might not have seemed like a lot of time, but she knew from experience that it could make the complete difference in an investigation. You could do a lot of damage in fifteen minutes.

"Can they continue the surveillance?"

"Yeah, that's not a problem," Miller replied. "I'm about a quarter mile behind the lead car."

"Okay, I got a terrible feeling about this. I'm going to make my way in that direction now. Keep me posted."

"Yes, ma'am."

Alex hung up the phone and dialed a number.

"Major Crimes, Blackshear."

"Tom, tell me you guys have a bird in the air up here," Alex said.

Something about the tenor of her voice made him realize that she wasn't joking.

"Hold on, Alex, let me check."

After what seemed like an eternity, he came back on the line.

"Negative, it's down in Raymond on a perp search from a carjacking."

"Fuck me," Alex muttered.

"What's wrong?" he asked.

"Vermont just called; my suspect packed up and headed out of town, in the direction of the border."

"Wish I could help you out," Blackshear said.

"Don't worry about it, Tom," Alex said. "I guess it's time to go to plan B."

"At least you have one; happy hunting."

"10-4, talk to you later," Alex said and hung up the phone.

"Hutch!"

"Yeah, Chief?"

"It's time to earn your pay," she said as she got up from the desk and grabbed her jacket. "You just became my plan B."

"What do you need?" he asked.

"I need you to get me to Vermont and I need you to break a whole lot of traffic laws while doing it."

"You don't have to ask me twice," he said, grabbing his jacket.

"Abby, you have the fort. Call in someone to cover the road."

"Yes, ma'am."

CHAPTER FOURTEEN

Ricky Childers glanced up at the highway sign as he made his way north on I-91. He turned on his signal, as he got off the highway at exit 28, making a right turn onto US-5, before pulling into a gas station.

He knew he was close now, and he didn't want to make any more stops until he was there. Ricky got out of the truck, unscrewed the gas cap, and slid the dispensing nozzle into the gas tank. He sat back down in the pickup to examine the map one last time.

Out of the corner of his eye, he caught a movement in front of him and glanced up from the map. He watched as a state police car pulled into the parking lot.

Ricky felt his body tense up as the car turned in his direction and he could feel his heart pounding in his chest. As he continued to watch, the vehicle turned away at the last moment and pulled into a spot in front of the station. The trooper got out and headed inside without even noticing him.

"Fuck me," he exclaimed, as he dropped the map onto the seat next to him.

A second later, Ricky jumped in his seat, startled by a loud, metallic *clang* over his left shoulder. He jerked around to see what was happening, half expecting to come face to face with the barrel of a gun. It took a moment for it to register that it was the automatic shutoff on the gas pump. Ricky felt his body slump back into the seat.

That's it, I'm done with this shit, he thought.

He took a deep breath, composing himself, before getting out of the truck and putting the nozzle away.

Once he was finished, he got back in and started the engine. He fought the urge to race out of the parking lot, signaling as he pulled back onto the road. At this point he didn't need to get stopped for some bullshit infraction by some cop trying to make his quota.

Traffic was light as he made his way toward Braeden, and he glanced around at the rural community. It was an eclectic mix of businesses and farm land with a smattering of homes thrown in. In many respects, it wasn't all that much different from Penobscot.

For a moment, he wondered if he would ever make it back to Penobscot, but chased the thought from his mind. That was his past, and right now he needed to focus on his future.

He came to an intersection and turned left, heading north. A short time later he was driving through the country. The roadway was lined with trees, their bright fall colors painting the landscape for as far as the eye could see. Up ahead he saw the overpass for I-91, which he had just been traveling on, and knew he was almost there. Ricky reached into the console to remove the pack of cigarettes and lit one up. He took a drag as he lowered his window down and exhaled, the wind quickly drawing the smoke out.

A few minutes later, he spotted the squat skyline of the small town that marked his destination. He took one last drag on the cigarette, flicking it out the window as he approached the rural border crossing station.

Ricky pulled the pickup up behind another vehicle and put it in park. Up ahead, a Canadian customs agent was having a conversation with the driver of a van, as another agent inspected the interior. They were never this meticulous at this rural crossing, but he reasoned that they appeared to be more conscientious because it was a commercial vehicle.

After several minutes, he glanced down at the pack of cigarettes, wondering whether he had enough time to light one. Before he could decide, he heard the *very* distinctive sound of a shotgun being racked.

He turned around *slowly* and gazed down the black abyss of the Mossberg 500's barrel.

"Hey there, Ricky," Alex said with a smile. "Are you planning on going somewhere?"

CHAPTER FIFTEEN

"This is fucking bullshit," Ricky Childers fumed as he sat inside the interrogation room at the Vermont State Police Barracks in Derby. "I want my fucking attorney."

"Glad to see that he has lost none of his charm," Vanessa Miller noted as she and Alex stared at the agitated man through the one-way mirror.

"Oh yeah, he's a peach," Alex said sarcastically. "Any luck with the truck?"

"They just towed it in. They'll start doing an inventory shortly."

Alex had hoped that they would find something at the scene, but the vehicle appeared clean. There were just a couple of pieces of luggage tossed in the back, along with some tools.

"Hey, boss," Hutch said as he joined the two women. "I just got off the phone with Childers' union supervisor over at the construction site."

"What did he say?" Alex asked.

"Said that all he knew was that Ricky never showed up this morning."

"So Ricky didn't submit a request for time off?"

"Not according to his boss," Hutch replied.

"Did he say that he was having any problems? Any work issues?"

"No, according to him, Ricky was one of his better employees. He said that he knew that he drank a lot and hung out at titty bars... Uh, sorry, I mean strip clubs."

"Yeah, we got it the first time," Alex said with a smile. "What else?"

"Nothing, he said that every once in a while he'd go on a bender, miss a day or two of work, and then he'd be straight as an arrow for months. He just figured it was Ricky being Ricky."

"Did he say anything else?"

"Just that he was his best electrician, so he cut him some slack."

"Did we get anything from the motel?" Alex asked.

"Nope, he paid his bill in full this morning and left."

"So this wasn't planned," Miller said.

"It doesn't seem so, Sarge," Hutch replied.

"Well then, I guess I need to go have a little chat with Mr. Childers."

"Do you want me to come in with you?"

"No, not right now, Vanessa," Alex replied. "I need to gauge how far I can push him. I'll start drumming my pen on the desk if I need an interruption."

"It's your party."

"I don't think he's going to enjoy my *party favors*," Alex said, as she opened the door.

Childers sat fuming behind the metal table, his left foot nervously tapping the floor, as he watched Alex come into the room.

"I want my fucking attorney. Right now, bitch."

"Really, Ricky?" Alex asked, as she took the seat across from him. "After all we've been through?"

"When my attorney gets finished with you, I'm going to own fucking Penobscot. Then you can come crawling to me on your hands and knees for a job."

"I bet you'd love to see that, wouldn't you?"

"We'll see who's laughing when my attorney gets a hold of you."

"Wow," Alex replied. "You know, if I had a dime for every time someone threatened me, that they were going to 'have my job,' I'd be laying out on the beach of the tropical island I owned. So unless you'd like to just keep sitting there, fantasizing about me crawling on my hands and knees, why don't you just shut the fuck up and listen for a change?"

"Am I under arrest?" Childers asked.

"No," Alex replied.

"So I'm free to leave?"

"Not exactly."

"This is bullshit."

"I'm trying to find your missing son, Ricky. You'd think you would want to be more *cooperative*."

"I need a cigarette," Childers said.

"Christ, so do I," Alex replied, as she removed the pack from her pocket.

"Can I have one of those?" he asked.

"Will you talk to me about your kid?"

Ricky stared at her, then down at the cigarette pack in her hand.

"Yeah," he said resignedly.

Alex passed one over to the man, holding the lighter up for him as he lit it and then lit hers. She knew that someone, standing outside, was having a heart attack about this egregious break in public health code policy, but she also knew that niceties like that went to the bottom of the list when you were interrogating someone.

"I'm curious, Ricky," she began. "It seems like I'm the only one interested in finding Cory. So would you like to tell me why you chose to take an international joy ride while I'm out there busting my ass?"

"I was bored," he said. "I needed a change of scenery."

"Was that a short or long term decision?" Alex asked.

"Don't know," Childers replied, blowing a smoke ring into the air. "I hadn't gotten that far yet."

"I'm having a hard time buying into that, Ricky."

"That's your problem, sweetheart, not mine."

"I just can't believe you'd walk away from Sapphire like that. I thought you two made such a cute couple."

"Sapphire? Hell, she was just another *port in the storm*," Childers replied.

"Oh, so what, your some sort of half-assed pirate now?"

"Something like that," he laughed. "Don't get me wrong, she was fine while it lasted, but then they all start talking about the future and I just don't need that kind of aggravation. Been there, done that, and lost the shirt off my back."

"So what about your job?" Alex asked. "I mean you didn't come all the way out here to just chuck that away."

"What does it matter?" Childers asked. "Anything I make that bitch back in Penobscot takes. I'm just sick and tired of being Karla's goddamn punching bag."

"So you'd just pack up and leave?"

"Why not?" Childers replied. "I figured she could go to court and get all the bullshit orders she wanted, but it wouldn't matter to me if I lived in another country."

Alex took a drag on the cigarette as she stared at the man.

"I hate to break the awful news to you, sparky, but the United States government is part of an international convention concerning enforcement of child support. If a non-paying spouse, that means *you*, resides in a country, like Canada, where the US has a bilateral agreement, they can still come after you. In other words, you're up shit's creek without the proverbial paddle."

"Seriously?"

"Seriously," Alex said. "You should probably have talked to a lawyer, before you rubbed those two brain cells together to formulate that plan, Ricky."

"Fuck it. Let her try to find me."

"Does that same sentiment go for your son?"

"You keep trying to lay this guilt trip on me about Cory, but it isn't going to work," Childers said. "I tried to be a good dad, but that cunt wouldn't allow it. I have a clear conscience."

"Did you ever think he'd be better off away from her?"

"Every goddamn day," Childers replied.

"How come you didn't fight for custody?"

Childers took a drag on the cigarette, the ash building up on the tip, and held it up to Alex.

"Not my fucking shop," she replied as she tapped hers on the edge of the desk. "State police seem to have a good cleaning crew."

Ricky followed suit.

"It wasn't like I didn't try," he said. "Her old man had more money than he knew what to do with. She got herself some hotshot bitch attorney from Concord who bled me dry in court appearances. She paraded a bunch of women I'd been with to discredit me."

"Strippers?"

"I don't judge," Childers replied. "Anyway, I ran out of money trying to clear my reputation long before we ever got to the issue of custody."

"That had to be a tough nut to swallow."

"I'm a guy," he said. "I figured I didn't have a snowballs chance in hell of getting custody anyway."

"What about helping us to try to find him?" Alex asked.

"You ever think that maybe he's better off gone?"

"Why would you say that?"

"Because his mother is a manipulative fucking man-hater, that's why. The kid probably ran away just to quit listening to her bullshit."

"I imagine that as a parent that had to be hard on you."

"Yeah, of course, it did," Childers said, "but life's hard. It's probably better that the kid learns that early."

"And the thought never crossed your mind to help *liberate* him?"

"You mean kidnap him?" Childers asked.

"Well, if the kid had as tough of a life as you say he did."

"Look, tough life in your mom's house is one thing; tough life in prison is something completely different."

"People have done a lot more for someone they love."

"Lady, I love my son; but I love my freedom a lot more."

"You're a helluva nice guy, Ricky," Alex said as she got up and headed to the door.

"And you have a helluva nice ass, chief. Too bad you've got that broom handle shoved so far up it."

Alex turned to look back at the man, a smile on her face. "Did you ever think maybe it was just *you* that Karla hated?"

"That's funny, because no one else has bitched about me," Childers proclaimed.

"Yeah, because women like Sapphire and Destiny are such amazing judges of character."

"Fuck you," he hissed.

"Sweetheart, you'll never have enough dollar bills to make that fantasy come true."

Alex opened the door and walked out of the room.

"That went well," Miller said.

"Yeah, he missed his calling. Asshole should have opened up a charm school."

"Should we cut him loose?"

Alex looked down at her watch. It was getting to the point that they would be hard pressed to justify holding him any longer. "We get anything on the car?"

"Nada," Miller replied. "It looks like he was doing exactly what he said, skipping town."

"I'm not fucking buying it, Vanessa," Alex said. "Guys like Ricky live for two things, beer and broads. Last I checked he wasn't independently wealthy, so where is he going to get the funds to support his immediate needs?"

"Maybe he has a job lined up in Canada that he doesn't want us to know about."

"Maybe," Alex said, "doubtful, but maybe. Where is his truck?"

"Parked out back. I'll show you."

Alex reached into her pocket, removing the pack of cigarettes and lit one up, as the two women made their way to the parking lot behind the building.

What did you hope to find? she wondered. *Did you really believe that Cory Childers would be huddled under a blanket in the back seat? But none of this makes any sense. Why would Ricky just throw everything away, if he wasn't involved in anything?*

"What are you looking at, boss?" Hutch asked as he walked up to them.

"A whole lot of nothing, junior."

"I'll say," Hutch replied. "The best thing on that piece of shit is the spare tire."

Alex took a drag on her cigarette and eyed him curiously. "Come again?"

"I said the spare tire is the best thing on it," Hutch replied. "I did an inventory of the truck and its contents. The spare looks brand new."

"Where is it?"

"Mounted under the bed," he replied. "Why?"

"Show me," she replied.

Hutch led the two women over to the back of the pickup. Then he got down on his knees and pointed up toward the spare.

"Right there, boss," he said gesturing to the tire.

Alex kneeled down and peered up at the brand new P245/70R16 tire that was mounted to the underside of the vehicle.

"*Sonofabitch*," she exclaimed, a huge smile growing on her face. "I swear to God I'm gonna make a detective out of you yet, Hutch."

CHAPTER SIXTEEN

"Can I fucking go now?" Ricky fumed when Alex returned to the room. "I'd planned on eating something French for dinner this evening."

"I'm sure some poor Canadian stripper will be sorry she missed out on *that* opportunity," Alex said as she took the seat across from the man.

"So, can I go?"

"Listen, Ricky, I'm going to give you one last chance," Alex said. "We are talking about an innocent young boy, your son. He is out there somewhere and I need to find him. So I'm asking you, one last time, is there anything you can think of that can help me find Cory?"

Ricky Childers gazed at her, his face devoid of any emotion. Her voice had a pleading tone to it and there was desperation in her face. He was her only hope and she knew it. The stuck-up, hot-shot cop from the big city was begging for his help.

"I've got nothing," he replied with a grin. "Besides, even if I did, I wouldn't do a damn thing to help that bitch."

Alex shook her head somberly as her fingers drummed on the desktop nervously. "Ok, then I guess I'm done with you, Ricky."

"*Finally*," Childers said, slamming his palms down on the desk as he stood up. "Get ready to have your ass sued, *Chief*."

"I'll be waiting with bated breath," Alex muttered, as the man walked out of the room and slammed the door shut behind him.

She closed her eyes and sat there, listening to the silence.

How many times have I been in a room like this? she wondered. *Hundreds at least, perhaps even a thousand.*

It was always the same game. Like some sort of half-assed, criminal justice dance, where you had to weave in and out between the truth and lies. It was a place where all the rules and procedures they taught you to follow in the academy were more like *guidelines*. All in the pursuit of the one clue, the one confession, that would bring a rightful conclusion to the case. Sometimes you were the windshield and sometimes you were the bug. It was just that kind of game.

Alex let out a sigh as she got up and headed out the door.

Outside, Ricky Childers was in handcuffs, screaming like an organ grinder's monkey, his mouth running in *four quarter* time.

"You, fucking, bitch!" he yelled, when he saw Alex. "What the fuck are you arresting me for? I had nothing to do with Cory's disappearance."

"I'm not arresting you, dip-shit," Alex said. "They are."

"For what?"

"If I had to fathom a guess, I'd say *Possession with Intent to Distribute* for starters," she replied. "I assume the feds will look to take it over, seeing as you attempted to crossover into a sovereign country with it. They tend to frown on such activities."

The color immediately drained from the man's face.

"You know, for as smart as you think you are, you really are a dumb fuck, Ricky," Alex said. "All you had to do was play the game. Be the hapless, worried dad and I'd have patted you on the back and sent you on your way with my sympathies. But no, you had to get an attitude; try to play the tough guy. You know what happens when you do that to a cop? It's like slitting your wrist and jumping into shark-infested waters."

"The way I see it, let your anger toward Karla cloud your better judgment," she continued. "Every month you pissed your paycheck away on beer and broads, thinking you were fucking over your ex. Then, when you knew you were on the verge of getting your ass tossed in jail, you miraculously came up with a lump sum payment. So I asked myself, 'how did you do that, Ricky?' Back in the interview room, you said you ran out of money when you were fighting to get custody, so how exactly do you come up with a couple of thousand dollars at a time? Not to sound mean, but you ain't exactly got the looks or the body to work a street corner and you don't strike me as the *investor* type. No, someone who lives for beer and broads doesn't just toss away a perfectly good job. So when your boss said you had an occasional habit of being a no-show, it made me wonder where you were going. Then I remembered that you are currently in arrears and it hit me. You found yourself new friends, ones who had that kind of cash, if you were willing to take a risk from time to time."

"That's a nice story," Childers replied, "but stories don't send people to prison."

"No, you're right, stories don't, but Niko does."

"Who the fuck is Niko?" the man asked.

Alex glanced over as a trooper walked in, holding the leash of a German shepherd.

"This is Niko, Ricky," Alex said. "And just for the record, when you have a piece of shit truck, that you like to ride through the mud for shits and giggles, it's probably a good idea to have a semi piece of shit spare tire and not a brand new one hanging from the underside of your truck."

"Fuck me," the man exclaimed.

Alex took a step forward until she was face to face with him.

"If I were in your shoes, Ricky, I'd do myself a big favor and start singing like a goddamn canary," Alex said. "Because when they start rounding up the rest of your *merry band of idiots*, I promise you that someone will talk and that is the one who is going to get the deal."

"I want my lawyer," the man said.

A mischievous smile grew on her face. "Good luck with that hot-shot, I hear the federal prison in Marion is lovely this time of year."

She pivoted and began walking toward the exit door. When she got there, she paused and turned around. "Hey, Ricky, look at the bright side. At least you don't have to pay that *bitch* child support anymore."

"Fuck you, Taylor," Childers swore.

Alex chuckled as she opened the door and stepped outside.

It was getting late and the sun hung low in the western sky. She found Hutch leaning against the patrol car drinking a cup of coffee.

"So how did it go, boss?" he asked.

Alex lit a cigarette and sat up on the hood of the car.

"I guess we won a battle," she said, taking a drag.

"Did we?"

"I don't know, it just sounded like the right thing to say," she replied. "At least we got him off the street. That was a good pick-up on the tire."

"Eh, I just told you about it, you were the one who made the connection."

"That's what most police work is, junior. Taking the pieces of the puzzle and making the connections. Learning how to do it just takes time and practice, but you have to learn to *see* the pieces first. You did that today, you should be proud of yourself."

"Thanks," Hutch said. "So, do you think he knows anything?"

"No, he doesn't."

"How can you be so sure?"

"It's all about human nature. Childers knew he was toast the minute he saw the K9. If he had any information, he'd have been begging to make a deal. No, the only card he has left is flipping on the folks he's running for and he knows I can't help him with that, so he will wait to talk to his attorney."

"So we are back at square one," Hutch said.

"No, not really," Alex replied.

"What do you mean?"

"Well," she said. "Today we figured out who *didn't* do it."

CHAPTER SEVENTEEN

Alex sat on the couch, sipping a cup of coffee, as she stared at the files strewn across the coffee table.

She'd taken the day off, needing a break from the daily nonsense she had to contend with at the office, but now she only felt frustration. While it wasn't exactly back at square one, she was much closer to the beginning of the investigation then she was to the end and the clock was still ticking.

Her potential suspect list was one name shorter, but it had also been her most promising one. After they had gotten back, she had driven out to Karla Grayson's place to break the news. It was one of the hardest things she ever had to and the woman had not taken it well. She, like Alex, had held onto the belief that Ricky was involved. Now, with that hope gone, the reality that she might never see Cory again hit her like a ton of bricks.

The look of hurt and pain in Karla's eyes was like a stinging rebuke to Alex's efforts to find the missing boy. Even though she knew that it wasn't intentional, it was there.

It was one o'clock in the morning before Alex left the woman and headed home. It was almost three o'clock by the time she finished the bottle of wine and went to bed.

She picked up the pack of cigarettes from the coffee table and lit one. Alex knew she had to quit, but it was the only thing that seemed to calm her down enough to think.

With Childers gone from the list of potential suspects, she needed to refocus on who was left. She picked up her cellphone and called Hutch.

"Morning, Chief," he said when he answered the phone.

"Are you in the office?"

"Yeah," he replied. "What do you need?"

"I know you checked the pedophile list already, but I want you to pull the old ones and check out those who were sentenced. See if any of them may have gotten released early and failed to report in."

"Sure thing," he replied. "Anything else?"

"Yeah, I need you to email that paperwork on Childers' parents."

"Ok, I'll send them over to you in a minute."

"Call me back if your search turns up anything."

"Will do, boss."

Alex hung up the phone, knowing it was most likely going to be a dead-end, but at this point she was running out of options. She took a drag on the cigarette and set it down in the ash tray. She opened up the laptop and selected the email program. A minute later she heard the ping announcing that she had a new message.

Alex began reading the documents that Hutch had sent her on Joellen and Mark Childers.

Karla Grayson had it partially correct; Ricky's mother was indeed dead. After her husband was sent to prison, Joellen Childers made her way out of town, eventually making it as far as Manchester. There, she got hooked up with a member of a local motorcycle gang who turned her on to some new *fun*. Her alcohol problems soon took second place to the new drug habit she had acquired.

Joellen had desperately wanted to become someone's *old lady*, but that position required trust. Her habit, coupled with a tendency to spread her legs for any patched member looking for some fun, made her a *knock-a-round girl*. Someone to have a good time with, but not someone you'd risk taking responsibility for.

A few years back she was discovered in a seedy motel room; dead from an apparent heroin overdose. The local cops surmised that she had simply done herself in, but Alex read it a different way. At the time of her death, Joellen was no longer a casual user. Judging from the amount in her system, it made Alex wondered if someone else hadn't *helped* her along on her trip to oblivion. Not that it would have mattered to the locals. The motel was a local dive, the kind of place where no one saw or heard anything. So, in the end, Joellen Childers became just another closed case that the detectives filed away before moving onto the next one.

Mark Childers was another story completely.

Prison life seemed to agree with him, at least in terms that it offered a structured life and removed the temptation of alcohol. While he served his prison sentence, he found God and received a degree in Divinity from an online university. Upon his release he was sent, as a condition of parole, to a substance abuse rehabilitation center in Plymouth. The staff there was so impressed with his ability to counsel his fellow residents that, when his parole was completed, they offered him a job as a counselor.

Alex picked up the paper listing the information for the rehabilitation center and scanned it for a contact number. When she found it, she picked up her cell and placed the call.

"Guiding Light, this is Tanya, How may I help you?"

"Hi, can I speak to Mark Childers?" Alex asked.

"Sure," the woman replied. "May I say who is calling?"

"Alex Taylor."

"One moment please," the woman said, putting the call on hold.

Alex waited as the call was transferred.

"Hi this is Mark Childers," the man said. "How may I help you?"

"Mark, my name is Alex Taylor; I'm the chief of police in Penobscot. I was wondering if I could ask you a few questions?"

"Sure, what's this about?" the man asked.

"I'm investigating the disappearance of your grandson, Cory, Mr. Childers."

"My God, what happened?"

"That's what I am trying to find out," Alex replied. "His mother reported him missing a few days ago."

"I don't know what to say," Childers replied. "I'm honestly not sure how I can help you, Chief Taylor, the truth is my son and I have been estranged for many years."

"So you knew that you had a grandson?"

"Yes, Ricky told me about him the last time we talked."

"When was that," Alex asked, trying to contain her excitement.

Is this the break you've been searching for? she thought.

"Oh, it had to be at least a half-dozen years ago," the man replied.

Alex felt the euphoria come shattering down around her and she crushed the cigarette out in the ashtray.

"Can you tell me what sparked that conversation?" she asked.

"Well, I'm sure that you are aware of my past," Childers said. "After they sent me to prison, I struggled with my life. It was as if God and Satan were fighting over me. After my release, I realized that I would not be able to help others, until I came to terms for all the wrongs I had done in my life."

"So you called Ricky to make amends?"

"Yes, at least in theory," the man replied. "Reality was a bit different."

"How so?" Alex asked.

"I was never a good father, Chief," the man said. "I felt that I needed to contact Ricky to try to make peace for what I had done and the things I hadn't."

"He wasn't receptive to your peace offering?"

"I don't know what I expected, but it certainly wasn't that," Childers said. "Understand that this was a dark period of my life I am speaking about. My wife, the good Lord bless her soul, and I were too busy enjoying the carnal pleasures of life to be tied down with children."

"Yet you still had them," Alex said pointedly.

"Yes," the man admitted somberly, "and we let those precious babies slip through our fingers as we enthusiastically embraced our sinful nature."

"So what did Ricky say when you spoke to him?"

"What *didn't* he say?" the man replied. "In a torrent of anger he unleashed on me all the fury he had kept wrapped up inside all those years. That's when I first learned about Cory."

"What did Ricky say about him?"

"How he was a different father to his son. How, unlike me, he was there for him and how his child would always know that his father loved him."

"That had to hurt," Alex said.

"Just because the truth is unpleasant, doesn't make it any less the truth."

"That is very true," she replied.

"I asked if there was a chance to meet him," Childers said, "but Ricky wouldn't hear of it."

"Did he say why?"

"Sadly, yes," the man replied. "He told me that since I had never wanted anything to do with him, when he was growing up, that he would return the favor."

"And that was the last time you spoke?"

"Spoke? Yes, but I didn't give up trying to extend the olive branch," he replied.

"How so?"

"Well, I still know a few people back in Penobscot," Childers said. "I found out where Ricky lived and would send out letters and cards, doing everything I could to keep that window open."

"How'd that go over?" she asked.

"The first few went through, but then they started coming back 'return to sender.'"

"And you have had no other contact?" Alex asked.

"No," Childers said, "but I keep trying. I know that I have not always led an exemplary life, but that was the past. The trials we endure, while unpleasant as you are going through them, teach us humility and allow us to grow deeper in our faith as we trust in the Lord. "

"Well, thank you for your time, Mr. Childers," Alex said.

"You're quite welcome, Chief Taylor," the man replied. "I do have one request though."

"What's that?"

"When you find Cory, please let me know. I will pray for his quick return."

"I will," Alex said. "Oh, just for the record, where were you last Friday?"

"I was down in New York City attending a conference on substance abuse and the role of the church," he replied. "I drove down Thursday night."

"Okay. Do you remember where it was being held?"

"Yes, it was at the Marriott Downtown," Childers replied. "I didn't leave till Sunday evening. I can send you the bill from my hotel stay if that would help."

"It would," Alex said, giving the man the fax number to the office.

"Okay, I'll send it right over," he said.

"Well thank you for your time, Mr. Childers," Alex said. "If you can think of anything else, please contact me."

"I will, Chief."

Alex hung up the phone and tossed it onto the coffee table.

"*Fuuccck!*" she screamed.

She picked up the pack of cigarettes and lit another one. Then she got up and made her way to the kitchen and poured herself a *tall* glass of wine.

Maybe you just lost your edge, she thought.

She walked back to the couch and sat down, staring vacantly out the window. Her frustration was almost palpable and she felt herself struggling to stay connected to the case.

Alex knew that this wouldn't be the first time an investigator got burned out; it happened all the time. Investigators spent years *listening* to the clues, letting them lead the case to its rightful conclusion, and then, one day, the clues stopped talking. Perhaps it was their way of testing ones investigatory skills; seeing whether or not a cop had it in them to be a *real* detective.

Right now, it was a test she was failing miserably.

She took a drag on the cigarette and picked up one of the folders off the coffee table. She began flipping through the documents, hoping that something would *jump* out at her. They were the *pieces of the puzzle* she had told Hutch about yesterday, only they were all painted white, with no discernable patterns for her to match-up. What she needed was an edge piece, something that would at least help her set up the borders.

"There you go," she hissed, as she sent the folder flying across the room, papers scattering in every direction. "You're a fucking pathetic detective, Taylor. You're looking for the fucking clues to come crawling to you!"

A feeling of rage welled up inside her as she fumed.

"*Great*," she mumbled, looking at the mass of papers strewn across the floor. "That's just fucking great."

Alex finished the glass of wine and got up. She went to the kitchen and poured herself a refill, then walked over to the bay window and sat down, staring out at the lake. It was a beautiful fall day outside. The water was like a mirror and it held the reflection of the crisp, clear blue sky and colorful trees that dotted the shore line.

Most people loved to come up to the northeast to enjoy this festive time of year. They traveled hundreds, even thousands, of miles to take in the vibrant, wonderful colors of this paradise, but it was a false image.

The colors weren't meant to be warm and inviting, but a warning. A harbinger of what was to come. Soon the picture postcard scenery would be replaced with dark and foreboding skies. The leaves would fall from the trees, leaving everything barren and lifeless. The cold would settle in, seizing the area in a frigid, vice-like grip, until spring could finally break its hold.

It was on days like that, that Alex wished she could be somewhere else. A place where the sun shone brightly in the sky above, where she could bury her toes in the sand while sipping on one of those *frou-frou* drinks with a little umbrella in it. That was *her* paradise.

What fool wouldn't love to be there right now, she thought.

She took a drag on her cigarette and then knocked back the wine.

Alex turned away from the window and looked back at the papers lying on the floor.

"*Sonofabitch*," she whispered, getting up from the seat.

She got down on her knees and began sifting through the documents until she found the one she was looking for. Then she got up and sat back down on the couch.

She *googled* the name and began searching through the entries. Given the amount of time that had passed, it took her about eighteen pages before she found an entry from something called the *Outer Banks Sentinel*. She clicked on the link and waited for it to load.

Error Code 404: *We're sorry, this page could not be found.*

"Oh for fucks sake," Alex screamed. *"Really?"*

She hit the back button and looked at the link. There was a date on the entry from May 7th, 2003. She ran the name and pulled up their webpage. It was for a local newspaper and she clicked on the *contact us* link.

Alex grabbed her phone and dialed the number, listening to it ring.

"Outer Banks Sentinel, this is Mandy, how can I help you?"

"Hi, Mandy, my name is Alex Taylor; I'm with the Penobscot Police Department up in New Hampshire. I was wondering if you could help me out."

"Sure, officer, what do you need?" the woman asked.

"Well, you see, we are a *really* small town here, and the mayor thinks I have nothing better to do than work on his pet projects. We have a teacher that came from your area and it's his tenth year here. The mayor wants to do a *Nag's Head loss is our gain* type of thing. I found a link to an article about him resigning from a school down there on May 7th, 2003, but it comes back as an error, saying it cannot be found."

"Oh yeah, we had a major overhaul of the website and removed a lot of old content."

"I was wondering if you guys kept hard copies and if you might be able to send me a copy of the article."

"Sure, I can pull up a digital one for you."

"Could you? That would be so awesome," Alex said.

"Do you want me to fax it or send it to you by e-mail?" the woman asked.

"Email would be great," Alex said. "And thank you so much."

"Oh, no problem," Mandy replied.

Alex gave the woman her email address and hung up the phone. She crossed her fingers, hoping she had finally found an *edge piece* that would help her to start to put this puzzle together.

A half hour later she heard the *ping*, signaling that she had a new email, and opened the program. A wave of excitement filled her when she saw it was from the newspaper.

Officer Taylor, here is the article you asked for. Please let me know if there is anything else you need, Mandy.

Alex clicked on the attachment and began reading it.

Kill Devil Hills Teacher Resigns.

Outer Banks Sentinel – May 7th, 2003: *The superintendent of the Kill Devil Hill's school district reported that fourth grade history teacher, John Connolly, resigned his position with the Kill Devil Hill's Elementary School, effectively immediately. When questioned as to why Mr. Connolly was leaving before the end of the school year, Principal Gordon Monroe would only say that the resignation was by mutual agreement and that Mr. Connolly was leaving to pursue other opportunities. Principal Monroe said that, while the school was saddened to lose such a valuable member of its faculty, it was planning on conducting interviews to seek a suitable replacement immediately.*

Alex leaned back in the couch and rubbed her eyes. "Who the hell quits their job a month before the end of school?"

She pulled up the website for the elementary school and grabbed her cellphone, dialing the number that was listed.

"Kill Devil Hill's Elementary School, this is Joanna, how may I direct your call?"

"Hi, Joanna, my name is Alex Taylor. I'm the chief of the Penobscot Police Department in New Hampshire. I need to speak to whoever handles personnel matters."

"Sure, that would be our assistant principal, Brian Adams," the said replied. "If you'll hold on for a moment, I'll transfer you to his line."

"Thank you," Alex replied, as the woman placed the call on hold and music streamed from the phone's speaker.

Seconds ticked by as the shrill instrumental melody played out on a continuous, and exceedingly annoying, loop. She was convinced that it was designed to get callers to hang-up, rather than wait for their call to go through. Alex was seriously considering doing just that when she heard the music end and a voice come on the line.

"Hi, Chief Taylor, this is Brian Adams, how can I help you?"

"Hi, Brian, the mayor tasked me with doing updated background checks on all our city employees," Alex said. "This includes the teachers and staff at our schools. It's more of a formality than anything else. You know what I mean, a *dot the I's and cross the T's* sort of thing."

"Busy work," the man said with a laugh.

"Exactly," she replied. "Anyway, all of the teachers here are locals, except for one that came from your school. I hoped that you might help me out with some information on him."

"Sure, can you tell me who it is?"

"Yeah, his name is John Connolly. My information says he left there around 2003."

"I don't know him," Adams replied. "He was before my time. I didn't get here till 2008. Let me go pull the old records down in storage and I will get back to you. Is there a good number to reach you at?"

"Yeah, I'll give you my cell number," Alex said. "It's the easiest way to reach me."

She heard the man copy the number down as she gave it to him and he recited it back.

"Yep, that's it," she replied.

"Ok, I'll go take a look and get back to you in about a half hour."

"Great, Brian, I appreciate it."

"No problem, I will talk to you soon."

Alex began sorting through the paperwork as she waited to hear back from the man. She pulled all the reports and records that pertained to Connolly and began putting them in a separate folder. There wasn't a lot to go on, but at least the records from North Carolina would give her a better picture. It might just prove to be a dead-end, but until she had another name to consider, she would have to focus on him.

After she had re-organized the paperwork, Alex got up and went to the kitchen, opting for a cup of coffee instead of wine. She lit another cigarette and headed back over to the couch, checking her watch. It was nearly an hour since she had spoken to the man.

How long does it take to find personnel records? she wondered.

A half hour later she tried to call back, but he was apparently out to lunch. She left her name and number again, then went to make herself something to eat. She was just finishing when she heard the cellphone buzz. She grabbed it and quickly answered it.

"Hello?" Alex said.

"Hey, boss," Hutch said. "I got that information you wanted."

"That's great," she replied.

"Try not to sound so excited."

"I'm sorry. I've just been waiting for another call. What do you have?"

"Okay, well according to the database and court records, we've had fifteen arrests for charges relating to pedophiles. Of them, only four are still in prison."

"Nice to know you can get an early release after you ruin a kid's life," Alex said.

"Ain't that the truth," Hutch agreed. "Anyway, I tracked down the remaining ones. Of the eleven, four are dead and five moved out of the state. I checked out the last two with parole."

"What did they have to say?" Alex asked.

"One of them, an Antonio Martinez, has been in a residential addiction treatment center outside of Manchester since September. His original charge was for raping a minor, but when I looked into it I found out he'd knocked up his sixteen-year-old girlfriend when he was twenty."

"Young love," Alex replied.

"Yeah, that's why I'm never having kids," Hutch replied. "But the other one, Charles Goodwin, is listed as currently residing in Penobscot. His record shows that they arrested him for possession of child pornography materials. Apparently he'd been parked outside of a school when a neighbor noticed that the car was *moving*. She called the cops, who discovered exactly *why* the car was moving and they collared him for indecent exposure. When they inventoried the car they found Polaroid's of some students and a bunch of other photos."

"Charming little fucker," she replied. "I've always wondered how they ever make it out of prison."

"That is one of life's little mysteries."

"Has he had any recent contact with his parole agent?"

"No, he missed his October appointment," Hutch said. "So I took a ride over to the house he was living at and interviewed the home owner, a Mr. Cooperman. Goodwin told him that his mom had just died down in Florida and that he was leaving to go to the funeral. He told her he would be gone for a few weeks."

"*Sonofabitch*," Alex replied. "When was that?"

"According to Mr. Cooperman it was on the 16th, two days *before* Cory Childers disappeared."

"That's too much of a coincidence for my liking."

"That's what I thought as well," Hutch replied. "I notified his parole officer and he is going to revoke him."

"Lot of good that does us now," Alex said. "We have to find him first."

"Any suggestions?" he asked.

"Yeah, get back with the parole officer. I bet that he's got a shit load more on his investigative plate than just a dickie-waver. Ask him if he'll give you copies of his folder regarding his previous contacts and residences. I'm sure he'll be more than happy to have the help. Follow down the leads and see if you can come up with anything."

"You got it, boss," Hutch said.

"Oh, one other thing, did the landlord mention if he owned a car?"

"Yeah, he said he drives a 1988 Hyundai Excel. I got the plate information."

"Put out an alert on him and the vehicle," she said. "I doubt that piece of shit would make it out of New Hampshire, let alone all the way to Florida, so make some calls to Amtrak, Greyhound, and the TSA. Find out if they have any record of him traveling to Florida."

"I'll get on it and let you know."

"Good work, Hutch," Alex said and hung up the phone.

Great, I lose one suspect and I gain a new one, she thought. *I hate this fucking game.*

At one o'clock, Alex put a call back into the school to speak with Brian Adams. After waiting on hold for fifteen minutes, she heard someone come on the other line.

"Hello, this is Principal Truitt," a woman stern voice said. "Who am I speaking with?"

"This is Chief Taylor of the Penobscot Police Department. I'm trying to reach Assistant Principal Adams."

"He's gone for the day."

"Then maybe you can help me. I'm looking for information on a former teacher, John Connolly."

"The Kill Devil Hill's Elementary School does not release school personnel records without approval."

"So," Alex said. "You're the principal, approve it."

"*I* don't approve it without the district superintendent's approval."

"Are you for real?"

"Is there anything else I can help you with, officer?"

"It's Chief, and no, I doubt there is anything you'd be willing to help me with anyway. Feel free to get on your broom and scare some children," Alex said, before ending the call.

What the fuck was that all about? she wondered. *So much for 'sure, let me look and I'll get back to you?'*

Clearly there was something more going on beneath the surface.

She pulled up the website for the Kill Devil Hill's district superintendent's office and placed a call.

"KDH District Superintendent's Office, how may I help you?"

"Yes, I'm trying to reach the superintendent, is he available?"

"Yes, may I say who is calling?"

"My name is Alex Taylor; I'm the chief of the Penobscot Police Department up in New Hampshire."

"Ok, please hold."

Again, Alex was left to hear the same droning music while she waited. Several minutes later, a man answered.

"Superintendent Monroe."

Judging from the chilly tone of his voice, there were a lot of angry people in Kill Devil Hills.

"Good afternoon," Alex said. "My name is Alex Taylor; I'm the Chief of Police in Penobscot, New Hampshire."

"Yes, what can I do for you?" he asked brusquely.

"I was hoping that you could provide me with some information about one of your former employees, John Connolly."

"And what is this regarding?" the man asked.

"Well, I'm doing a routine background check on city employees. I saw that your school district had previously employed Mr. Connolly, but we have nothing on file."

"I'm sorry, the district doesn't release personnel information," Monroe replied. "That information is available from the school where Mr. Connolly was employed."

"That's funny," Alex said. "You see, I just got off the phone with the principal, a Ms. Truitt, who said I needed approval from the district to obtain that information."

"She's clearly mistaken," the man said. "Local administrators handle the release of employee personnel information.

"Listen, I'm not sure what kind of communication issues you folks have down there, but I'm just trying to do my job and I'd appreciate a straight *goddamn* answer, if it isn't too much of a bother."

"As am I, Chief Taylor," the man replied. "As I said, the responsibility for releasing employee information rests in the hands of the local administrator. I recommend that you contact Ms. Truitt for the information that you are seeking."

"And if Ms. *Warm and Fuzzy* refers me back to you?" Alex asked.

"As I have said, all information on employee—"

"Yeah, yeah, I heard you the first and second time," Alex snapped. "You have some fucking game going on there. You two should consider a career in politics."

She ended the call and pitched the phone across the room.

"Asshole!" she roared.

She grabbed the pack of cigarettes and lit one, her fingers drumming an angry beat on the arm of the couch, as she tried to come to terms with the circle jerk conversations she just had.

Something wasn't right in North Carolina, and someone was doing their best to cover it up. There was no other way to explain Connolly's sudden departure, before the end of the school year, and the lame excuse they had given to the media. No, you don't have that kind of falling out and then, a year later, you're giving him a glowing fucking recommendation for a job, a thousand miles away, but won't release his employee records.

Alex looked down at her watch and crushed out the cigarette. She got up and retrieved her phone. It was a nasty habit she had, pitching her phone when she got pissed-off, and Alex was glad she'd invested in the extra sturdy case. She scrolled through the contacts and selected a number.

"Hey, Chief," Abby said, when she answered the call.

"Abs, if anyone asks I'm sick, *cough-cough*."

"Okay, anything I need to be aware of?"

"I need to take a little road trip down south," Alex replied. "Call it a long weekend."

"You need me to do anything?" Abby asked.

"Stay by the phone and have bail money available."

"Oh, so you're planning on having *fun*?"

"Yeah, I'm planning on *educating* a couple of teachers."

"Good luck," Abby said.

"It's not me who will need the luck, Abs."

CHAPTER EIGHTEEN

Alex had driven throughout the night.

Her journey had brought her to the doorstep of the coastal town of Kill Devil Hills, located in Dare County, North Carolina, shortly after eight o'clock in the morning.

The drive had taken her back through New York City for the first time in months. She'd chuckled to herself when the thought crossed her mind to go bang on Maguire's door just after midnight, but with everything they had been through in recent months, she figured that it wouldn't be a smart idea; especially given the strong potential for heavy weaponry to be involved.

The last part of the trip had been through a desolate expanse of land that made northern New Hampshire appear vibrant in contrast. Alex was almost giddy as the car navigated its way along the Caratoke Highway and over the Wright Memorial Bridge, signaling that the drive was nearly over. She glanced over at the choppy waters of Albemarle Sound and the cold gray October sky that hung over it.

She hoped that it wasn't a sign of what lay ahead for her.

On the other side of the bridge, she turned right onto North Croatan Highway and followed the signs for Kill Devil Hills. The town was part of a two hundred mile long string of narrow barrier islands, known as the Outer Banks, which ran north along the coast of North Carolina and into the lower portion of Virginia. It was a wildly popular summer vacation destination that was known simply as OBX to the locals.

During this time of year, the local population of Kill Devil Hills was less than seven thousand residents, but that number would swell substantially once the summer crowds descended upon it.

The town's name dated back to the Colonial era. At that time, shipwrecks were a common occurrence and locals would loot the ships before they would sink. Often these vessels would carry rum and the scavengers would bury their finds in the surrounding sand dunes. Since rum was known as *kill devil* by the English, these sand dunes became known as the Kill Devil Hills. It would be from these same sand dunes where the Wright Brothers would later take flight in the first airplane.

The nearly fifteen hours she had spent traveling here had given her a lot of time to reflect on the case. There was nothing like a black sky and the monotonous drone of your own wheels to force you to focus.

She had been deep in thought when the cellphone had rung just before eight o'clock. Hutch had followed up with her request to check with the transportation entities. An inquiry with TSA officials over at Manchester-Boston Regional Airport had determined that Charles Goodwin had hopped a Southwest flight to Fort Lauderdale on the morning of October 17th. A check of the ticket information showed that he was scheduled to fly back on the 22nd, but was a no-show.

Hutch had then contacted the Londonderry Police Airport Division, who found the man's car in the long term parking lot and impounded it. If Goodwin returned, and tried to report his car stolen, they would detain him and contact Hutch. It would get him off the street, but it also cleared him of the missing child.

Even before Hutch had called her last night, she had been certain that the key to unlocking the mystery of Cory Childers disappearance in Penobscot awaited her here in Kill Devil Hills.

As she drove along North Croatan Highway, she spotted a Dunkin' Donuts and pulled in. It gave her the time to hit the bathroom, get some good coffee, and figure out exactly where in the hell she was.

Fifteen minutes later, she sat in the parking lot, drinking a hot cup of coffee and eating a toasted coconut donut, as she searched the internet on the car's computer screen, trying to locate the KDH Elementary School. It took her about ten minutes to get her bearings before she headed off to the location. She hoped that a personal appeal would be enough to get some information regarding the mysterious John Connolly.

Alex pulled the Charger into the school's parking lot, finding a place near the front door. She walked up to the one story brick building, then pressed the intercom button and waited for a response.

"Yes, can I help you," a woman's voice asked through the speaker.

"Yes, I'm here to see Mr. Adams," Alex said.

The buzzer rang and Alex opened the door, making her way over to the reception desk.

"Do you have an appointment with Mr. Adams?" The woman asked.

"No, I'm new to the area. I was told to speak with him regarding registering my daughter as a new student."

"Okay and your name is?"

"Abby," she said. "Abby Simpson."

"Please have a seat, Ms. Simpson, while I call him."

Alex sat down in a chair and leafed through an old issue of Good Housekeeping magazine. A few minutes later, a man emerged from a corner office.

"Ms. Simpson, I'm Brian Adams, please come in," he said, flashing a warm smile.

Alex put the magazine down and stood up, returning the smile as she accompanied the man into the office.

"Have a seat," he said as he shut the door behind them. "How can I help you today?"

Alex took the nearest chair and waited till he had sat down behind the desk.

"Well, Brian, for starters you can tell me why you didn't call me back yesterday regarding John Connolly, and why I had to drive my ass down from New Hampshire to find out why the Kill Devil Hill's School District is doing its damnedest to impede a police investigation?"

She could see the panic in the man's eyes as he realized who she was. He tried to speak, but ended up just stammering.

"Easy, Brian," she said. "I'm not mad at you."

"Chief Taylor, I am truly sorry you made the trip down here, but I can't tell you anything."

"Because of Principal Truitt?" she asked.

The man squirmed uncomfortably in his seat as he tried to plan his response.

"It's complicated," he finally blurted out.

"Brian, my relationship with my former partner is *complicated*; this is an organized attempt by this school district to keep me from finding out information about one of its former employees. I'm just curious why everyone seems so angry when I bring up the man's name, yet no one wants to talk about him."

"You don't know what you're asking me to do," he whispered, as his eyes darted back and forth nervously. "I about had my head chopped off yesterday when I asked Ms. Truitt about him."

"Why did you have to ask her?"

"Because there was no file on John Connolly in the old records," he replied. "Since he was before my time here, I went to her to see if she knew anything. What I got was a fifteen minute *lecture* on divulging employee information. Then she took your information and said that she would handle it."

"And you're sure that there was nothing at all in the files about Connolly?"

"I went through the whole file cabinet, thinking maybe it somehow got misplaced. If Connolly worked here, then someone intentionally removed his folder. It's just not there, Chief Taylor."

"That's amazing," she replied.

"I wish I could help you, really I do, but this is well outside my abilities and I doubt that you will get any help from in there," the man said, pointing toward a wooden door, which Alex assumed led to the principal's office.

"Ok, well I appreciate you trying," Alex said as she got up from the chair.

Adams stood up and came around the desk to walk Alex out. When they got to the door, he put his hand on it, holding it shut.

"Look, something is going on here. Even I could figure that out. If the folder isn't here, there should be a duplicate over at the superintendent's office. That's your best shot at finding out what they are trying to hide."

"Thanks, Brian, I appreciate that.

Adams opened the door and Alex stepped outside.

"It was a pleasure to talk to you, Ms. Simpson. Once your husband and daughter come down, I'll be happy to help you get her enrolled."

"Thank you, Mr. Adams," Alex replied and headed for the front door.

Once she was back in the car, she pulled up the website for the district superintendent. On the staffing page she found a photo of the superintendent, Dr. Gordon Monroe. The man appeared to be in his mid-forties, with a badly receding hair line that only seemed to highlight his slightly pudgy appearance. If that wasn't bad enough, he had a pencil-thin mustache which looked as if some small, wooly garden animal had taken residence on his upper lip.

The site's map indicated that the superintendent's office was located about a mile down the road from her current location. She followed the directions and located the office at the far end of a small strip-mall complex. Most of the stores didn't open until ten o'clock, so the parking lot was relatively empty except for two cars near the office. Alex parked next to one of them, facing the front door of the building. She reached down and picked up the cellphone.

"KDH District Superintendent's Office, how may I help you?"

"Hi, this is Chief Taylor, from the Penobscot Police Department. Yesterday I called to speak with Superintendent Monroe about a personnel matter. I will be in town in about a half hour and was wondering if he'd be available to have a meeting with me? I'll only be around for a few hours and then I'm heading back to New Hampshire."

"Hold on please, while I check his availability."

Alex once again sat listening to the mind numbingly annoying music as she waited.

"Chief Taylor," the woman said, when she came back on the line. "I'm sorry, but I just checked Superintendent Monroe's schedule and he won't be coming into the office today. He is scheduled for a professional development course in Elizabeth City and won't be back until Monday."

"Damn," Alex replied. "Oh well, I'll stop by in a bit and drop off my business card."

"Oh, okay," the woman said. "That will be fine."

"Okay, see you soon," Alex said and hung up the phone.

She slouched down in her seat, lowering the window, then reached down and picked up the pack of cigarettes from the console. She lit one up as she stared at the front door. A moment later she watched as a harried looking man, juggling papers and briefcase, came rushing out the door, making a beeline for the car parked next to her.

Just as he approached the car door, Alex took a long drag and exhaled, sending a cloud of smoke into the man's path. He stopped dead in his tracks as he tried to figure out who had just violated his space.

"Morning, Monroe, running a bit late for your course, aren't you?"

"Excuse me," the man said. "Do I know you?"

"Yeah, I'm the pain in the ass cop you're trying to avoid this morning," Alex replied, as she opened the car door and stepped out, blocking his way to his vehicle.

"You've wasted your time coming here, officer. They handle personnel matters at the local level. There isn't anything more I can say to you."

"That's funny, Monroe. That didn't seem to stop you from giving him a *glowing* recommendation a few years back."

"Well, we've instituted new policies since then," he stammered, as he moved backward, in the direction he had just come from.

"Oh, I see," Alex replied as she followed him. "So, you *could* talk about it, but now you *won't* talk about it. That makes perfect sense. No wonder our kids are idiots."

"You need to speak to Ms. Truitt regarding any personnel matters at her school. There are ramifications that need to be considered—"

"Ramifications my ass," Alex growled. "Stop jerking my chain, Monroe. What the hell is it that you people are trying to hide?"

The man stumbled backward over the curb, catching himself on one of the support posts that held up the roof above the walkway.

"I'm sorry, I can't comment any further, you need to speak with the principal," the man replied. "We have nothing further to discuss. You have no school business to attend to here. If you come inside, it will force me to call the local police and report that you are trespassing. Good day."

Alex watched as the man hurriedly opened the front door and walked inside, locking it behind him. She stood there a moment longer, staring in amazement at the door.

Are you fucking shitting me? she thought. *Am I in fucking Oz? Did I miss the tornado?*

She turned and made her way back to the car. She took one last drag on the cigarette and pitched it out the window, bouncing it off of Gordon's car.

"Guess it's time for plan C," she muttered as she dropped the car into gear and pulled away.

CHAPTER NINETEEN

Alex sat on a wooden bench at the Avalon Fishing Pier, the wind whipping through her hair. She stared out at the Atlantic Ocean, watching as the roiling seas crashed with a thunderous roar onto the sandy beach below.

The beach was nearly deserted, save for a few brave couples walking hand-in-hand along the shoreline. She tried to remember the last time she had been to the beach, but couldn't. The water wasn't a lucky place for her. It just brought back memories of the night she had let everything slip through her fingers.

Which only made the call that she was making seem so much harder.

"I need your help," Alex said when he answered the phone.

"Don't you ever get tired of asking that?" Maguire asked.

"Nah, it's my second favorite thing to say," she replied, taking a drag on the cigarette, "right after 'kiss my ass, rookie.'"

"So what do you need? Advice or bail money?"

"The former," she replied, "but the day is still young."

"Okay, shoot," Maguire said, turning off the television and laying the remote on the desk.

"Remember our talk about my missing kid?"

"Yeah, you were having a juggling match with your suspects, anything pop?"

"I've ruled out the dad; he got busted on an *intent to distribute* charge. If he had anything valuable to trade, he would sang."

"What about the mother's boyfriend," Maguire asked.

"That's the reason I'm calling you," she replied. "I started delving into his past and I hit a brick wall. He was originally from North Carolina and was a teacher down there. When he first came to Penobscot, a decade ago, they gave him a glowing recommendation, now they're acting like the guy is hotter than a nuclear reactor leak on an August afternoon in Chernobyl."

"That is odd," he replied. "What's in his folder?"

"That's the problem," she said. "There is no folder, at least none that I am aware of. The school in Penobscot was in a bind and he came highly recommended, so they hired him, but there is no paperwork. The local newspaper down there said that he left a month before the school year ended. I reached out to the locals and they are giving me the old circle jerk. I even came down here to see if my charming personality and good looks would motivate them, but nada."

"Charming what?" he asked.

"*Anyway*......," she continued, ignoring the jab. "I was wondering if you knew anyone in Kill Devil Hills who could shed some light and perhaps intercede on my behalf."

"Not there, but I know a detective who works in Nag's Head. I can reach out to him and see if he knows anyone in the local department that can help you."

"I'd appreciate it," Alex said. "Oh, and there is one other thing."

"If this keeps up, you might as well just have me come and work for you."

"I'm just making you pay me back for all those days I had to carry you in the Seven-Three."

"What else do you need," Maguire asked. "It's starting to get *deep* here and I'm not wearing boots."

"Can you reach out to the Marriott Downtown and have them pull a bill for a Mark Childers?" she asked. "He stayed there last weekend."

"Sure," he said. "He a potential suspect?"

"I thought so, but he was staying at the hotel when all this went down. He sent me the bill already, but I want to make sure it wasn't fudged."

"No problem," Maguire said. "I'll take care of it. Stay by the line and I'll get right back to you on your current predicament."

"Sounds good," she replied. "By the way, it doesn't look good for me being able to make Gen's baby shower."

"Trust me, they'll both understand," he said. "I'll let them know."

"Thanks," she said and ended the call.

Alex went back to watching the people on the beach down below.

What would have happened if you'd just stayed sober? she wondered. *Could that have been you down there?*

She chased the thoughts away. That was then, and there was too much time that had passed to worry about it now.

Two cigarettes and twenty minutes later her phone rang.

"What do you have for me?" she asked.

"You're going to meet a Detective Martin O'Neil from the Kill Devil Hills PD for lunch," Maguire said. "Over at a place called the Black Pelican at noon. It's in Kitty Hawk on North Virginia Dare Trail. He should at least be able to give you some background on the players you're dealing with."

"Thanks, James, you're the best."

"You owe me a beer," Maguire said. "In fact, you owe me a lot of beers."

"No problem," she replied. "You can have all the ones I have in my fridge."

"I'll remember that when your state *thaws out*," he said. "Call me back if you need anything else."

"Will do, stay safe."

"You too, Alex."

She looked down at her watch; it was a quarter to twelve. She searched for the restaurant and found the location. Alex got up and made her way down the pier to the parking lot.

The Black Pelican was only a two mile drive from the pier and she got there with ten minutes to spare. She took a seat on the outside deck, which overlooked the parking lot, and ordered a beer. At five minutes after twelve she saw the unmarked Chevy Tahoe pull into the parking lot below, taking the spot next to hers. She watched as the man got out of the car, put on his suit jacket, and made his way toward the restaurant.

"O'Neil?" Alex asked as the man reached the door.

"Chief Taylor?" he replied.

"Please, call me Alex," she said, standing up to shake the man's hand.

"I'm Marty, it's nice to meet you, Alex," he said, shaking her hand and taking the seat across from her.

The man looked like he'd just walked straight out of *central casting*. He was tall, with sandy blonde hair, gray-blue eyes, and a bright smile. If the man's chiseled jaw and broad chest didn't give you an idea of his strength, his firm grip certainly did.

"So what brings you to the lovely Outer Banks?"

"I'd like to say I came down to work on my tan," she said, "but the truth is I'm trying to follow-up on a lead, regarding a missing child case, I have. Unfortunately, the locals are not being particularly *cooperative*."

"I've got to tell you that seems odd to me," O'Neil replied. "Usually everyone here is tripping over themselves to help the police."

"I would have thought the same thing, but all I keep getting is the runaround."

Just then the waitress approached the table.

"Hey, Marty, are you guys ready to order?" she asked.

"Yes I am, Teri," the man replied. "How about you, Alex?"

"Yeah, I'll have the tuna salad sandwich," Alex said.

"Excellent choice," O'Neil replied. "I think I'm going to have the tuna steak sandwich and a nut brown ale."

"Sound's good, I'll get your orders in."

"So, what is it you need?" O'Neil asked.

"Well, like I said, I have a missing kid," she said. "The mother's a teacher and it looks like she is in a relationship, with one of her colleagues, that she is trying to keep secret. It made me a bit curious. When I looked into it, I found out he was originally from here and had left his teaching job suddenly. The school by me hired him on a good recommendation, but there was no paperwork from his time here. I was just trying to get a look at his personnel folder to get more information."

"And the district wouldn't provide it?"

"No, I'm in the middle of a circle jerk with them. The principal says that only the district can allow the release of information, and the district says it's the principal's call. I spoke to the assistant principal, who told me that the file was missing."

"I know Ms. Truitt and Dr. Monroe, they are both stand-up people. Maybe if I went over there and asked, I could find out something for you."

"I'd really appreciate that," Alex said.

O'Neil pulled a pen and a notepad out of his pocket.

"What's the name?"

"Connolly, John Connolly," Alex said. "He supposedly left in…."

Alex watched as the man closed the pad and slipped it back in his pocket. The previously cheerful look on his face had turned into a scowl, as if he had just been given *terminal* news.

"Seriously? Not you too?"

"No," O'Neil said, "but now I understand why you're hitting that brick wall."

"I'm glad you know," she replied. "Do you mind sharing it so I don't feel as if I am losing my mind?"

The waitress returned, setting the beer down in front of O'Neil.

"Food will be up shortly."

"Thanks, Teri," he said, picking up the glass and taking a drink as he watched her walk away.

"Everything I am about to tell you is strictly *off the record*."

"I'm okay with that," she replied.

It wasn't true, but she had nothing else to go on, so she would have to accept it.

"I remember it well because I'd just been promoted to detective, maybe three or four weeks," he said. "I got a call from an anonymous source that said she witnessed an eight-year-old being sexually accosted at school by his teacher."

"John Connolly?" Alex asked.

"No names were given, but your day job is secure," O'Neil replied. "According to the source, the kid was getting some after-school *tutoring* when it happened. She said that the kid and the teacher both had their pants down and that she believed that there was physical contact between them."

"What a sick fuck," Alex said.

"Yeah, that's an understatement," the man said, taking a sip of his beer. "I opened up a case. Then I took a ride over to the school to talk to the principal, which was Gordon Monroe."

"This is getting good."

"Yeah, well, apparently Gordon was already aware of the *allegation* against Connolly," O'Neil replied. "He didn't seem overly pleased about what had happened, but confided in me that his *hands were tied*."

"Was there an arrest made?" Alex asked.

"Nope," he said.

"You're shitting me?"

The waitress returned, cutting off their conversation as she set their plates in front of them. "Can I get you anything else?"

Both said no and waited for her to leave before resuming their conversation.

"It never got that far," O'Neil said. "Shortly afterwards I was called into the chief's office and told that the case had been closed. He said that an internal investigation, signed off by the district attorney's office, had determined that no children had come forward to claim that Connolly had ever done anything wrong or inappropriate to them. Since the complainant was *anonymous*, there was nothing more to investigate."

"And you just let it go?"

"No, not exactly," he said. "I did an administrative subpoena for the phone records to see if I could get a number for the anonymous complainant who called me. It came back to a pay-phone a half mile from the school. I then proceeded to have my ass chewed out by my chief who wanted to know whether I understood the concept of a closed case or if I needed a refresher course back on patrol. I was told to let it go and not bring it up again, or the department could be sued for defamation."

"So this was a cover-up," Alex said.

"Clearly someone got to someone else," he said. "Unfortunately, I'd be lying if I said I knew who it was."

"I can't let it go, Marty," Alex said. "I can't turn my back on a potential child molester, especially when he is in a relationship with the mother of my missing kid."

"You will not get an argument from me, but I'm not sure what direction to give you for your answers."

"You got a weak link that I can exploit?"

"If you were so inclined to push buttons, I'd say start with Gordon Monroe," O'Neil replied. "I could tell that this entire thing never sat well with him. In all the dealings I had he was a solid, upstanding man. This seemed to break him."

"He hasn't seemed enthusiastic about helping me out so far," Alex said, as she picked up her sandwich and took a bite.

O'Neil pulled out the notebook and began writing. When he finished, he tore the page out and slipped it across the table toward Alex.

"You didn't get that from me," he said. "But if I were you, I'd put some distance from the professional persona and see if a more *personal* appeal might jar his memory."

Alex picked up the paper and slipped it in her pocket.

"Thanks," she said.

"Don't thank me," the man replied. "If I had done my job better, you might not be here."

"We're adults, Marty. You and I both know that that not everyone is treated equally under the law. Sometimes you work the system and sometimes the system works you. It's just the nature of the job."

"Yeah, but that doesn't do much good when you wake up with nightmares about not being able to help."

"True, but it has been my experience that only the honest ones have the nightmares," Alex said. "It's the ones who don't that worry me."

"Well, I think Monroe has probably had his share of nightmares over the years," O'Neil replied. "Not sure who got to him, or what was said, but I think if you figure out the right button to push, you just might be able to get him to open up."

"That's the trick, isn't it," Alex said. "Trying to find the right button that opens them up, while praying you don't push the one that shuts them down."

"Hey, it's all part of the twisted little game we play," he said, taking a bite of his food.

Alex looked out over the railing, past the sand dunes, to the angry surf that rolled in, relentlessly crashing against the beach head. She could hear the sound of seagulls crying out over the deafening roar of the breaking waves.

"I guess that makes us the lucky ones, huh?" she asked.

"If it was easy, everyone would do it."

"Don't you ever tire of it, Marty? The endless parade of victims, the system that seems more inclined to handcuff us instead of the actual perpetrators?"

"Only on the days that end in Y," he replied. "Other than that, I'm good."

Alex laughed a cynical, knowing laugh.

"Sometimes I feel as if the world has changed," she said. "That I'm living in a place where the pursuit of justice has become politically inexpedient and where the perpetrators rights trump those of the victims."

"I hope I'm not overstepping myself here, Alex, but do you mind if I tell you something?"

"No, go right ahead."

"When I got the call asking me to talk to you, they said you'd been with NYPD, so I'm not telling you anything that you don't already know, but I think we sometimes need a friendly reminder. We do the things that terrify everyone else, but they are the first ones to judge us. They're more than ready to jump up on their soapbox and spend days or weeks criticizing what we did in mere seconds. But when no one else is around, they look into the mirror and know it's a lie. They don't have the stomach for the battle, they fear the fight; they hold their lives more precious than those around them."

"But you and I are different, Alex. We long for the hunt; it's what drives us. Whether we are chasing criminals or clues; or putting ourselves in harm's way for the same people who criticize us. We're not the pundits or the politicians. We don't sit in cubicles or push pencils; not that there is anything wrong with that, but that's just not who we are."

"So, you're saying that we're like some wild animal, stalking the high grass of society, hunting for evil people?"

"Everyone wants to be a lion, Alex," O'Neil said. "That is until it's time to do lion shit."

"God, I'll drink to that," she said, raising the beer glass in a toast.

"Here's to happy hunting," he replied, tapping his drink against hers.

CHAPTER TWENTY

Alex glanced down at the paper that O'Neil had given her and then back up at the house number, making sure she had the right place.

It was a quaint, two-story home, about a block from the beach in Southern Shores, which had been converted from an old bungalow. The house had wood clapboard siding, painted a warm yellow color with white trim and storm shutters. The home sat about eight feet off the ground, on thick wooden stilts. Given its proximity to the ocean, they had probably saved the house from flooding on several occasions.

Alex pulled the charger over to the opposite side of the street, which allowed her a better view of the home, and waited.

O'Neil's background on Connolly was intriguing, but it was only a *story* at this point. Anonymous complainants and unknown victims were hardly a solid bargaining tool in an interrogation. She needed something tangible to use against the man, and this was her last opportunity to get it.

It was just after five when she saw Monroe's car pull into the driveway. She pulled her car up behind his, getting out just as the man stepped from his vehicle.

"This is harassment, Chief Taylor," the man retorted. "I plan on reporting your behavior to the powers that be, back in Penobscot."

"Please, just give me two minutes, Dr. Monroe."

"Two minutes or two hours, the answer will still be the same," the man replied, removing his briefcase from the vehicle and shutting the door. "I am not at liberty to discuss personnel matters. Take up your issues with Ms. Truitt."

Monroe turned and started walking toward the staircase.

"Ms. Truitt wasn't the principal when John Connolly did what he did, you were, Dr. Monroe."

The man stopped in his tracks and turned to look back toward her.

She could see the emotion raging inside him. Now he knew that someone had talked and they had opened a door which had been closed for a decade. It was a fleeting moment and she jumped at it, not wanting to let it slip from her grasp.

"I have a missing eight-year-old boy, Dr. Monroe, and the only lead I have to follow right now puts me on your doorstep. I need your help."

The man looked around nervously, making sure there was no one around that could overhear their conversation. He then took several steps toward her and when he finally spoke it was in a hushed voice.

"I'd love to help you, officer, honestly I would, but you just don't understand. I *can't* discuss it."

"You can't or you won't?" Alex asked.

"Does it really matter?"

"Someone once said that the only thing necessary for the triumph of evil is that good men do nothing."

"Then maybe you have me mistaken for a *good* man," he replied.

Their conversation was interrupted by the sound of a screen door slamming shut, followed by the sound of tiny feet scampering down the wooden staircase.

"Daddy!" a small voice cried out, as a small boy flung himself at his father's leg, wrapping his arms tightly around it. "You're home!"

An uneasy silence gripped the air.

"Is he mistaken too?" she asked.

Monroe stared down at the boy's golden mop of hair, then back up again at Alex.

"You have your boy, Dr. Monroe," Alex said. "All I am asking for is your help to find mine."

"We should talk, inside," he whispered. "Follow me."

"Thank you."

CHAPTER TWENTY-ONE

"Here you go, officer," Lori Monroe said, setting a mug of coffee on the table in front of Alex.

"Thank you, Mrs. Monroe," she said. "That's very kind of you."

"It's my pleasure," the woman replied as she took the seat next to her husband on the sofa across from Alex.

She took her husband's hand in hers as he told the story of John Connolly for the first time in a decade.

"It was mid-April, toward the end of my second year as principal at the elementary school," he said. "I'd originally come here from Greenville. Until then, there had been no problems with the students or the faculty. Then, one Monday afternoon, toward the end of the school day, I was sitting in my office when my secretary said that one of the teacher's aides, a woman named Julie Briggs, wanted to speak with me about a personal matter. Julie was a young girl, in her twenties, who'd gone back to school to get her degree to be a teacher. She was doing TA work as part of her college program."

"I'd assumed it had something to do with that, so I had her sent in. From the moment she walked into my office, I could tell something was wrong. She had always been a bubbly person, but now she looked positively ill. I asked her if she felt all right or if I should call the nurse. She said no, that she was fine, but needed to speak to me about something that had happened, something that she had witnessed."

Lori Monroe continued to hold her husband's hand, as if she was giving him the strength to continue.

"Julie said that on the previous Friday, after school had ended, she was in her car when she realized she had left a folder, containing some test papers that needed to be graded, back in the classroom. She walked back to the room, opened the door, and stepped inside. Julie said that she heard a noise and that it had startled her, because she thought everyone was gone for the day.

She turned and saw John Connolly in the room's corner fixing his pants. She was about to apologize for the intrusion when she noticed a young male student, named Bobby Allen, behind him zipping up his pants. At that point she realized what was going on."

Monroe reached down, picking up his coffee mug, and took a sip before continuing.

"She said that she confronted him, but he made an excuse that the boy had gone to the bathroom and his zipper had broken. He'd only been trying to help fix it, so that the boy wouldn't be embarrassed, when she had come barging in."

That's not a new story, or even an original one, Alex thought.

During her career, she'd heard a ton of them. Many involved the adult innocently *helping* the minor out. By that time, the child had already been brainwashed into believing that they, not the adult, would get in trouble if it was ever found out. Other times the adult might even threaten to hurt them or their family members if they said anything. So they were always willing to go along with whatever story the adult told. It wasn't until you got the child alone that you stood a chance of getting the truth out of them.

"Julie spent the weekend agonizing over what she knew she had *seen* and what Connolly had told her had happened. By Monday she was a physical wreck. At lunchtime, he caught her in the hallway and made light of the misunderstanding, saying how he realized just how badly it must have looked. He thanked her for making him understand that, in the future, he'd have to be more aware of appearances and not try to be so *helpful*. When she heard him refer to the future, she realized that it would most likely happen again and that's when she decided to tell me what she had seen."

Alex took a sip from the coffee cup and set it down on the table.

"What did you do?" she asked.

"At first I didn't know. I mean they *tell* you what you're supposed to do, but when you have it happen for the first time it is all overwhelming. I guess I sort of panicked. First, I thanked Julie for coming forward and then told her to go home and wait for a call from me. I said that I would call her as soon as I spoke to the police."

"Did you call the cops?"

"I was going to," Monroe said. "I planned on calling, but I wanted to make sure I was doing everything right, so I called the district superintendent's office first."

"Who was that?"

"Mary Sinclair," the man said with disdain. "She came from what could best be described as an educational *legacy* family. Up till then I hadn't realized just how deep her academic roots went. It seemed *everyone* in her family had been teachers. Her grandfather was a *professor emeritus* at UNC Chapel Hill, and both of her parents had been teachers. Her father was a professor at Methodist, and her mother was a principal at a high school in Fayetteville. Even her brother was a teacher."

"John Connolly?" Alex asked.

"Yes, John Connolly," Monroe confessed, taking a sip from his coffee mug. "Although, at that time, I didn't know that they were related. Mary was married to Archibald Sinclair, the president of the powerful, and very influential, North Carolina Teachers Union."

"Let me guess, Mary Sinclair said she would handle it?"

"Yes, she did," he replied. "As principal, I felt my notification obligation had been fulfilled by notifying my superior. So I waited for the police to contact me, and I waited."

"They never contacted you because Sinclair never called them."

"After a week I realized that," he said.

"What did you tell Julie Briggs?"

"A few days after she had reported the incident to me, Ms. Briggs sent me a letter stating that she had been reassigned to a school closer to her home. I tried to call her, but her phone was no longer in service. Then I tried to send a letter to her at the address on the envelope, telling her I needed a contact number, but the post office returned it saying the addressee had moved and left no forwarding address."

"I assume you thought that was odd," Alex said.

"That's an understatement," he replied. "Then, when I didn't hear from the police, I called Sinclair's office. She informed me that her office had been in contact with the State Board of Education and that they were looking into the matter. She said that Connolly was now on paid administrative leave and that she would get back to me to let me know what action would be taken."

"Did she?"

"Oh yes, she did. Three weeks later she informed me that the investigation had cleared John Connolly of any wrong doing. She said that their investigators had already spoken to both the boy and his family and they had confirmed that it had all been a misunderstanding. However, given the seriousness of the allegation and the lapse of judgment he had shown, Connolly would resign effective immediately."

"So they just swept it under the rug," Alex said.

"That's what I believed," Monroe said. "I knew something wasn't right. If it had been investigated, why hadn't anyone talked to me? So I started asking what I thought were innocuous questions of some of the older staff members. That's how I learned that Mary was John's older sister. I knew someone who was good friends with Dr. Carrie Ford, who, at the time, was on the State Board of Education. I asked them to look into it and get back to me. A week later, my friend came to see me. He told me, in no uncertain terms, to drop the matter, that there was nothing more to look into."

"What did you do?" Alex asked.

"I protested. I said that was bullshit because I had been told by a reliable witness who had seen Connolly with the boy. My friend said there was *no witness* and there was *no complainant* and if I continued to push the issue I would have *no job*. He told me that Connolly was untouchable; that he was protected by the union. Archibald Sinclair owned the SBE board, including the lieutenant governor, Bob Bradley, who had received sizeable campaign donations from the union. I was told that the union had paid off the parents, going so far as to move the entire family to Raleigh where they could get better care for their special needs child. They even got the father a job working in the maintenance department at Chapel Hill."

"Were you ever able to speak to the young boy's parents?" Alex asked.

"The Allen's? Oh, I tried," Monroe replied. "I went to their home, before they left town, but they had signed a confidentiality agreement barring them from discussing the matter. I later found out that Ms. Briggs had signed one as well."

"That was convenient," Alex said.

"Very," Monroe replied. "Trust me, Chief Taylor; I did everything I could think of."

"So who called the police?"

The man looked at his wife nervously and then back at Alex.

"I didn't know what else to do," he said. "Lori knew something was wrong. I hadn't been eating or sleeping. One day I couldn't take the guilt anymore and I told her what had happened."

"I said we needed to report it to the police," Lori said. "That he just couldn't let this go without reporting it."

"So you were the woman who made the anonymous call?"

"Yes," she replied. "I thought by contacting the police it would get it out in the open, that someone would have to look into it, but it didn't seem like they were keen to investigate."

"They tried," Alex said, "but the investigation got shut down."

"By who?" Gordon asked.

"The chief of police said that the matter had already been investigated and that the district attorney had signed off on it."

"Well, that explains everything," he replied.

"What do you mean?" Alex asked.

"Our illustrious chief of police, Winston Hale, is married to our district attorney's sister. I doubt he even goes out the door in the morning without checking to make sure his brother-in-law approves."

"I guess that explains why *he* put an end to the police investigation, but why would the D.A. want to turn a blind eye? Usually a case like this is a feather in a prosecutor's cap."

"Because our district attorney is Jonas Bradley," Gordon said.

"*Bradley?*" Alex asked. "You mean as in Lt. Governor Bob Bradley, *Bradley?*"

"Uh huh, and little brother Jonas does everything his big brother tells him to do."

"Holy shit," Alex said. "Talk about your cloudy gene pools."

"I can tell you one thing," he said. "This entire place is in dire need of a *bleach bath*."

"So that was the end, huh?"

"Mostly," he replied. "I resigned myself to the fact that he had gotten away with it, but Several months later, when I got the request for a recommendation, I came unglued. I went to Sinclair and told her we couldn't allow this. She explained to me how the union had already said that if we did anything to impede Connolly's career that they would haul us into court and sue the district. Sinclair said that the district was borderline solvent and it could not survive a lawsuit that it had no hopes of winning."

"The same union her husband ran?" Alex asked "And the same one who had paid off the family and witness?"

"Like you said, it's a cloudy gene pool, Chief Taylor."

"It's criminal," she replied.

"Down here it was just business as usual," Gordon said.

"So how did you wind up with the superintendent's job?" Alex asked. "That sounds like a nice promotion for all the *waves* you were churning up."

"You'd think so," Monroe said, "but it was a tactically planned *quasi*-demotion."

"What makes you say that?"

"Sinclair got tapped to be on the SBE board," he explained. "Prior to her resignation, she nominated me for her slot. Of course, it was rubber stamped immediately by the school board. No one would question her chosen replacement, especially since she was going to be at state, which meant we'd get priority when it came to funding consideration."

"So why do you think it was a demotion?"

"Because, just prior to her leaving, she drafted up new rules and regulations which gave complete autonomy to the principals in all matters relating to personnel under them; then she hand-picked my *successor* who was also approved by the board."

"Ms. Truitt," Alex said.

"The *protector of secrets*," he said.

"Couldn't you just get rid of her and put someone else in?"

"Are you serious?" Gordon asked with an incredulous look. "Do you have any idea how difficult it is to get a teacher terminated *for cause*, let alone because you don't see eye-to-eye with them?"

"I'm getting the feeling it might be difficult," she replied.

"My dear, *difficult* is pulling a royal flush in Vegas while sitting on a million dollar pot. Firing a teacher is damn near *impossible*."

"If it is that hard, it makes me wonder why they just didn't let him stay," Alex said.

"Honestly, I think his sister wanted it that way," he said. "Sort of like the whole *black sheep of the family* thing. I wondered if she knew it was only a matter of time before he did it again and that perhaps the family of the next child wouldn't cave in to some union money. With him gone it was now someone else's problem."

"I guess everything comes down to the almighty dollar."

"You either have them or you want them," Gordon replied.

"It seems like a helluva price to pay for your soul," Alex said.

"I have a feeling that, in this case, most of those involved had sold theirs off a long time ago," he said. "So where does this leave you? I mean, all of this is just a *story* without any corroboration."

"At least I have the story," she said. "That's more than what I had when I arrived this morning. One thing I have learned is that these sick bastards live in fear of their secrets coming out, hopefully I can use the threat as leverage to find out what he knows."

"A word of advice, Chief," Gordon said. "John Connolly is a very smart, very charming person. Don't underestimate him or his intellect."

"Oh, don't worry, I'm counting on him being intelligent," Alex said. "I'm hoping that he underestimates mine."

"Then I wish you good luck and I hope that, at least in some small measure, you can find a way to serve justice, even if it is *belated*."

"Thank you," Alex said as she stood up. "And thank you for the coffee, Mrs. Monroe."

"You're very welcome," she replied.

"Have a safe trip back to Penobscot," Monroe said as he walked Alex to the door and stepped out onto the porch with her. "And thank you."

"For what?" Alex asked.

"For giving me the chance to break my silence," the man replied. "And for giving me a small part of my soul back."

"You're not like Mary Sinclair, Doctor. The fact it has bothered you all this time proves that you never lost your soul."

"I hope you're right," he said. "I'd like to think the nightmares will go away one day."

"Just remember, soulless people don't have nightmares," she said as she headed down the staircase and walked toward the car.

"Godspeed to you, Chief Taylor," he said. "Now go find your boy."

CHAPTER TWENTY-TWO

Hutch was standing on a ladder in his living room, carefully applying a strip of the blue painter's tape along the crown molding, when his cellphone rang.

He laid the roll of tape on the top step and removed the phone from the clip on his belt.

"Hey, Boss," he said.

"What are you doing right now?" she asked.

"I'm just taping up the walls for tomorrow night's painting party," he said. "What are you doing?"

"I'm in the car coming back from North Carolina," she replied.

"North Carolina *state*?" he asked.

"That would be the one," she replied.

"Why are you down there?"

"I came down here to speak to a man about a teacher."

"Connolly?"

"Yep, and it is one hell of a story," Alex replied. "It seems our teacher of the decade loves to do more than just *teach* his students."

"Are you serious?" Hutch asked, as he climbed down the ladder and made his way into the kitchen.

"No, apparently he was caught red-handed, but he also has a highly connected family. Those connections, along with some liberally applied cash payoffs, made it all go away and Connolly left town with a clean record."

"Ain't that some shit," Hutch said, as he removed a can of soda from the fridge.

"It's something all right," she replied. "Anyway, I'm on my way back, but I will not be able to make it straight through. I'm going to have to crash somewhere along the way and catch a few z's."

"What do you need me to do?"

"Well, for starters, I hate to break the news to you, but I think we might have to put the painting party on hold."

"That's fine," he said. "It didn't seem like anyone was overjoyed about doing it anyway."

"Look at the bright side, when you reschedule it for next week no one will have an excuse."

"I hadn't thought about that."

"Thinking outside the box has some perks," she said, lighting a cigarette. "Right now, I need you to get in touch with Abby and whoever else is free. I want someone on Connolly from the time I get off the phone with you until I get back into town."

"You think someone might tip him off and he'll run?"

"I don't think so," Alex replied. "But I won't bet my life on it either. This is one of those 'err on the side of caution' things. Just put a body on him in a private car. I don't want to spook him before I've had a *heart-to-heart* with our little freak."

"I'll go sit on him first," Hutch said. "Then I'll arrange for someone to take my place overnight so I'll be free when you get into town."

"Good, hopefully he'll remain clueless till I get back there."

"What happens if he leaves?"

"Just tail him and see where he goes," Alex said. "It might be nothing."

"What happens if he gets spooked and packs up?"

"Follow him till he breaks the law and arrest him."

"What happens if he doesn't break the law and tries to leave Penobscot?"

"Hutch, John Connolly might be the only lead we have left to finding Cory Childers. If it looks like he is planning on getting out of Dodge, then when he *breaks the law*, stop him."

"I understand, but chances are the judge will just throw it out of court when they arraign him."

Eight hundred miles away, Alex rolled her eyes and took a drag on her cigarette.

Hutch was a good kid, but sometimes he couldn't see the forest for the trees.

Was I ever like that? she wondered.

"It's Friday night, Hutch," Alex replied. "We'll worry about whether or not the charges stick when Monday rolls around."

"Copy that," he replied. "Let me grab my stuff, then I'll head right over there."

"Okay, pass the word along to keep me posted if he leaves the apartment or if there is any other activity there."

"Will do, Chief. I'll see you when you get back," Hutch said and ended the call.

CHAPTER TWENTY-THREE

It was shortly after noon when Alex arrived back in Penobscot. She pulled her car up behind Hutch's, which was parked diagonally across from the apartment building. She grabbed the two coffee containers, along with a bag of donuts, and made her way over to his pick-up truck.

"Welcome home," Hutch said as she climbed up into the vehicle.

"Have you ever thought about installing a step ladder in this beast?"

"There's a handrail," he replied as he took the bag from her.

"You're gonna get married one day and she'll make you trade this monster in for a Prius."

"In your dreams," Hutch laughed. "Toasted coconut?"

"Would I get you anything else?"

"You're the best, boss."

"That's what it says on my business card," Alex said as she opened the lid on her coffee cup. "So what's our little pervert been up to?"

"Nothing, really," Hutch replied. "He went over to Lucy's Diner for breakfast this morning, then grabbed a paper and came straight back."

"Any visitors?"

"Not unless they were there prior to me getting here last night. No one came or went from the time I arrived, but I guess they could have slipped out when he went to breakfast."

"I doubt it," she said, as she took a sip of coffee. "If he is in a clandestine relationship with Karla Grayson, then I would think that he would go there, rather than risk someone seeing her at his place. News spreads too quickly in small towns."

"So what's your plan?"

"Well, after you're done, I think we'll go knock on his door and ask him to take a ride with us."

"And if he doesn't want to go?"

"Oh, I think I'll just have to insist," she said with a smile. "Besides, you know just how charming and persuasive I can be when I want to."

"Yeah, like a sledgehammer driving home a carpet tack," he said.

"Speaking of the devil," Alex said. "Look at who just stepped out of his hovel."

"What the hell is he wearing?"

Alex picked up the binoculars from the console and peered through them as the man made his way down the stairs.

Connolly was wearing a pair of green trousers and a khaki colored shirt adorned with brightly colored patches.

"*Jesus H. Christ*," she said, handing the binoculars to Hutch. "It's a fucking scout uniform.

"Oh, if that isn't just creepy as hell," Hutch replied as he watched the man get into the car. "What do we do?"

"Follow him," she said as she opened the door to the truck. "I'll follow you in case we need two cars."

"Yes, ma'am," he replied and started up the truck.

Alex quickly made her way back to the Charger and got in, watching as Hutch's truck pulled away from the curb. She trailed behind, keeping a safe distance, as they headed across town toward Lake Moriah.

Where the hell are you going? she wondered.

The answer to that question came fifteen minutes later as they pulled into the parking lot of the Anderson Wildlife Refuge.

As Alex watched, Connolly's car drove toward a cluster of other vehicles parked near a large, covered picnic area. Connolly got out and headed over toward the assembly of scouts and adults gathered around the benches.

Alex pulled next to the pickup, on the far end of the parking lot, next to a popular hiking trail. It allowed them to maintain visual contact on Connolly without sticking out. She got out of her car and rejoined him in the truck.

"What do you want to do?" he asked as she got in and shut the door.

"We'll just watch him for now," Alex replied. "Unless we see him head off alone with any of the kids, then we snatch him up."

Over the course of the next hour and a half they watched as Connolly led the group in activities. Then the meeting broke up and the parents began ushering their kids out to the cars. Soon Connolly's vehicle and another were the only two left on that side of the parking lot.

As they watched, a female parent, with child in tow, walked out toward her vehicle chatting with the man. As they talked, Connolly reached down and patted the young boy on the head.

"That's just wrong," Hutch said.

"Probably grooming his next victim," Alex replied.

"With the mother right there?"

"Sure, he's signaling the child that he's *safe*," she replied. "She might be a single mom who's just looking for a good male role model for the kid. She doesn't realize that she's leaving the front door unlocked for the thief."

The two continued to talk for a few minutes until Connolly turned and headed toward his car.

"Okay, let's follow him back to town," Alex said. "You follow me. If he heads directly back to the apartment, we'll snatch him up there. If he heads anywhere else, I'll go and do a car stop. Either way I think it's time that we have a chat with our little *libertine*."

"Sounds like plan," Hutch replied, as she got out of the truck.

A moment later, Alex watched as the Ford pulled out of the parking spot and headed out of the lot. She followed it, keeping enough distance so he would not spot her vehicle. It was touch and go as to where he was heading, and Alex feared that he just might go toward Grayson's house. At the last moment, she finally saw him turn in the apartment's direction.

As the man pulled into a parking spot at the apartment building, Alex stopped her car immediately behind his and got out.

"Mr. Connolly," she said, approaching the man.

"Chief Taylor," he said, startled by her sudden appearance. "What are you doing here?"

"Oh, I was just in the neighborhood," she replied. "I have been meaning to stop by and speak with you."

"Oh, is this about Cory?" he asked.

"Yes," she replied. "I hoped that you might be able to come into the office and give me a statement."

"Regarding...?"

"Just how you know Karla, any interaction you might have had with the family before Cory went missing."

"Do we have to do this right now?" he asked.

"Well, you know what they say, no time like the present."

"I don't know," Connolly said, looking uneasy. "I have plans this evening and, well, obviously I need to change."

"Trust me, we're looking at a half hour, an hour tops," Alex replied. "I'll make sure you're back in plenty of time."

"Can't we do this another time?" he asked. "Perhaps tomorrow? I have nothing going on tomorrow."

"Mr. Connolly, I'm trying to find your *friend's* missing son, don't you think there just might be a sense of urgency to that?"

The man stared nervously at the waiting patrol car and then back at the apartment. Alex sensed that there was a palpable fear gripping him. Something didn't feel right, like he was getting spooked, so she took another path.

"Listen, I know that you are a very busy man, but I just need you to talk to me about what you may know about Ricky Childers," she said, lying to the man.

Alex saw the tension drain from his body at the mention of the other man's name.

"Right now, he's being held on a charge that, personally, I don't see sticking," she continued. "If I can't develop a fresh lead, they will let him go and I think he will flee the country."

"I thought Karla said that you guys had ruled Ricky out as a suspect?" Connolly asked with a quizzical look.

"We've ruled out his *immediate* involvement," Alex explained. "However, we haven't concluded that he wasn't involved in some type of peripheral participation. Just because he may not have snatched Cory, doesn't mean that he didn't arrange it. We are still looking into his background and connections. All you have to do is answer a few questions, look at a couple of photos, and I'll bring you back here myself."

"Well, I certainly want to do everything I can to help you guys find Cory," he said. "Are you sure that it won't take too long?"

"The quicker that we start, the quicker I will get you back."

"Ok, then let's get this over with."

"Outstanding" Alex said as she led the man toward her car.

CHAPTER TWENTY-FOUR

Hutch had arrived back at the office a few moments earlier and was already at his desk, sorting through some paperwork, when Alex walked in with Connolly.

"Hey, Hutch," she said as she led Connolly into the office.

"Yes, Chief?"

"Can you take Mr. Connolly here to the interview room and grab him a cup of coffee?"

"Sure thing," he replied.

"Officer Hutchinson will get you settled," Alex said to the man. "I'll be with you in a few minutes; I just have to gather up some things."

"Please follow me, sir," Hutch said, escorting Connolly to the interview room.

Alex went to her office and sat down. She pulled out the pack of cigarettes and lit one up, taking a long drag as she contemplated the interview that awaited her. She knew that she only had one shot at this and there was no room for error. Surprise was on her side, but that was the only decent card she had to play.

A moment later Hutch appeared in the doorway. "I got him setup in the back, boss."

"Thanks," Alex replied.

"So how are you going to handle this?"

"I'm not sure," she said, taking a drag on her cigarette. "I'm trying to figure out the direction to go right now."

"Seriously?"

"Yeah, interviews are an odd thing, Hutch. Most of the time you go in with a limited amount of information, but you want them to believe that you know more than you do. If you sell it right, they talk, because they think you already know it; but if you push too hard, they clam up. No two interviews are ever the same. It's a very fine balancing act."

"Do you think he will be tough?"

Alex frowned as she twirled the tip of the cigarette on the edge of the glass ashtray.

"He could be," she said. "Connolly's smart and, by all accounts, a very charming individual. He's already survived one battle with the system, so he is most likely going to have learned from his mistake."

"And if he doesn't talk?"

"Then, barring a miracle, I'm afraid that Cory Childers name is just going to end up being one of the half million other kids in the NCIC database."

"Then let's hope he gives us something interesting to work with."

"Oh, I have no doubt that it will be interesting," she said.

Alex stood up and crushed the cigarette out in the ashtray.

"Watch the interview. When I ask him to tell me about how Karla is as a mother, knock on the door and tell me I have an important phone call from the state police."

"Okay," Hutch said, "but why?"

"That will be my *intermission*. I'm going to be leading him down a path and I want him to get comfortable before I spring my trap."

"What happens if you don't ask that?"

"Then just keep watching," she said with a smile, "but now it's show time."

"Good luck," Hutch said.

"Thanks."

Alex grabbed the file and her coffee mug before heading out the door. She stopped by the coffee pot, filling the mug, and then opened the door to the interview room.

"I'm so sorry," she replied as she walked into the small room. "I get pulled in twenty different directions the minute I walk through the door."

"Oh, no problem," Connolly replied. "I completely understand."

"Do you need more coffee?" Alex asked.

"No, I'm good."

Alex laid the folder on the desk and took a seat. She began thumbing through the papers inside as she took a sip of coffee from the mug.

"So, how long have you known Karla Grayson?"

"Oh, it has to be almost ten years now. She was one of the first teachers I met when I got here."

"That's right," Alex said. "You're a transplant like me. You're from the south, right?"

"Yes, I'm originally from North Carolina."

"Must be nice," she said.

"It was, but I decided that I needed a change of scenery. I figured New Hampshire would qualify."

"Isn't that the truth," she agreed. "So did you know Karla when she was single?"

Alex watched as Connolly thought about the question for a moment.

"No, I don't think she was single," he replied. "I think when I got here, she was dating her husband. Then she got pregnant and they got married pretty quickly."

"What did you think of him?"

"Ricky? Oh jeez, I'm probably the wrong person to ask about him."

"I take it you weren't a fan?"

"Honestly, I never understood what she saw in him. I mean Karla is a smart, attractive woman, and Ricky, well he was about one step ahead of Neanderthal man."

"That bad, huh?" Alex asked.

"Trust me, I'm being generous," Connolly replied. "Personally, I think he intrigued her, you know, that whole bad-boy thing, but when she got pregnant it all came crashing down on her. The rest of the faculty could see it, she was a wreck."

"How so?"

"Karla was trying to live in two different worlds. She was a respected teacher and mother-to-be, and then you had Ricky who was constantly trying to drag her into his *seedy* little world. She looked awful back then, like she was physically drained."

"You think Ricky was abusive?"

"Mentally abusive? Absolutely," Connolly said. "I witnessed several of their exchanges. He would just constantly harangue her until she finally caved in. Physically, I'm not a hundred percent positive, but I certainly had my suspicions."

"After Cory was born, did you notice any change?"

"Yeah, Karla became sad," he replied. "I think the magnitude of what her life had become finally hit home."

"Did you ever see Ricky around his kid?" Alex asked, taking a sip of coffee.

"Not that I can remember. If memory serves me correct, I don't think they were together too much longer after Cory was born. Rumor was that Ricky wasn't quite finished *sowing his oats*, if you get what I mean."

"I've heard that Ricky had a reputation for being a ladies man," she said.

"I'm not exactly sure if the women he fooled around with could be classified as *ladies*."

"So you never actually saw the father and son together? You don't know if they ever had a relationship."

"No," he said. "If I ever did, it would have been at some type of social gathering, like Founder's Day, but never just the two of them out together. Ricky didn't strike me as being one of those *hands-on* parents."

"What about the people he hung out with?"

"That's hard for me to say," Connolly replied. "I didn't keep the same company as Ricky. I knew some of them as parents from school, but we didn't enjoy the same social circles."

"You think Ricky might have been angry at Karla?"

"Oh, almost certainly," he replied. "Karla vented a lot about Ricky. I think she felt as if he knocked her up and then continued living his life, while she got tied down with their son. So she hit back the only way she knew how, through his wallet. She said that it infuriated Ricky."

"So you don't think it would have been out of the realm of possibility for him to try to get even?"

"Oh, I think there was a part of him that *lived* to get even with Karla."

"Revenge is a powerful motivator." Alex replied. "What can you tell me about Karla?"

"Karla?" Connolly asked. "What do you want to know about her?"

"Anything you know," Alex said. "What kind of person she is, how she was as a mother."

"I guess I don't understand why you are asking about Karla," he said, his face visibly showing the level of concern he felt at the sudden change in questioning. "I thought you were interested in her husband."

"Oh, I am," Alex replied. "It's just that I always try to get an overall *picture* of who I am dealing with. Knowing what kind of woman Karla is, from those around her, might help me figure out how someone might exploit that."

"Oh, I see," Connolly replied with a tone of relief.

Suddenly there was a knock at the door.

Alex turned around just as Hutch opened the door.

"Sorry, boss," he said. "The state police are on the phone. They say it's important."

"It's okay," Alex replied. "Tell them I'll be right there."

She turned back around to look at Connolly.

"I'm so sorry," she said. "I promise, not too much longer. Just whatever you can think of that might help determine if there is anything someone could have been able to use against her."

"I'll try," Connolly replied.

"Thanks," Alex said as she got up, grabbing her mug, and headed toward the door, closing it behind her as she left the room. She walked over to the coffee pot and got a refill.

"How's it going? Hutch asked.

"Good, they are always good when they think they are *helping* you," she said, as she took a sip of coffee. "They listen to your questions and they think you're the village idiot, going down some dumb line of questioning. So they tell you what they think you want to hear."

"So he's lying to you?"

"No, he's feeding me *information* that he thinks I want to know. Right now I've convinced him I'm still on a Ricky Childers hunt and he will tell me everything I need, to keep me on it."

"I don't know if you realize this or not, but you left the case folder in there. Aren't you afraid that he'll look inside?"

"No, I left *a* case folder in there, not *the* case folder. If he gets up the nerve to look, he will only see stuff that pertains to Ricky. It'll solidify in his mind that I'm focused solely on hunting down Karla's ex."

"Sneaky," Hutch replied.

"Remember, Hutch," Alex said as she lit up a cigarette. "This job is a game. Yes, it has life or death implications, but, at the end of the day, it is still a game. The choice is up to you whether you play it like checkers or chess."

"Well, then I'm glad it is you who is asking the questions and not me," he replied.

"Then you had better pay attention and learn," she replied, taking a drag on the cigarette. "Because one day you will sit in that chair and not have a choice."

"I'll start taking better notes."

"Speaking of taking notes, did you get Sgt. Miller's phone number like I told you?"

"Maybe," Hutch replied.

"Have you called her yet?"

"Maybe," he said with a sheepish grin.

"See, you can be taught," Alex replied. "So when did you talk to her?"

"Last night," he replied, "while I was babysitting the pervert."

"Aw, that's so cute. What did you two love birds talk about?"

"It wasn't *that* kind of talk," he sputtered as his cheeks reddened. "I was just thanking her for her help on the Childers' case."

"Well then, I guess you still have a *lot* of learning left to do," she snickered. "Did she say anything about our misogynistic little shit?"

"Yeah, she said, the DEA is involved now," Hutch replied. "When Childers found out how much jail time he was looking at, he shit himself and started singing like a bird."

"Nice," Alex said, taking a drag on the cigarette and then crushing it out in the ashtray next to the coffee pot. "I bet the thought of spending several long years away from his beloved booze and broads was a great motivator."

"It seems that way," he replied. "Vanessa said that it turned out that Ricky was only one of a dozen different couriers they were using. The case has exploded into a major narcotics investigation. They even setup a task force with the state police, DEA, and RCMP."

"And all he had to do was smile and play the concerned father," Alex said. "We would have asked him a few questions and sent him on his way, but they always think they're smarter than us."

"Like the pervert?" he asked.

"Time will tell," she said. "So, how's this long distance relationship going to work out?"

"We're not dating, boss."

"Not yet," Alex said, "but the weeks still young."

"You're not funny."

"I'm a little funny."

"No, you're not," he said.

"Eh, maybe it's a woman thing," she said. "After the interview I'll call Vanessa and see if she thinks I'm funny."

"Don't you dare," Hutch said.

"Take it easy, junior. I'm just messing with you."

"I really do like her, Chief"

"No?" Alex gasped. "I'm shocked. Here I thought it was strictly professional."

"Not that I think anything will come out of it," he said.

"Why do you say that?"

"Uh, for starters, she lives in a different state."

"What the hell are you talking about? We made that trip in just over two hours. Hell, if I knew that I was gonna get lucky, I bet I could make it faster than that."

"Chief," Hutch said, his cheeks turning bright red.

"What? I'm just saying you have to get your priorities straight here."

"Don't you have an interview to do?"

"Yeah, you're right," she said. "Besides, I bet you two could find a nice little motel, just over the state line in St. Johnsbury."

Hutch shook his head at her light-hearted ribbing.

"Keep the coffee hot," she said as she turned and headed toward the interview room.

John Connolly looked up as she walked into the room, closing the door behind her.

"I'm so sorry," she said, "but that's the problem with bigger departments, they have all the time in the world to just talk."

"No need to apologize" Connolly said. "I've been on one or two of those types of calls myself.

"So where were we?" Alex asked.

"You wanted to know about Karla," he replied.

"Yes, that's right," she said as she reached down to pick-up the folder.

She knew he'd taken the bait, as the folder had been moved from the position she had left it.

Good, she thought. *Let him live in blissful ignorance a few moments longer.*

"So what can you tell me about Karla?"

"What do you want to know," he asked. "She's a fantastic teacher, mother, and friend. I can't say that I have ever met someone as amazing as her before."

"How long did you say you've known her?"

"She was one of the first teachers that I met when I came to Penobscot," he replied. "So it's going on ten years."

"So you have known her through the entire saga with her ex?"

"Oh yes," he replied. "I've seen the entire thing unfold."

"Before I go into that, I wanted to ask about the other people around Karla. Did you notice anyone that you may have had questions about? Maybe someone who you didn't feel was a good person?"

"About Karla? No, nobody," the man replied. "Like I said, the only one that I ever thought was the wrong person in her life was Ricky."

"So you don't think there was anyone else that could have been angry with her, someone who might have wanted to get some measure of revenge?"

"Oh, God no," Connolly replied.

"You don't think there was a problem with anyone, maybe someone from her past?"

"She's one of the sweetest people I have ever met. I doubt she's ever crossed anyone in her life. Well, except for Ricky, but he brought that all on himself. I'm sure that if there was anything going on with someone else, she would have let one of us know; the teacher's lounge is a kind of peer-to-peer therapy lounge."

"So what do you know about the issues with Ricky?" Alex asked.

"Just what Karla shared with us in the teacher's lounge," he replied. "I don't think she had anyone else to talk."

"Wasn't she originally from here?" Alex asked. "Didn't she have any friends?"

"Being a teacher sort of separates you from the rest of society," Connolly said. "You're in charge of people's kids and they don't want to know that you're having troubles at home. It makes them feel *uncomfortable*, like we might snap in the classroom. So we tend to shut the world away, just put on a happy face and then talk amongst ourselves."

It was actually something Alex could relate to. Cops were the same way. They saw humanity at its worst, dealt with horrific scenes day after day, and when it came time to vent, they did it behind closed doors with the people they felt safe with.

"So what did she vent about?"

"Mostly Ricky and the latest bullshit he was putting her through," Connolly said. "Occasionally it would be about one of the parents."

"Was there anything unusual about that?"

"No, that's an occupational hazard we all deal with," he replied. "You can't make every parent happy. They all think their little Johnny or Susie is the next Einstein and blame the teacher when those aspirations don't manifest themselves in the kid's grades."

"Did she ever say that there was anyone in particular?"

"Not that I recall," he replied. "It's a small school, so the problem just moves from grade to grade. I don't recall any specific parent being someone I'd be concerned with."

"But you teach fourth grade, correct?" Alex asked.

"Yes," he replied.

"So if a new student came in, and started after fourth grade, you would not have had any interaction with them or the parent?"

"That's true, but I don't remember any in recent years."

"And Karla never mentioned having any problems with anyone outside of school, did she?"

"No, no one," Connolly said. "Karla was pretty much a homebody. If she wasn't at school, she was at home. I guess it is tough to have a young child to watch after all the time."

"So she had no one to leave him with?" Alex asked.

"Not that I knew of," he said. "You saw where she lives; it's far enough out of town that it makes it hard to have a babysitter available."

"I'd imagine it would be."

"It was easier for her when her mother was alive, but now she rarely has any alone time."

"I bet that must make it hard on you two love birds?" Alex asked matter-of-factly.

Connolly's jaw dropped and his eyes went wide in shock as he fought to regain his composure.

"Wait,… What,… I don't understand," he stammered.

"Oh sure you do, John," Alex said. "Or do you routinely go around locking lips with your co-workers?"

"I wa,… wa,….was just being friendly."

"Oh, I'll say," she replied. "Any *friendlier* and I would have needed a cigarette and a cold shower."

"I think I need to go," Connolly said as he stood up.

"You know, there is one thing I can't figure out though," Alex said. "Maybe you could help me out."

"And what's that?" he asked.

"How exactly did Penobscot's teacher of the year handle the fact that you like little boys on the side?"

The color drained from Connolly's face and his knees buckled. He grabbed the edge of the table as he fought to steady himself and collapsed into the chair.

"I don't know what you're talking about."

"Oh, don't play coy, Johnny," Alex laughed, as she reached into her pocket and withdrew the pack of cigarettes. "Here, let me refresh your memory, it's a sultry May day in the Kill Devil Hills' elementary school, one of your students pants are down around his ankles—"

"Stop!" Connolly screamed.

Alex lit the cigarette and took a long drag. "What's wrong? Are you going to tell me your tastes have matured?"

"Where did you hear these lies?"

"Oh, so Bobby Allen is a liar now?"

"You... You..., spoke to Bobby?"

"You know, the funny thing is that no one considered that Bobby would grow up one day. I mean you could make a deal with his parent's, but what if when he turned, oh I don't know, say eighteen, he might not have the same desire to honor a non-disclosure agreement. How long has it been since you left there? Oh yeah, ten years."

"I don't think I want to talk to you anymore."

"Oh, it's too late for that, cupcake," Alex said. "You're either going to occupy my time or I will start making house calls, first with Karla Grayson and then with Terry Owen. I'm sure they will be very interested in hearing how you managed to evade sexual abuse charges in North Carolina. I doubt that it will go over well here in Penobscot."

"Karla knows," Connolly said.

"Does she?" Alex asked. "Did you have a come to Jesus moment while you were eyeing her son?"

"No, it's not like that," he replied. "Look, I know I had some problems, but I'm not that way anymore."

"Oh, please, spare me the sob story about how your daddy didn't tell you he loved you enough, so you twiddled some kid's dick to make you feel better about yourself."

"No, really, I got help. I was seeing a doctor in Berlin for years. He helped me to understand what was wrong with me and I'm not that way anymore."

"Oh and was Karla so understanding?" Alex asked. "I mean she had to love the fact that her son was going to be around you. I wonder if it made her jealous to think you might be more attracted to him than you were to her?"

"We talked about it," Connolly replied. "Karla is very understanding and supportive about my illness. She knows that I have worked very hard to overcome those obstacles?"

"I wonder how hard Bobby Allen will have to work to overcome what you did to him?"

"Look, I'm sorry about that, I was a different person back then."

"Oh, so because some shrink in Berlin gave you the medical all clear, everything is good, huh? Karla is going to just allow you to tuck Cory into bed at night?"

"No, we talked about that, she knows that I can't allow myself to be exposed to that kind of environment. I go to great lengths while I am teaching to be professional and keep my distance. It's the reason I always volunteer to be partnered with the new teaching assistants or even recruit class moms."

"That's very magnanimous of you," Alex scoffed, as she took a drag on the cigarette and crushed it out onto the floor. "I bet the PTA would love to know the lengths you go to hold your devil at bay."

"You'll never understand," he said.

Alex looked at the man with hatred in her eyes. Her face had grown dark and her jaw clenched tightly.

"You're right, you little fucking piece of shit," she growled. "I'll never understand how you could steal the innocence of a young child and then sit there pretending to be some goddamn victim."

Connolly felt a cold chill run down his spine, and he knew that his physical wellbeing was now in extreme jeopardy. He thought about making a run for the door, but knew that would only give her the reason she was looking for.

"But I'm not that person anymore," he said meekly.

"So how exactly was this *relationship* between you and Karla Grayson going to work out, if being around Cory would be so *hard* on you?"

"We discussed finding a babysitter who could look after Cory overnight, allowing me and Karla to have time alone."

"Well, that would work for a while, but what about when it got really serious, did you guys ever discuss that?"

"We did," he replied.

"Oh, I can't wait to hear this plan," she said.

"Our relationship had only gotten serious over the course of the last few months. When it did, it took us both by surprise. We thought about the future and how we could work around things. Karla had proposed that Ricky could take Cory for a while."

Now it was time for Alex to be shocked, and she fought to maintain a calm exterior as she struggled to process what Connolly had told her.

"She was going to consider allowing her *ex* to have custody of Cory?

"Yes," he replied. "Karla has grown increasingly frustrated with the situation. Between Ricky not being involved with Cory and always making the child support a game, she wondered why she was fighting it. She said that she had raised him for the first half of his life and maybe it was time for Ricky to step up to the plate."

"Did she actually talk to him about that?"

"She told me she had and Ricky had been open to the idea," he said. "It was something we discussed not too long ago, maybe three or four weeks ago, but then he started jerking her around again for the child support, so I don't know what happened with it. Ricky had a habit of saying one thing and doing the opposite."

"And you would be okay with that? Letting a mother give up her kid to a deadbeat dad, because you can't be trusted to control your urges?"

"Look, I love Karla," he said, "and she loves me. I wouldn't have asked her to do that, but she knows that I can't allow myself to be in that position."

"You're a pathetic little fuck, you know that?"

"I'm just being honest," he replied.

"Wow," she said with contempt, rapping her knuckles on the desk for emphasis.

"Am I free to go now?"

"Not just yet," Alex snapped, as she got up and opened the door. "Just cool your jets for a bit and I'll get back to you."

"I could ask for a lawyer," he said. "I know my rights."

Alex spun around and glared at the man. "You do, huh? You know all about your rights, do you? How about the one about keeping silent? Cause right now that's the fucking one I would suggest you use."

"If you know so much about me, then you know my family has connections, very powerful connections," he said defiantly. "Ones that would eat up and spit out a hick cop like you."

Alex studied the man and saw that he had changed. Any fear that might have gripped him was gone. Now all she could see was a look of contempt. As if he realized that he could make all this go away with a phone call, just like he had before.

She closed the door and walked back toward the table, resting her palms down on the table top and stared menacingly at Connolly.

"Let me set the record straight here, slick," she snapped. "First, you don't know me and you certainly don't know what I'm capable of. I've been threatened by people a thousand times more dangerous than you, or your *well-connected family*, and I'm still standing. So pardon me if I don't tremble at your pathetic attempt at trying to grow a pair of balls to threaten me with. I'm not an eight-year-old that you can push around. Second, and pay really close attention, John, because this is fucking important. You see, I can also make a phone call. Unfortunately, the folks I'd share your little secret with aren't the most understanding people in the world. In fact, I'd go so far as to say they'd be downright *hostile* to a little fucking pedophile like yourself. So, I think it's in your best interests to humor me, instead of trying to pretend to be some little badass. You're people would send me a *cease and desist* letter; my people will send you back home in small pieces. Do I make myself clear?"

"Yes," Connolly said, swallowing hard.

"Good, now you just feel free to exercise your right to remain fucking *silent* until I get back to you," she said and stormed out of the room.

CHAPTER TWENTY-FIVE

"How's it going in there, Chief?" Hutch asked as he watched Alex close the door to the interview room.

"He's a fucking piece of shit," she groused as she refilled her mug and lit a cigarette.

"He didn't break?" Hutch asked.

"Weren't you watching?"

"Yeah, I was, but then one of the board members called asking if we had Connolly here," Hutch replied. "Word travels fast in small towns."

"What did you tell him?"

"I said he was here helping us out on the missing kid case. I figured that would buy us a little time."

"Good thinking on your feet," Alex replied.

"So he didn't break?"

"No, he broke," she said, taking a long drag and exhaling slowly. "It's what he said that has me worked up."

"Bad news?" he asked.

"Well, I don't think Karla Grayson has been as forthcoming as she pretends to be," Alex replied. "The two of them have been in a romantic relationship for months."

"But you already had an inkling about that," Hutch replied. "What did he say about his history down in North Carolina?"

"He said he told Karla all about it," Alex replied, taking a sip of coffee.

"You believe him?"

"Actually, I do. He said he was honest with her about his past and that he had gone to get help from a doctor in Berlin."

"Why didn't she tell us about that?"

"That's an excellent question," Alex said. "One that I plan on asking her after you drag her scrawny ass in here."

"I mean, I get it," he replied. "If they were trying to keep it secret, then I guess she couldn't have said anything about him."

"Yeah, that's fine," she shot back, "if you are trying to keep your relationship a secret from your co-workers. It's not okay when you are in the middle of a friggin' abduction investigation."

"You want me to go bring her in now?" he asked.

"Yeah," Alex said. "I have a feeling that *she* is who he was planning on meeting tonight, so she should be at home. I will keep lover boy under wraps till you go get her, I don't want the two of them talking."

"Okay," Hutch said, grabbing his jacket from the back of his seat. "What if she isn't there?"

"Then swing by his apartment and see if her car is there. If you don't see it, call me and we'll figure something out."

"10-4," he replied as he headed for the door.

Alex walked into her office and sat down in the chair. It wasn't the first time an investigation had taken a left turn on her, but it was the first time that she had hit a wall like this.

Why didn't she say anything about talking to Ricky? she wondered. *For that matter, why didn't he?*

"Evening, Chief," a voice called out, pulling her back from her thoughts.

Alex looked up to see Paul Murphy standing in the doorway.

"Hey, Paul," she said. "You're in a little early for the midnight, aren't you?"

"I swapped shifts with Bobby," he replied. "My daughter, Liz, is on the girl's traveling basketball squad, they have a match over in Colebrook tomorrow."

"Lovely," Alex replied. "I've got to hand it to parents today, my folks wouldn't have pulled the car out of the driveway to travel to one of my softball games in high school."

"Yeah, well, sometimes I think that's because they were smart. Two weeks ago my wife had to travel down to Conway on a school night. They didn't get home till almost midnight. It's ridiculous what they put these kids through."

"Small towns are all about their sports."

"Yeah, tell me about it," he said. "There are times I wish my daughter was anti-social."

"Good luck with that," Alex said with a laugh.

Murphy turned to walk out and then paused.

"Oh, I forgot to mention that Mona Richards called," he said.

"The fish fry lady?" Alex asked.

"Yeah, she said that someone from here had left a note on her door while she was on vacation, it said that we wanted to speak with her."

"Okay, I'll take a ride over," she said. "Can you hang out here till Hutch returns?"

"Sure," he replied.

"When he gets back with Karla Grayson, you can cut John Connolly loose," she said. "He's waiting impatiently in the interview room. I just don't want them talking until I have a chance to speak with her first."

"No problem, Chief," the man said.

Alex got up, grabbing her jacket, and headed for the door.

CHAPTER TWENTY-SIX

Alex made her way up the steps of the old wooden wraparound porch and knocked on the front door. From inside the house, she could hear the high pitched barking of a small dog. A moment later the door opened.

"Mrs. Richards?" Alex asked.

"Ah, Chief Taylor," the woman replied. "I hadn't expected you to come over to speak to me."

"Well, it's a small department, ma'am. Everyone has to do their share, even me."

"Please, come in," the woman replied as she opened the screen door.

Mona led Alex into the living room, as the small dog excitedly ran around in circles.

"Cute dog," Alex said. "What breed?"

"Oh, that's my precious little *Peaches*," Richards said. "She's a Yorkie. Go lie down, sweetie."

Alex watched as the dog ran over to a small bed near the fireplace. She made a mental note to avoid that particular breed if she ever had the desire for a pet. She couldn't imagine listening to that incessant *yapping* with a hangover.

"Please, have a seat," Mona said, motioning Alex to the sofa that sat in the middle of the room. "Would you care for some coffee?"

"That would be very nice," Alex replied. "Black is fine."

"I'll be right back."

Alex looked around the room, taking it in. It was a quaint little house, overflowing with knick-knacks and collectible figurines. On one side of the room was a large, three-sectioned bookcase, filled from top to bottom with hundreds of books. Across from that was an old, white-washed brick fireplace.

Mona emerged from the back of the house carrying a tray, with two mugs and a plate of cookies, which she sat down on the coffee table in front of Alex. She then sat down in one of the leather club chairs across from her.

"Thank you," Alex said as she picked up the mug and took a sip.

"So what can I do for Penobscot's finest?"

"Well, I just wanted to talk to you about Cory Childers," Alex said.

"Oh, it's such a dreadful thing," she replied. "I cannot imagine what that poor woman is going through."

"I understand you worked that evening at the dinner?"

"Yes, I was on cashier duty when Karla came to order her food," Richards said.

"Do you remember anything, did you two talk?"

"Oh yes, her little boy came up while she was in line, asking if he could go to his friend's house to get him," Richards replied.

"You heard that?"

"As clear as day."

"What did Karla say?" Alex asked.

"Well, I don't think she was particularly happy," the woman replied. "As much as any mother, that is trying to get dinner, would be."

"Do you remember anything that they said?"

"After he asked if he could go, she asked if he wanted to eat," Richards said. "He said something about not being hungry and she told him to come right back."

"That was it?" Alex asked.

"Yeah, he left and we talked for a few more minutes before she got her food."

"Did she say anything out of the ordinary?"

"Oh, just about how he looked like his dad, and how much that worried her," Richards said. "I knew Ricky growing up and I could never imagine him being father material."

"What about Karla? Did you know her too?"

"Somewhat," she replied. "I knew her parent's, Jonas and Margaret, from church. They were a lovely couple, good Christians. Karla used to go to church when she was younger, but when she hit her teen years, she slipped away. Like most kids, I guess."

"Did you see any problems with her? Hear anything unusual?"

"No, nothing like that," Mona said. "I *knew* most of the bad kids, Karla wasn't one of them."

"How'd did you know?" Alex asked.

"I worked at the high school for over forty years," the woman replied. "You learn all about the trouble makers, the slackers, and the goodie-two shoes."

"I bet you saw a lot of things over the years," Alex laughed.

"Oh my, the stories I could tell you," she said, "especially ones about that pompous ass who sits in city hall. What a little conniver he was."

"Still is," Alex said as she took a sip of her coffee.

"Zebras don't change their stripes, sweetheart."

"Did you know Karla when she began teaching?"

"No," Richards said, "she came in the year after I left, but from everything I have heard, she is a remarkable teacher."

"Yes, that's what everyone says," Alex agreed. "So, tell me what you know about Ricky."

"Everyone *knew* Ricky," Richards said. "Sad story, really."

"How so?" Alex asked.

"Well, being the son of Joellen and Mark Childers, for starters," she replied. "Not sure what would have been worse, being abandoned at birth or having them for parents."

"They seem to have quite the reputation," Alex said.

"Then there was that horrible custody battle. I swear that was all that some folks here in town lived for."

"Some people revel in others misfortune."

"That is very true," Richards said. "I'm not sure what the ultimate reason was, but by the time he started school, Ricky was already lost."

"Why do you say that?" Alex asked.

"His behavior, mostly. Teachers can tell when a child is acting up to gain attention, but Ricky was different. He seemed to actually enjoy being disruptive."

"How did his grandfather handle it?"

"He tried, but I think it overwhelmed him. I honestly believe that he thought that by showering the boy with love that Ricky would change. I don't think he understood that the damage had been done long before he got custody."

"You think he was born that way?"

"I most certainly do," Richards said. "Genetics are a powerful thing."

"From what I have experienced, I'd have to agree with you."

"Yes, police officers often have to contend with the same issues that we do," she said. "The decline in the family environment has caused all of us problems."

"This is very true," Alex said. "I remember when I would get in trouble I would get two ass whooping's; one from whoever caught me first and the second when I got home."

"And the world seemed so much better for it," Richards said with a laugh.

"Yes, although I didn't exactly believe that back then."

"So, I take it you think Ricky is involved in this."

"Well, I'm trying not to focus solely on him," Alex said, "but until I find a better suspect, he is still on my radar."

"I'd like to say he wasn't, but people sometimes do horrible things and I know that there was no love lost between him and Karla."

"One more question and I'll let you go. It's a long shot, but did you happen to notice any people that didn't look like they fit in?"

"That's a loaded question, my dear. The Founder's Day event brings in a lot of *odd* folks, both from within Penobscot and from the outside. That being said, no I don't recall anyone that made me concerned."

"Yeah, Karla said she didn't see anyone that looked out of place while she was eating."

Richards gave Alex a quizzical look. "Karla didn't eat at the pavilion."

"Are you sure about that?" Alex asked. "In her statement she said that it was when she got done with dinner that she had realized that Cory hadn't returned."

"She must be misremembering things," Richards replied. "Although I can't say as I blame her, with everything she has gone through, but I got off-duty shortly after she placed her food order. I had to come home to let Peaches out and I saw Karla walking toward her car as I was leaving."

"Are you absolutely sure it was her?" Alex asked.

"I'm positive," she replied. "I'd just had a conversation with her."

"That's very interesting," Alex said as she stood up. "Thank you so much for your time, Mrs. Richards."

"Like I said, I'm sure that with everything going on in her mind, it was a simple mistake."

"Oh, I'm sure it was. I have a hard enough time trying to remember what I had for breakfast."

"It doesn't get any easier when you get to my age," the woman replied as she and Alex walked toward the front door. "If there is anything else you need, please don't hesitate to ask."

"I will, and you have a wonderful evening," Alex said as she stepped out onto the porch.

"You too, Chief Taylor."

Alex walked down the steps, removing the pack of cigarettes from her pocket and lit one up as she headed toward the car.

She had gotten so much information from the interviews with Connolly and Richards. Now she had to process it all before she sat down to interview Grayson. She had hoped that a clue would emerge, one that would put her on the path of finding out who was responsible, but she only felt as if she had hit another wall.

Alex started the car and pulled away from the curb. She headed back to the office, slowly cruising through the quiet streets of Penobscot. The ride took her past Billy Turner's home, the last place that Cory had been seen.

Where are you Cory? she wondered as she turned down the alley, taking a shortcut to city hall. *I could really use your help right about now.*

CHAPTER TWENTY-SEVEN

"Hey, Chief," Murphy said as Alex walked into the office. "I was just about to raise you on the air."

"What's up?" she asked.

"Mr. Connolly is getting agitated," he said. "He's been threatening to call a lawyer and sue us for false imprisonment."

"Why is he still here?" she questioned.

"You said not to let him go until Hutch got back with Karla Grayson," the man replied.

Alex looked around the office, realizing that Hutch wasn't there.

"I swear, he gets sidetracked faster than a raccoon on garbage night," she said. "Raise him on the radio and find out if he thinks he can make it back here before dinner."

"Yes, ma'am," Murphy replied, picking up his portable radio. "M-11-8 to M-11-3, M-11-3 are you on the air?"

The radio crackled with static, but there was no reply.

Alex reached over and picked up the base transmitter mic. "M-11-1 to M-11-3, are you on the air?"

Again there was a burst of electronic static followed by silence.

"The Grayson farmhouse is in a bit of a dead zone," Murphy said. "You want me to ride out, see if he's having car problems?"

In the background, she could hear Connolly's voice calling out from the interview room.

"Hey, officer, I need to use the bathroom, now!"

"No, I'll head over," she said. "If Connolly sees me, he's just going to go bat-shit crazy. I'll just do the interview over there."

"What do you want me to tell him?"

"Lie to him," she said as she walked toward the door. "Say that you spoke to me and I need to have him sign something. Tell him I was on my way back and had to respond to a call. I'll let you know when I get there and when you can cut him loose."

"Yes, ma'am," Murphy replied.

Alex rode over to Grayson's place, thinking about what Richards had told her. If Ricky had re-written his own history, then it was conceivable that Karla's idea, to have Ricky take custody of Cory, could have set him off. Maybe he felt as if Karla was abandoning Cory, just like they had abandoned him.

She made a mental note to reach out to Sandy Oberti, and see if she had any luck in identifying Ricky's other siblings, when she got a free moment. As unlikely as it was, perhaps Ricky had re-established contact with them. One thing was for certain, this case had taken so many twists and turns that she was thinking she had developed whiplash, but she couldn't let any potential lead go unaddressed.

Alex pulled the car off the county road and headed up the gravel driveway. She pulled up behind the marked patrol car parked in front of the house.

"Hutch?" she shouted as she approached the front porch.

She climbed the stairs and peered into the house through the screen door.

"Karla?" Alex asked in a loud voice as she opened the door.

Everything was quiet inside.

She felt a cold chill run down her spine and felt the hair on the back of her neck stand up. It was a sensation she hadn't felt since her days back in New York City; a sixth sense that cops developed, which often made the difference between going home and going to the hospital, or worse.

She reached for the semi-automatic on her hip, drawing the gun out of the holster as she entered the house. Alex held the gun close to her body as she cautiously made her way inside. She worked her way alongside the living room wall, on the far side, which gave her the widest field of vision. As she inched forward, she kept glancing back, *checking her six* as they called it in the military, as she approached the rear of the house. There was a staircase she had passed on the way in, which led to the second floor, but Alex wanted to make sure that the bottom floor was clear before she searched upstairs.

Tactical room clearing was an art form, a choreographed dance that was best accomplished with several heavily armed friends. You could do it alone, but it took much more time. Move too fast and you could miss the threat, which would likely end badly.

As Alex approached the door to the kitchen, she cut a wide berth, slogging her way along the back wall toward the room, trying to see as much as she could before she committed herself to entering. As she drew closer, she could see a dark form lying prone on the floor.

"Oh fuck," Alex exclaimed. "Hutch?"

There was no reply.

Alex fought the instinct to rush in, knowing that someone could lurk just inside the room, beyond her sight, waiting to ambush her. She had to call for help first.

"M-11-1 to base, *emergency transmission*," she said into the radio mic clipped to her shoulder. "I have an officer down. Send back-up to the Grayson residence, forthwith. Also have fire rescue respond."

"10-4, Chief," Murphy's rattled voice exclaim over the air.

Immediately she heard Steve Harper's voice come over the radio, "M-11-7, show me responding."

"M-11-6, I'm in route," Abby Simpson said.

Now that the cavalry was responding, she took a deep breath and committed herself.

Alex made her way into the kitchen quickly, remembering the layout from her last visit. As she crossed into the room she slid along the left wall, scanning from right to left with her gun as she searched for any potential threat that awaited her.

Every fiber of her being wanted to rush to Hutch, to render aid to her injured officer, but whoever had caused the injury was still out there. It would do neither of them any good if she also fell victim.

Once she was certain that there were no immediate threats, she moved over to Hutch's side. He had a large gash to his head and a pool of blood had gathered under his mop of blonde hair. Next to him, lying just under the kitchen table, was a discarded iron fireplace poker.

Alex reached down to his neck, feeling for a pulse. It was there, but it was weak.

"Hold on, Junior," she said as she reached over and grabbed a kitchen towel from the oven handle, pressing it against the head wound.

In the distance she could hear the wail of sirens as they approached the location.

Alex began examining him, looking for any secondary wounds. It was then that she noticed the empty holster on Hutch's gun belt.

"Oh, Christ," she muttered.

Her eyes scanned the kitchen, looking for clues. A chair had been knocked over and the table was pushed against the back wall. The remnants of a ceramic bowl littered the floor, along with several pieces of fruit. Alex glanced over and could see that the back porch door was open.

Was there a struggle? she wondered. *Who left?*

A minute later Alex heard Abby call out from the front of the house. "Chief?"

"In the back, Abs," Alex said. "Watch your six, the upstairs isn't cleared yet."

Seconds later Abby appeared in the doorway.

"Oh fuck, is he—"

"He's alive," Alex said, "but I need you to stay with him and keep pressure on this head wound till rescue gets here. I'm going to continue searching the house."

"Yes, ma'am," Abby said as she kneeled down beside Hutch, taking the towel from Alex and held it firmly against his head.

"Watch the backdoor," Alex said as she got up and headed back into the living room. She reached the staircase and proceeded up cautiously.

The second floor wasn't large, just two bedrooms with a bathroom between them, and it only took a few minutes to search them. By the time she'd finished her search, Steve Harper and the fire rescue guys were entering the home.

"What happened, Boss?" Harper asked as she came down the stairs.

"I don't know, Steve," she replied, "but Hutch is injured, his gun is missing, and Grayson is gone."

"You think she's involved?"

"I have no idea," she said. "For all I know, she could be another victim. Put out an alert on Karla Grayson and tell them to approach with caution. Then I want you to contact the state police and have them send us their crime scene people. I want you to stay here till they finish and keep me updated on anything they tell you."

"Got it, Chief."

Alex walked back toward the kitchen. She watched as they loaded Hutch onto the gurney and strapped him in. She motioned for Abby to come over to her.

"Yeah, boss?"

"I know you were off-duty," Alex said. "Thanks for responding."

"I was just heading home from the market when I heard the call," she replied. "That's why I got here as fast as I did."

"Thank you, but can you do me another favor?"

"Anything," Abby said.

"Can you follow them to the hospital and stay with Hutch? I don't want him alone and I need someone there to ask him what happened when he regains consciousness."

"Absolutely."

"Thanks, Abs," Alex said as they watched the firemen remove him. "Call me as soon as you know something."

"Will do," Abby said as she followed them outside.

Alex walked out, watching as they loaded Hutch into the ambulance. Once they were finished, the ambulance headed down the gravel driveway, with Simpson's patrol car following.

She removed the pack of cigarettes from her pocket and lit one.

"Need anything else, Chief?" a firemen asked.

"No, I'm good, but thanks," she replied. "How is he?"

"I'm no doctor, but I think he'll be fine."

"I appreciate the quick response," she said.

"Anytime," the man said and headed toward the waiting fire truck.

Alex took a drag, watching as the fire truck headed down the driveway.

What the fuck happened? she wondered.

"State police are on their way, boss."

Alex turned around to see Steve Harper standing in the doorway.

"Thanks, Steve," she said, taking a drag on her cigarette. "Any idea on how long?"

"They said they had a team finishing up a job in Lancaster and should be here in about an hour."

"Ok, I'm heading back to the office and have another chat with John Connolly to see if he can shed any light on this," she said. "Keep an eye out here and let me know when they show up."

"Yes, ma'am," Harper said.

Alex walked down the steps as Harper headed back inside. She walked over and got into her car, starting the engine up as her mind continued to process what had just happened. She rolled down the window, taking a final drag, and flicked the cigarette out onto the gravel, glancing over at the barn as she did so. It was highly unlikely that anyone would have remained behind, but it was always better to be safe than sorry.

She got out of the car and walked over to the barn door, pushing it open. Alex took the flashlight out of her pocket and shone it inside. The brilliant light flooded the cavernous building, chasing away the darkness. She searched around, looking for a light switch, and found it just inside the doorway. Alex flipped the switch and it flooded the interior with bright light. Alex glanced around, looking for anything that might seem out of place.

The barn was filled with a variety of old farm vehicles and implements, but Alex wasn't interested in those items, as much as she was in what *wasn't* in the barn. She scanned the room, but the dark green quad-runner was nowhere to be found.

"*Sonofabitch*," she exclaimed.

Alex rushed over to where the other four-wheeler sat. She searched for the keys and found them dangling from a chain attached to the handlebar.

Alex climbed up on the Honda, slipping the key into the ignition and started the machine up. She pulled out of the barn and roared off past the police vehicles, cutting across the front yard.

Steve Harper came rushing out of the house to see what was going on, but he was too late.

"Chief!" he shouted as the quad went roaring past him and into the adjacent field.

The last thing he saw was the red glow of the taillights as she headed off toward the Birney River.

CHAPTER TWENTY-EIGHT

Alex carefully made her way over the unfamiliar terrain as she headed toward the River.

She knew that it was nothing more than a hunch. There were any number of reasons the other quad was missing from the garage, but it was the only thing she had going for her right now.

Up ahead, the sun was just beginning to set across the western sky, painting the blue horizon with streaks of bright pinks and reds. But the tree line was already cloaked in shadows, and it was a darkness that hid a potentially deadly threat.

The high-pitched roar of the four-wheeler shattered the stillness as she traversed along the open field. Alex knew that it was a dangerous gamble. Whatever awaited her up ahead would know she was coming long before she ever got there.

The Birney River started high in the rugged mountains along the border of New Hampshire and Maine. Peter Bates loved to fish it and she had, at his instance, accompanied him on several trips. On one occasion he had gone into significant detail to explain the geography of the river. The upper part of the river was steep, with fast moving water that wasn't suitable to fishing. However, there were several sections where it slowed down before it emptied into Lake Moriah.

Two of those locations were on the northern edge of town, and you would have to cross over a major road to get to it. Alex dismissed those as they were in the opposite direction she had seen the woman head off in before. That left two other potential spots ahead of her.

Alex *guesstimated* her location in relationship to the area where she believed was the first suitable fishing area. She veered off, making a beeline for the forest's edge, and pulled the four-wheeler into a break in the tree line. Alex turned off the machine and dismounted it. She made her way on foot, following the edge of the river and using the sound of the flowing water to mask the sound of her approach.

The sun had set over the horizon and the woods were bathed in darkness. For most people, the thought of pursuing an armed adversary in this environment would have been an unnerving experience, but chances are those people hadn't had a partner who'd been a Navy SEAL.

Maguire had taught her long ago that the darkness was an ally, if you knew how to use it.

"You don't fear the night, Alex," Maguire said to her. "You fear what hunts in the night. So always make sure you are the biggest, baddest mother-fucking hunter out there."

She'd gone about a hundred feet, listening to the ambient sound of nature, when she stopped dead in her tracks. She crouched down low and closed her eyes. A gentle breeze was blowing through the oak trees and for a moment she wondered if she had been mistaken, but then it hit her again, the pungent smell of a cigarette being carried by the wind.

Alex turned her head in the direction that the scent had come from and opened her eyes. She peered into the darkness, allowing her eyes to take in everything. The seconds ticked away and then she saw it, the faint glow of an ember off in the distance.

With her target now in sight, she continued her way along the water's edge, using every bit of the environment that she could to remain unseen. She drifted to a location just beyond the point where she had seen the burning cigarette, and then moved up into the woods, coming from the direction that would be least expected.

The dark figure was squatting down low, their back against one of the enormous oak trees, as she approached. Just off to the side, Alex could make out the four-wheeler.

When she was about ten yards out, she stopped. Alex squeezed her fingers tightly on the pistol's grip, activating the pressure pad that sent a stream of red laser light out, landing on the target in front of her.

"Police, don't move," Alex called out.

She saw the body go stiff as she continued to work her way around, moving into a better position to see her quarry.

"Let me see your hands," she said, "slowly."

As Alex watched, two hands rose in the air.

"Now get up," she said.

As the figure stood up, Alex kept the laser's red dot focused on the chest area. "So, do you want to tell me what you're doing out here, Karla?"

"I was just enjoying nature, Chief Taylor," the woman said nervously. "Would you mind telling me why you're pointing a gun at me?"

"Where were you an hour ago?"

"I was here," Grayson said, "getting some fresh air. It's been a terrible day, so I figured I would ride over here and unwind a bit."

"That's convenient," Alex said. "Down here all alone."

"I didn't think I needed a witness for me to drive around my property," Karla replied angrily. "Now do you mind telling me what is going on?"

"I'm trying to figure out why one of my officers was lying unconscious on your kitchen floor, Karla."

Grayson let out a gasp.

"Oh my God, are you serious? Who? How?"

"I hoped that you'd be able to shed some light on that for me," Alex replied.

"I have no idea," Grayson said. "I wasn't supposed to be home tonight, I had plans to meet a friend. But when I didn't hear from them, I just assumed that something came up."

Alex thought of Connolly sitting in the interview room back at the station.

"And you didn't see anyone around your place tonight?" Alex asked.

"No, no one," Karla replied. "The only person who came by today was Kevin, the postman. He dropped off a package around noon, and that was the only person I saw. When I didn't hear from my friend, I ate an early dinner and decided to take a ride out here to watch the sunset."

Alex felt a chill run down her spine.

Is there someone else out here? she wondered.

Alex's eyes darted back and forth, scanning the area for any visible threats. If Grayson had been out here for the last hour, that meant someone else had assaulted Hutch.

"We can discuss all that later," Alex replied, "but for now, I need you to gather up your stuff and take a ride with me."

"Sure," Karla said. "I just need to grab my blanket."

Grayson bent down, grabbing the edge of the red flannel material.

Alex lowered her weapon as she continued to scan the forest, listening for any unusual sounds.

Out of the corner of her eye, Alex saw a blur of activity. She had only an instant to react, hurling her body to the left and rolling as she hit the ground. Almost immediately she heard the thunderous roar of the gun, its bright muzzle flash lighting up the woods for the briefest of moments.

Her momentum carried her body forward for another moment before she came to a stop and scrambled into a defensive position behind another tree.

She brought her own gun up, but deactivated the laser. She needed every benefit that the darkness afforded her now.

"Aw, are you okay, Chief?" Karla asked sarcastically.

You dumb sonofabitch, she chided herself. *You almost bought the farm at the hands of a fucking teacher.*

"Why don't you come find out for yourself, Karla?"

"Oh, I don't think that is such a good idea."

"You know it's over, don't you?"

"Almost," the woman said.

"And where are you going to go, Karla?"

"I have some options. I just have to take care of one last problem."

"Oh yeah," Alex asked, "and what's that?"

"You," Karla said matter-of-factly.

"I hate to break the news to you," Alex said, "but that's not going to happen."

"I bet that Hutch would have said the same thing."

Alex reached around the tree, leveling the .9mm toward Grayson and fired off a rapid volley of several rounds.

The night air was once again filled with brilliant flashes of light and a thunderous roar. Alex used the distraction as cover to reposition herself to another location, several yards away, as Grayson let out a terrified scream in the distance.

"Put the gun down, Karla," Alex called out. "You're a teacher for Christ's sake; you don't know what you're doing. There's only one way out of here for you."

"You're right," she replied. "There is only one way out for me. Only one of us is leaving here, Alex. Surely you, of all people, know that."

"It doesn't have to end this way."

"Doesn't it?" she asked. "What, are you just going to let me walk away?"

"You know I can't do that," Alex replied.

"Then we have a problem," Karla said. "Because there is no way that I'm going to jail."

"You need help, Karla."

"I'm beyond help, thanks to you."

"No one's beyond help, think about Cory and John."

Alex heard the woman laugh. There was no humor in it, just a hard, cynical laugh of someone who knew better.

"John was fine while everything was going good, but he doesn't exactly have a steel backbone in him. No, I'm on my own now."

"Then let's focus on Cory," Alex said. "Help me find him and we can take care of all the rest later."

"Cory's fine, Chief," she replied. "It's the rest of us who are fucked."

"Where is he, Karla?"

"Here, there, everywhere," she exclaimed as she randomly pointed in different directions. "I guess you'll just have to work harder to find him."

Alex closed her eyes for the briefest of moments, as the words sunk in.

"Why, Karla?"

"You're asking me why?" the woman scoffed. "You could never understand."

"Try me," Alex replied.

"You have a life," she said. "Something that was stolen from me; long before I even had a chance to enjoy it."

"What about Connolly? He really cares for you. Doesn't that count?"

Grayson laughed again. "He's just another part of the problem. I guess I have just made poor choices with the men in my life."

"What about Cory?" Alex asked. "He was innocent. Didn't he deserve a life?"

"There are no *innocents*," Karla sneered. "Cory is better off now. Far better off than any of us are."

"That's heartwarming, Karla. Glad you were considering his best interests when you ended his life."

"What would you know about it?" she hissed. "I *loved* my son."

"Let me fathom a guess here," Alex said. "The way I see it, you and old John had a thing going on, but then he told you about the little *problem* he had down in North Carolina. It's kind of hard to have a steady relationship with a guy if you have to question whether he likes your kid better than he likes you."

"Fuck you," Grayson raged, firing another shot toward the sound of Alex's voice.

"I guess I hit a nerve," Alex replied. "So you came up with a plan, you'd let Cory go live with his outstanding example of a father, only surprise, surprise, good old Ricky kicked your idea to the curb."

"That cocksucker ruined my life," she said. "Then he picks his bimbos over his own child."

"So your pedophile boyfriend is afraid he can't resist your kid, and your ex won't play nice with you, because you've been playing fuck-fuck games with him all these years, so you just got rid of your son?"

"Society loves mothers, especially ones who are victims," Grayson replied, "but then you had to play super sleuth, didn't you?"

"You're a special type of sick fuck, aren't you, Karla?"

"Why couldn't you just let it go? Why did you have to go digging into John's past?"

"Hutch told you we had John, didn't he?"

"Yeah, right before I opened up his skull," she replied. "Then I heard you calling on the radio and I panicked."

"Why didn't you just run?" Alex asked.

"Because I had a feeling you'd come looking," she said. "I didn't want to spend the rest of my life looking over my shoulder, waiting for you to appear."

"Oh, I don't think you have to worry about that now."

Once again, the night erupted in fury as Grayson fired several more shots in Alex's direction. The tree bark above her head exploded as one of the un-aimed shots nearly succeeded in ending the stand-off.

Alex rolled off to her right, sliding down a small embankment. She scrambled to her feet, quietly navigating her way along the trees, until she had gone several yards.

She made her way up to the edge and peered over. It was too dark to see anything, but she could hear the faint sound of footsteps, just off to her left. Alex climbed over the berm and worked her way back in Karla's direction. She hunkered down behind a tree, waiting for the right opportunity.

A moment later she caught sight of the woman moving in between the trees, down by the water, and heading off to her right. Alex repositioned herself and when the woman reappeared, she brought up her weapon, activating the laser, put the dot on Grayson's chest.

"Drop the gun, Karla!" Alex cried out. "It's over."

Grayson stood, frozen in time, as if trying to figure out what she should do.

"Drop it!" Alex screamed. "Now!"

The woman exhaled sharply, as if the fight had suddenly drained from her body.

"Okay, okay," she said. "I'm done."

Grayson began to lower the gun to the ground, as the small red dot flickered across her chest. Alex rose up, waiting to move in and take the woman into custody.

Then everything slowed down.

Alex had felt it before, knew exactly what was coming. Years earlier she'd experienced it back in Brooklyn North, during the bank robbery.

If it had been lighter outside, she would have noticed the reflexive narrowing of her vision, the on-set of tunnel vision, as her peripheral sight diminished. All at once everything took on a muffled sound, as if she was underwater. The loud rush of her own blood coursing through her veins replaced the ambient noise of the outdoors.

Time stood still as she watched Grayson's body rise up, the gun still gripped firmly in her hand. It wasn't so much that she *reacted* to Grayson, it was more like she just allowed her body to rely on memory. The countless hours spent at the range running drills: draw, sight, acquire, and fire.

Alex leveled the gun; the green glow of the gun's *Trijicon* front sight resting on the center mass of her target. She took a deep breath and held it as she pulled the trigger. The first of two 124 grain bullets raced toward their intended target at just over 1,200 feet per second.

The woman's inexperience, coupled with her attempt to bring the gun into a firing position to quickly, caused her to fatally expose herself.

Tonight had been Grayson's first time firing a gun, and it was also her last. From a distance of less than twenty feet, the double-tap of .9mm rounds from Alex's gun sent Grayson's body tumbling backward.

The first round struck low, entering just below the woman's rib cage where it tore through her small intestine. Had it just been the one round, the odds were good that she would have survived. The second round, however, rendered the first one moot. It tore through the area of the fourth rib, sent shards of bone and bullet fragments ripping through the woman's heart.

It seemed like a lifetime, but the entire gunfight had taken less than two seconds.

Alex exhaled, fighting to control the effects of the adrenaline rush that was coursing through her body. She reached into her pocket, removing a small tactical flashlight, and illuminated the scene. The acrid smell of cordite hung like a mist in the damp night air as she cautiously made her way toward the woman.

She stared down at Grayson's limp body. She was lying face-up on the ground; the gray flannel shirt she was wearing grew darker with each passing second; as blood streamed out of the two bullet holes. Her eyes were open, staring transfixed at the night sky above. One arm was extended over her head, as if she was trying to reach the water's edge.

Alex reached down, pressing her fingers against the side of the woman's neck, checking for a pulse, yet knowing it was an effort in futility. She'd seen death to many times before to not recognize it.

When she was done, she reached into her pocket and retrieved a clear plastic bag. Alex carefully picked-up the gun that Grayson had taken from Hutch and slid it inside. He'd get it back, but for now it was evidence.

After she was finished, she slumped down at the base of the old Oak tree that Grayson had used for cover. Alex reached into her jacket, retrieving the pack of cigarettes and lit one up. She took a long drag, exhaling slowly as she allowed her body to calm down.

"You stupid *sonofabitch*," she said to the dead woman.

Off in the distance she heard the roar of an approaching four-wheeler.

CHAPTER TWENTY-NINE

The post-shooting circus had begun.

Alex sat atop Karla Grayson's four wheeler watching as a swarm of crime scene technicians dissected the location. The sound of gas generators, that powered a half dozen industrial size work lights, shattered the previous quiet of the evening and made the scene look like a movie set.

Since it was an officer involved shooting, the New Hampshire State Police had come in with their personnel to investigate. At some point she would have to provide a statement, but that would have to wait until the District Attorney's Office could send someone up. Karla's body was still there, lying under a waterproof covering, waiting for the technicians to get all their measurements. Alex watched as they set-up the 3-D laser scanning equipment that would digitally recreate the scene for all eternity.

Something had been gnawing at her the entire time she had been here, something Karla had said when she asked where Cory was. Her coming back to this place rubbed at her wrong.

Once they had enough personnel on the scene, she had directed them in a grid search, looking for anything that had seemed out of place. It was Officer Matt Christianson who had spotted it, a splotch of red flannel that floated in place as he walked along the river's edge. That was where they discovered the body of little Cory Childers.

It was another nightmare that Alex would add to the catalog she kept in her head; another innocent victim she couldn't save.

She took a final drag on her cigarette and crushed it out against the fender.

"Alex!"

She turned to see Peter Bates approaching her at a trot.

"My God, are you all right?" he asked as he began to check her for injuries.

"Whoa, whoa, whoa," she said, holding her hands up defensively. "Take it easy, Doogie Howser, I'm fine."

"They just told me you were involved in a shooting and I rushed over."

"I was," Alex replied, tilting her head in the body's direction. "I won, she lost."

Peter followed Alex's eyes and saw the bright yellow covering.

"Karla Grayson?"

"Yep," she said, fishing the pack of cigarettes out of her pocket and lighting another, "and that's not all."

"What do you mean?" Peter asked.

"Her son is buried over in the river."

"Oh Jesus Christ, no" he replied, "not Cory."

"He never went missing," Alex explained. "Karla just decided that she needed a permanent break from being a parent."

"She killed her own kid?" he asked, hoping he had somehow misunderstood what she was saying.

"Yeah, she did, Peter," Alex replied, taking a drag on the cigarette.

"I knew her for years," he said. "I would have never guessed that she suffered from any sort of mental illness."

"Personally, I don't think she suffered from it, Peter," she replied. "I think she enjoyed every bit of it."

"Why do you do this job?" he asked. "Why do you put your life in danger for people like Karla Grayson?"

"I don't do it for people like her; I do it for people like her son."

"But you couldn't save him, Alex."

"That doesn't mean you don't try, Peter. Someone has to stand in the breach."

"Why don't you quit?" he asked. "You've done your time in law enforcement. You could become my assistant."

Alex let out a laugh that was loud enough to startle the crime scene techs.

"Yeah, that would work out well with my *compassionate* bedside manner."

"I'm just saying..."

"That's sweet, Peter," Alex replied. "It really is, but you do your job and let me do mine."

"I just worry—"

"Don't," she said, holding a finger to his lips. "Not unless I lose."

"That's not very funny."

"Just don't get caught *messing around* with my corpse, Doctor."

"Alex!"

"I'm just saying," Alex said, taking pleasure in his obvious discomfort. "You're a guy; you might want to send me off with a bang."

"I swear, you're certifiably nuts," Peter declared. "You do know that?"

"You say the most endearing things."

"Chief?"

Alex turned to see Paul Murphy standing at the edge of the tree line with another man in a black trench coat and hat.

"I'll be right back," she said, getting off the quad. "Give you a chance to chase away all those nasty thoughts."

Alex walked over to Murphy. "What do you need, Paul?"

"Chief, this is Reverend Martin O'Malley from St. Benedict's Church."

He was an older man, probably in his late sixties, with a round face and ruddy complexion that hinted at a penchant for more wine than water at communion.

"Good evening, Father," Alex said, shaking the man's hand. "What can I do for you?"

"'Tis a terrible tragedy, Chief Taylor," the man replied with an Irish lilt. "Karla Grayson was one of my parishioners. I just came out to administer the last rites to her."

"I think it's a little too late for that," she said, "but I don't have a problem with it. Officer Murphy will escort you over and check with the techs."

"Thank you so much, Chief."

"Don't thank me, Father," Alex said. "I don't think she deserves any *requiem aeternam* for what she did, but that's your business not mine. Just when you're done with her, you might want to spread a bit of *requiescat in pace* to the little angel who's lying in the river bed."

"You and I both know that good people can do bad things," he said, "but that's for God to judge, not us."

"I didn't judge her, Father," Alex replied coldly. "I just arranged the meeting."

O'Malley stared at her, unsure of how to respond.

"Officer Murphy will take you down now," Alex said, ending the conversation.

"Thank you."

Alex took a drag on her cigarette as she watched the two men walk away.

"What was that about?" Peter asked as he rejoined her.

Alex watched the priest as he kneeled down and prayed over the woman. Suddenly, she felt exhausted. It was as if everything that she had been through this evening had finally taken its toll on her, crushing the tough façade, which she had valiantly held up for hours, under the massive weight of reality.

There had been no justice served tonight; no triumph of good over evil.

She had seen true evil during her career; had taken great pleasure in removing it from society, so it could no longer prey upon the weak and innocent, but tonight was different. She had been forced to taken the life of a tormented soul; a woman who seemingly had everything, but had lost her fragile connection to the world through a series of dysfunctional relationships.

Alex felt no joy in what she had to do. There was no moral high-ground that she could claim. Two lives were lost and there was no way to put a positive spin on it.

"I guess he's trying to save a lost soul," Alex lamented as she took a drag on the cigarette.

"Is that even possible, under these circumstances?"

"God, I certainly hope so, Peter," Alex replied.

"For her?" Bates asked quizzically.

"For all of us."

CHAPTER THIRTY

It was just after ten o'clock on Sunday morning when Bill Rodgers, the investigator from the state police, turned off the tape recorder.

Alex had spent the last two hours being interviewed in her office by Rodgers and the county district attorney, Scott Nichols. While it wasn't a particularly adversarial interview as both men knew the shooting was justified, it still wasn't something that she took great joy in. Admitting on tape that you took another person's life was serious business.

Even though she knew she had done everything right, she still had to measure her response, knowing the words she used could always come back to haunt her. There were countless *justified* shootings that ended up claiming the careers, not to mention the lives, of police officers.

Even after they concluded the criminal case, there was always the possibility of a civil one to be considered. Nothing drew *distant* relatives out of the woodwork faster than a potential payday brought about by the death of someone by the police. Civil cases tended to be wildly unpredictable, like 2.8 million for a coffee burn *unpredictable*. Juries got all sentimental when they were awarding other people's money.

"Thank you, Alex," Nichols said as he stood up. "I'm sorry that you had to go through this."

"That's why I get paid the big bucks," she replied.

"If you say so," he laughed. "I'm glad you can keep your sense of humor."

"It's either that or drink heavily."

"Well, if it is any consolation," Nichols replied, "I don't see that you had any other choice in the matter."

"Thanks, Scott," Alex said as she waited for the *but*; there was always a *but* when it came to lawyers.

"But I will still have to present it to the Grand Jury," he explained as he slid the paperwork into his briefcase.

"I understand."

"That being said, I can't imagine them coming back with anything other than a no true bill. Will you be willing to testify?"

"Sure," she said. "I have nothing to hide."

"There is a grand jury already empaneled. I'll get back to you with the date."

"Sounds good."

"Now go home and get some rest," he said.

"Soon," she replied. "Right now I have an injured cop to check up on."

"Okay, we'll talk soon."

She watched as Nichols gathered up the briefcase and headed out the door.

Alex sat back down in her chair and picked up the pack of cigarettes from the desk.

"Knock, Knock."

Alex looked up to see Abby standing in the doorway holding a cup of coffee. She waved her in as she lit up the cigarette.

Abby walked in and set the coffee cup down on the desk. "I figured you could use this. How you holding up, boss?"

"I'll live," Alex replied as she took a sip, "but this will certainly help. Have we gotten any word on Hutch from the hospital?"

"They're keeping him overnight for observation," Abby replied, "but there doesn't seem to be any serious damage."

"I'm sure he'll be happy to hear that."

"Probably not," Abby said, picking up the pack of cigarettes from the desk and removing one. "He'll get ragged on unmercifully for not having anything *up there* to hurt."

"Well, if it is any consolation to him, you have to be *around* to get ragged on," Alex replied.

"I'll try to remind him of that," Abby said as she lit the cigarette. "So what is going on with your shooting?"

"It's the usual dog and pony show," Alex replied. "They take days, weeks and months to decide that what you did in a split second was either good or bad. Right now, everything looks fine."

"I don't even want to imagine what it is like to go through something like that," Abby said.

"You do what you need to do, Abs," Alex said. "God forbid you find yourself in that position, you do what you know is right and you don't hesitate. If you do, you might not find yourself *around* to get ragged on by the peanut gallery out there."

"That's the part they never tell you about when they are looking to hire you," she said somberly. "That you could lose your life or take one."

"Yeah," Alex replied. "Along with the part about the crappy pay, rotating shifts, and all holidays spent away from your family."

"Guess then no one would take the job."

"Sure we would," Alex said. "Some of us are just gluttons for punishment. Besides, I'd make a crappy fireman."

"You look beat, boss," Abby said. "Why don't you go home and crash?"

As if on cue, Alex yawned and rubbed at her eyes. "I guess I'm not as young as I think I am."

"Go home," Abby smiled. "I'll call you if anything earth-shattering happens."

"I'm not even going to put up an argument, Abs," Alex said as she got up from her desk and crushed the cigarette out in the ashtray.

"It will all still be here in the morning."

Alex grabbed her jacket and put it on. "Ok, kiddo, I'll see you tomorrow. Call me if you need anything."

On her way out of town, she stopped off to pick-up some coffee and munchkins, over at Dunkin' Donuts and then swung by Memorial Medical Center. She had been getting regular updates on Hutch's condition out at the crime scene, but by the time she had cleared from it, it was too late to stop in and see him.

Alex pulled into the emergency room parking lot and walked inside. She couldn't help but notice that there was no one else in the emergency room. It never ceased to amaze her at just the overwhelming difference between medical care in Penobscot and what she had grown accustomed to back in New York City.

Life in an urban medical center, especially a level one trauma hospital, was like a well-choreographed ballet of chaos and confusion. Doctors and nurses scurried from one triage room to another as they evaluated the most serious cases, responding to cries and screams from behind the curtains. Most of the time they got it right, however, sometimes one would slip through the cracks. It was not unheard of for a *quiet patient* to be pushed down the list, only to find out later that the reason they were so *quiet* was because they had expired.

It wasn't just a chaotic place for the medical staff. Cops found that a trip to the hospital often included more work than they originally thought. Alex recalled one 4x12 shift that she had been working. It had been a brutally hot Saturday night in August. They'd followed the *bus*, NYPD slang for an ambulance, to the hospital to finish taking the complaint report from a narcotic involved shooting that had gone bad for one participant. While they were there finishing the report, they had a pick-up of a stabbing victim who'd just been brought in. As they took that report, one of the E.R. nurses ran in and notified them that there was a fight in the E.R. waiting room. When they got out there, they made two arrests for assault, after the wife and girlfriend of their shooting victim ran into each other at the hospital and attacked each other.

Life in Brooklyn North was never dull.

Alex walked up to the nurse's station, where several women sat around talking and drinking coffee.

"Hi, may I help you?" one of them asked.

"Yeah, I'm trying to find one of my officers, Chris Hutchinson. They brought him in yesterday evening with a head wound."

"Oh, Chris, yeah they transferred him upstairs already," the woman replied as she began tapping the keyboard in front of her. "It looks like he is in room E208."

"Okay, so what's the easiest way to get there?" Alex asked.

"Take that hallway over there," she replied. "Go through the double doors and you'll find an elevator bank. Go up to the second floor and it will be on your right, in the east wing."

"Thanks," she replied and headed off down the hallway.

Alex got on the elevator and pressed the button for the second floor. She was thankful that it was a short ride, as an instrumental rendition of Ozzy's *Crazy Train* played on the elevator's speaker. She got out and made her way through the east wing till she found the room.

"Knock, knock," she said as she walked inside. "Did someone order a sponge bath?"

"Hey, Chief," Hutch replied, sitting up in the bed.

"I got you some cop food," she replied, holding up the donut bag and coffee; then set them down on the bed-tray.

"Thanks," he said as he opened the bag. "The food here is pretty bad."

"That's probably on Sheldon Abbott's order," Alex replied as she sat down in the chair across from the bed. "Maybe he thinks it will make you want to leave faster and cut down the cost of the hospital bill."

"I wish I could leave right now. I just want to go home and sleep. They kept waking me up all night."

"Judging from that turban you're wearing, I'd say they wanted to make sure you didn't suffer any lingering effects of a concussion."

"It looks bad, doesn't it?" he asked.

"You're alive. Don't worry about how it looks. Although the folks back in the office might start calling you *Hajji* instead of Hutch."

"I heard Grayson's dead."

Alex nodded her head somberly.

"I'm sorry, Chief," Hutch said. "I feel like this is my fault."

"She must have hit you hard," Alex said. "Cause you're starting to sound like a babbling idiot."

"I just meant that if I didn't let this happen, you'd never have gotten into the shooting."

"Junior, first, you didn't *let* it happen, and second, the only one responsible is Grayson, plain and simple."

"Yeah, but I let my guard down," he said. "I just let her out of my sight for a moment and all this happened."

"Are you ever going to let anyone out of your sight again?"

"No," he replied.

"Then consider it one of the hard lessons of law enforcement," she said, "and be happy that you're up here in a hospital bed and not down in the basement on a slab."

"I know. I just can't shake the feeling that if it had gone anymore wrong, you could be down there."

"Me?" Alex asked with a surprised look on her face. "No, not me, Hutch; Heaven doesn't want me and hell is too afraid that I'll take over."

"It's easy for you to joke," he replied. "You didn't fuck things up."

"What, you think you're the only cop who ever screwed-the-pooch?"

"This was a pretty big one."

"Nah, in the grand scheme of things, this doesn't even register on the list," Alex said. "You know what a major fuck-up is? Getting stiffed with the wrong apartment number by a snitch, on a narcotics warrant, and killing an elderly grandmother who confronted the entry team with a gun because she thought she was being burglarized again. That's a major fuck-up."

"I get what you're saying," he said, "but I still feel bad."

"Oh well, suck it up, buttercup."

"Hello?"

Alex and Hutch both turned to look in the voice's direction.

"Hi, I'm Doctor John Ferry," he said. "I'm just doing a follow-up."

"Will he live?" Alex asked.

"He took a decent shot to the head, but I'll go out on a limb and say yes."

"Good, because I'm not done abusing him yet," Alex replied.

"When can I get out of here, Doc?" Hutch asked.

The man picked up the chart and began looking through the notes.

"Everything looks fine here," he replied. "I can't see any reason to keep you. I've got to finish my rounds, but I'll have them draw up the release papers. Figure it will be around noon, so you can enjoy another wonderful *Memorial Medical Meal*."

"That's what I was hoping to avoid," Hutch replied.

"I understand," Ferry said, looking at the items on the bed-tray. "I'd probably stick with the coffee and donuts as well."

"How soon before I can start having him earn his pay again," Alex asked.

"I'd say bed rest for a couple of days and then he should be able to go back to light duty," the man replied, "but no enforcement activity until after the stitches come out."

"Sounds reasonable," she replied. "I've got a ton of old files that need some love and attention."

"Not the basement, Chief?" Hutch asked morosely.

"A few weeks weeding through old records and I bet you'll never let anyone get out of your sight again."

"That's cold," he replied.

"Not as cold as your coffee is getting, hot-shot," Alex said. "Drink up."

"Well, I'll leave you two to bicker amongst yourselves," the doctor said as he turned and headed toward the door. "The nurse will be by later with the discharge papers and to set-up an appointment to have the stitches taken out. If you have any questions, just call my office."

"Thank's, Doc," Hutch said.

"Well, I'm going to head home to get some sleep," Alex said as she stood up. "Now that I know I get to abuse you for more years to come."

"Nice to know you care," he said.

"I care about all my little misguided children," she replied. "I just have a special fondness in my heart for a few of you."

"Awww, that's sweet."

"Don't get carried away," Alex said as she headed toward the door. "You still have to do the paperwork in the basement."

"Thanks for checking up on me, Chief," Hutch called out.

"Anytime, Junior," she said from the doorway. "Call Abby when they cut you loose and she'll get you a ride back home."

"Will do."

Alex made her way toward the elevator and hit the down button. She felt the cellphone in her pocket vibrate and she removed it, scanning the message that had just come in. A moment later she heard the electronic ping, signaling that the elevator had arrived and looked up, just as the doors opened.

"Chief Taylor," a surprised voice said.

"Sergeant Miller," Alex smiled. "Fancy meeting you here."

"Well, I, uhm...," the woman stammered. "I heard about Hutch and I just thought I'd come by to see how he was doing."

"I'm sure he will appreciate that, Vanessa," Alex said.

"We've got to take care of each other, don't we?"

"I was just thinking that," Alex replied. "By the way, they're cutting him loose in a little while and, with everything going on here, we are shorthanded at the office. I was wondering if he could con you into a ride home?"

"Oh, I'd be happy to help," the woman replied.

"Thanks," Alex said. "I would really appreciate that."

"Don't mention it."

"Hutch's room is just down the hall on the right," Alex said. "If you hurry, you might be able to salvage one of the donuts I brought him."

"Thank you," Miller said.

"Call me if you need anything," Alex said as she got into the elevator. "And enjoy your time in Penobscot."

"I will," she replied, as the elevator doors closed.

"Oh, I bet you will, Sergeant Miller," Alex smirked. "God, I so called that one."

CHAPTER THIRTY-ONE

Alex sat on the window seat, staring out at the cold, gray sky.

It was a miserable day outside, the kind that chilled you straight down to the bone. Even though she had a roaring fire going, it did very little to chase away the icy grip that had a tight hold on her.

The light rain that had fallen earlier in the day had now given way to a torrential downpour; which pounded against the glass of the bay window with enough force that most people would have cautiously moved away.

Alex didn't care. The weather outside was no match for the maelstrom of emotions that gripped her mind.

She glanced down at the amber liquid in her glass, swirling it around, watching as tiny waves cascaded over the ice cubes.

The whiskey was an old friend, one who had comforted her through many of life's toughest times, and today was one of those days.

They'd buried Cory Childers this morning.

It was a somber funeral, as one should be for a little angel, taken much too soon.

Since his father, the next of kin, was in the custody of the state of Vermont; the city of Penobscot came forward and picked up the funeral expenses. It was one of the few times that she hadn't heard Sheldon Abbott complain about an expense.

Alex had reached out to Ricky's dad to let him know what had happened. He thanked her, but he was a no-show for the funeral. It didn't surprise her; she had learned long ago that people were funny.

Father O'Malley officiated at the funeral held at St. Benedict's. The church was uncustomarily filled to capacity. They had canceled school for the day, and Cory's classmates sat in the first row. When the service was completed, several members of the police department served as an honor guard, carrying the tiny coffin from the church to the waiting hearse.

Alex led the funeral procession from the church, through the rain-soaked streets of the city, on their way to the cemetery. Along the route, folks lined the streets to say a final goodbye. They traveled past the school one last time and, as they headed out of town, the fire department set up their ladder trucks, suspending a flag between them.

Alex had heard several people at the gravesite talking, saying what a beautiful send-off it had been. She just bit her tongue and kept walking.

There was no *beautiful* way to bury a child.

Alex raised the glass to her lips and closed her eyes, taking a sip. She felt the familiar burn of the liquid as it went down her throat.

It had been months since she had felt the need to drink anything harder than wine, but today she needed it. She wanted to feel numb. Alex knew that tomorrow everything would still be the same, but for now she just wanted to chase away the demons.

She glanced at the case folder lying on the floor, Cory Childers school picture peeking out from beneath it. The blue eyes and wide smile seemed so surreal considering everything that had happened.

Alex reached over and slid the photo back inside the folder. She didn't need to feel his accusatory gaze upon her right now; not as she tried to *drown* her sorrows.

The cellphone on the coffee table vibrated.

Alex leaned over and picked it up.

"Yeah?"

"Is that anyway to greet your old partner?" Maguire asked.

"Consider yourself lucky I even answered," she replied.

"So how did you manage to get the broom-handle stuck up your ass this time?" he asked.

"I buried my missing kid this morning," she replied, talking a sip of whiskey.

"Fuck," Maguire replied somberly. "I'm sorry, Alex. I lost track of the days."

"It's not your fault, James," she said. "I'm just in a foul mood."

"I understand," he replied. "It's kind of hard not to be in a foul mood over something like that."

"I keep beating myself up," she replied. "Did I miss something that first night? Was there something I should have seen?"

"Don't do that, Alex," Maguire said. "You did nothing wrong."

"I didn't?" she asked. "There's an eight-year-old kid who's dead, and his mother led me around like the village idiot. Someone screwed up."

"You said the autopsy came back that he'd been strangled."

"Yeah, I know…" she said as she lit up a cigarette.

"Your kid was most likely dead when the psychotic bitch reported him missing."

"I keep telling myself that, but I can't shake the thought that if I had picked up on something, maybe he would still be alive."

"What, like when she tells you that her kids missing you drag her by the hair into the station house and interrogate her with a phone book?"

Alex chuckled at the inference. She'd been known to get a bit *hands on* from time to time.

"You're talking about the exception to the rule," Maguire continued. "When ninety-nine mothers report their kids missing, it's a true story. Unfortunately, you ran into the one percent psycho."

"In my mind I know you're right, but in my heart…"

"So, in retrospect, what would you have done differently?" he asked.

"Nothing," she admitted.

Karla Grayson was the poster child for fine upstanding citizen. Everything in the case pointed away from her, not toward her.

Still, it was never an easy pill to swallow.

This was the side of law enforcement that the rest of the world never saw. Where the men and women, who swore an oath to protect and serve, grieved privately over the ones they *couldn't* save.

"We both know that Cory Childers wasn't your first victim and he won't be your last," Maguire said. "Not unless you decide to hang up that shiny badge of yours."

"Maybe I will," she replied. "Maybe it's time that I stick a fork in this shit and call it a career."

That elicited a laugh on the other end of the phone.

"I'm serious."

"And what are you going to do?" he asked incredulously. "Wait tables? Be a bank-teller? I got news for you, you're not exactly the poster girl for people-person. In fact, you're the kind of woman that, when your feet hit the floor in the morning, the devil says 'damn, she's up.'"

"I was thinking about going into the adult film industry," she replied, taking a drag off the cigarette. "I figured if I am going to get screwed over at every turn, I'd at least get paid better."

"Wouldn't that go over big in the Seven-Three lounge?"

"I mean, don't you ever just get tired, James?" she asked, lying down on the window seat.

"Only every day," he replied.

"That's what I mean, what's the friggin' point? Lately it seems as if I have to work at justifying what I do for a living. I mean, let's be honest. Half the people we serve don't even like us and the other half only seem to tolerate us; until we write them a ticket."

"So what, now you want to be loved?" he asked.

"I don't know what I want," she said. "Maybe I just want to go to a party and not have people stare at me like I am some sort of pariah, or make a joke about how they can't have any more fun because 'the cops are here.'"

"Let me know when you figure out how to do that," he said. "I go to thirty-thousand dollar a plate dinners and I still get treated that way, Alex. People just don't like authority figures."

"Not until they need help," she replied.

"I've always thought their guilty consciences come out in the form of humor."

"So basically, what you're telling me is that, if I want to feel accepted for who I am, I have to start hanging out more with the knuckleheads like you?"

"In a manner of speaking," he replied. "We still judge, but at least we provide the drinks."

"Well isn't that just a lovely scenario?"

"Which, in a round-about-way, brings me back to the reason I called you."

"I'm all ears," Alex replied as she crushed the cigarette out in the ash tray.

"I'm throwing a party and I want you to come."

"God knows I can use a break," she said. "When?"

"December 14th," Maguire replied. "It's a Saturday."

"Sure, why not," she replied, sitting up and taking a sip of her drink. "What's the occasion?"

"I'm getting engaged," Maguire said.

"You're what?" Alex exclaimed, a wave of shock washing over her.

"I'm getting engaged, partner."

Alex jumped up from the seat, her hand clasping her mouth as the drink she had been holding dropped to the floor, spilling its contents all over the carpet.

Her eyes went wide, scanning the room nervously, as if some unseen threat had entered the house. A sense of panic gripped her and nothing seemed right.

"Hello? Are you there?"

"Yeah,… I'm here," she spluttered as she willed herself to regain her composure. "I'm just… I don't know,… shocked, that's all. I never had you pegged for the marrying type."

"Neither did I," he laughed, "but with everything that has gone on, I have come to the realization that life is just too short."

"I guess," she replied.

"Don't worry, someday, someone will come and sweep you off your feet too."

"Nope, never gonna happen," she replied, forcing a laugh, as she picked up the glass from the floor and made her way into the kitchen. "I'm a bachelorette for life."

"Bullshit," Maguire said. "I thought that way too, but there is someone for everyone, even you."

"Just because some fool took pity on you," Alex said, opening the whiskey bottle and filling the glass back up to the rim, "doesn't mean I'm going to make that mistake. Besides, I enjoy living alone. I don't have to choose a side of the bed to sleep on, the seat is always down in the bathroom, and the remote is always where I left it."

She took a long drink, praying that the numbing effect would take hold quickly.

"Yeah, whatever," he said. "So you will come, won't you?"

"I don't know. I have like two months to come up with an excuse."

"Get your ass down here by the 14th, otherwise I'll fly up there and drag you back."

"All right, I'll be there," she replied.

"Good," he said, "and you can bring a date."

"I'll have to check my social calendar," Alex replied.

"You do that. I can't wait to see you, partner."

"Yeah, me too," she said. "Hey, I don't mean to cut you short, but I have a board meeting tonight that I have to get ready for."

"Look at you, all professional and whatnot," he laughed. "Fine, go have fun at your meeting, *Chief.*"

"Okay, I'll talk to you later," she said and ended the call.

For a moment she stood at the island, staring out the window across the room, and let what he had just said sink in.

She lifted the glass up to her lips, finishing the last of it, and then refilled it, before making her way back into the living room.

Alex picked up the cigarette pack and lit another one, staring blankly out the window at the rain. The anger she had felt before was gone, replaced with an emptiness inside of her that hurt much worse.

As she stared out the window, her eyes focused for a moment on one solitary drop that trickled down the window pane, like a tear drop. For a moment, it seemed as if even the outside world grieved for her.

Then she felt the first tear stream down her cheek.

CHAPTER THIRTY-TWO

"So this is where it all started?"

"Yep, this is, *was*, my home," Hannah replied as she stared through the rain-splattered windshield at the old, Plantation style house, with the large white pillars.

"It's a lovely house," Tatiana said.

"Yes, my mother thought so too," Hannah replied. "I thought it was more like a *museum*, a place where she could showcase all the Waltham money."

It had been over a year since she had been in the home; one final time to make things *right* with her dear mother. Months earlier she had run away, trading in her former life as Susan Waltham for that of Hannah Kurtz.

Her mother, Rebecca Waltham, was a creature of habit, and one of the things on her daily *must-do* list was her beloved treadmill. In retrospect, it seemed reasonable that she kept herself in such good shape, what with the number of beds she was hopping in and out of regularly.

Ironically, she had gotten the idea from a book, *Arsenic and Old Lace*, which she had once read while trying to *escape* from her mother's incessant badgering.

Hannah recalled how, on several occasions, she had slipped inside the house to add poison to her mother's water bottle, then would hide inside the closest to watch. It had become a game to her, to see whether this time would be the one where she would finally succumb.

Most days her mother would finish her run and head to the shower, allowing her to slip out of the house undetected.

Sadly, when the day had arrived, and she watched her mother tumble off the treadmill, her enjoyment was curtailed by the arrival of the police. She had barely enough time to get out of the house and make her escape in her mother's car. It had always annoyed her that the entrance for the garage had been on the other end of the property, but when the time had come, it had worked to her benefit.

Hannah still didn't know exactly what had drawn the police back to the house, but she resented them for taking away the *moment* she had worked so hard for. The new police chief had more going for her than the last one, and it seemed that she had been closing in on her at every turn.

For a while, she had even considered just running away from it all, abandoning her grand plan for revenge and exchanging it for safety, but the anger and resentment was too deep. She had a score to settle with her father, her ex-boyfriend, and her best friend. So she had packed away her fears, focused on what mattered, and began to plan meticulously. It took time and patience, but one by one they all fell. What started off as a simple act of revenge had quickly turned into an obsession.

There was something cathartic about watching the life drain away from someone that had hurt you. But when her list was complete, she found that she couldn't stop. Soon she began moving from place to place, *creating* encounters, which she would then use to justify her acts.

While it was fulfilling, it had also been a lonely existence. That was until she met Tatiana. She was both a kindred spirit and a maternal figure. Someone she could trust with her life and surrender her most intimate desires to.

"Do you miss it?" Tatiana asked.

"Sometimes," she confessed, "but that was before all the hurt and the lies."

"It's too bad that we can't go back to those simpler times," Tatiana said.

Hannah looked over at the woman. She smiled and took her hand in hers.

"Yes, but if we lived in the past, then we would have to surrender the present."

"And the future," the woman smiled.

"And the future is filled with *endless possibilities*," Hannah purred.

"Shall we go then?" Tatiana asked.

The two women had traveled back north to restock.

Tatiana had a cache of supplies scattered throughout the northeast, courtesy of the late Keith Banning, and they had used the trip to revisit some of their old haunts. Tatiana also had an outstanding score to settle with someone named Susan Hadley.

They had developed a rhythm between the two of them. Each took turns luring in their victim, so that, in the off-chance anyone had noticed the person leaving with someone, the description always varied.

They had also adopted that philosophy with everything else, from hair color, to attire, to the methods they used to dispatch their victims to the afterlife. It was a twisted theme on the old board game: Clue.

One time it would be the sultry older woman, with auburn hair, in the park with a steak knife. The next time it would be the young vixen, with blonde hair, in the back of a car with a derringer.

There victims were as random as the weather. One day it could be a male tourist from France who was visiting D.C., the next it might be a Baptist preacher's daughter, who they picked up for some *fun* in a lesbian bar in Charleston, South Carolina. They acted sporadically, never committed another crime in the same place, and generally left the state long before the police even knew they had a victim.

Their only M.O. was that there was no M.O.

"Almost," Hannah answered. "I just need to make one more stop."

"Where do you want to go?"

"The police chief's house," she stated.

"Are you serious?" Tatiana asked. "Do you think that's wise?"

"Well, not to the house," Hannah said, "just near it. I know a spot, across the lake where we can sit and watch through binoculars. I just need to see who it is I am up against."

Tatiana understood what she meant.

As hard as it was to imagine, they each had a strong attraction to their individual antagonist; a sort of *moth to the flame* desire. There was always an inherent risk, but that was where the fun was.

"Tell me where to go."

Twenty minutes later they sat at the far end of a parking lot for one of the public marinas that serviced Lake Moriah. There were several other vehicles parked nearby, but the fogged up windows made it clear that those inside had other things on their mind than the occupants of the latest car to join the mix.

Hannah reached behind the seat and grabbed the 20x binoculars. A moment later she was gazing out across the lake at the small house that sat on the other side.

"God, I love these things," she whispered as she rested the binoculars on the edge of the dashboard. "It's like you can reach out and touch someone."

"I was just thinking the same thing," Tatiana chuckled as she reached down and caressed Hannah's leg.

"Mmmmm," Hannah purred. "I bet you were.

The interior of the house was brightly lit and afforded her a clear view as she peered through the bay window. She tried to hold the binoculars still as she searched for her prey. Something that proved extremely difficult as she felt Tatiana's hand slip beneath the edge of her dress.

"You have only yourself to blame, baby," Tatiana replied. "Look where you brought me."

"I could take you into a church confessional and you'd still want to make out with me," Hannah laughed as she continued to scan the house.

"Ooh, we haven't done it there yet."

"Add it to the bucket-list, sexy," Hannah replied.

"Haven't you seen enough yet?" Tatiana asked impatiently.

"Almost," she replied. "Oh wait,….. I see someone."

Hannah watched as a figure emerged from the back, wearing a bathrobe and a towel wrapped around her head. As she continued to stare through the binoculars, the woman poured a drink, then made her way toward the window and sat down on the couch.

"Fuck these things are awesome," she said.

"Let me see," Tatiana said, picking up on Hannah's excitement.

"Hold on," she replied.

The woman sat the glass down, then reached up, pulling the towel free, and began drying her hair.

"Wow, she's a lot hotter than old Chief Parker was," Hannah remarked.

"Now I have to see," Tatiana said as she took the binoculars.

She scanned the horizon, peering up from the lenses as she tried to get her bearings. After a moment, she located the house and focused on the window. She could make-out the figure sitting on the couch and gazed intently, like a voyeur waiting to capture the moment, as they worked the towel around their head.

Tatiana let out an audible gasp when the moment finally came.

"I told you she was hot," Hannah replied.

As Tatiana continued to watch, she saw the same blonde haired woman that had appeared at Keith Banning's cabin nearly a year earlier.

CHAPTER THIRTY-THREE

Alex tossed the towel onto the coffee table and picked up the pack of cigarettes. She took one out and lit it, taking a long drag as she reclined back on the couch.

The whiskey had done its job, and she was enjoying the blissful comfort that came with the familiar numbness.

She stared out at the cold, empty blackness that stared back at her through the window and laughed.

Isn't that the perfect metaphor for me? she thought. *Just another cold, empty, black-hearted bitch*.

Everyone around her seemed to have found love. Maguire had Melody, Hutch had Vanessa, Christ, even Sheldon Abbott had his *Juggs* Montgomery.

Ok, that isn't exactly love, she corrected herself, *but it's close enough for government work*.

What did she have?

"Frustration, that's what you have," she said, slurring her words as she raised her glass up in a mock toast.

She'd sacrificed everything for her career, putting the job before family, friends, everything. Now it felt that the very thing she had given it all up for was turning against her.

It didn't matter what they all said. It didn't matter that Karla Grayson was a psychotic bitch that had fooled everyone. Her job had been to save Cory Childers, and she had failed.

"You're a frustrated fuck-up," she laughed as she took another drink.

Alex heard a knock on the door.

"Really?" she said. "Now my misery needs a fucking audience?"

Alex took a drag on the cigarette and closed her eyes, hoping the distraction would go away.

She didn't want to entertain anyone, and she didn't want anyone to try to make her feel better. She just wanted to get drunk and pass out.

Is that too much to ask? she wondered.

A moment later she heard another knock on the door.

"Go the fuck away," she shouted.

The next knock was louder, as if whoever was outside was trying to telegraph some sense of urgency.

"Oh for fuck's sake, enough," she ranted as she finally relented and got up from the couch. "You should have turned the fucking lights out."

She set the glass down on the kitchen island before heading toward the door. Whoever it was had no idea the shit storm that was about to descend upon them.

Alex unlocked the door and swung it open violently.

"What the fuck?" she screamed.

"Jesus Christ," Peter said, taking a step backward. "I've been trying to call you."

"I wasn't available," Alex replied. "It wasn't an invitation to knock down my fucking door."

"I was worried," he said, watching as she turned around and headed back toward the kitchen, flipping the door closed as she went.

Peter grabbed the door before it shut and followed her inside.

Alex poured herself a refill as she watched him shut the door and take off his jacket.

"Don't get too comfortable," Alex said, "you're not going to be here that long."

"Why didn't you answer your phone?"

"I wanted to be alone," she replied. "*Hint, hint.*"

"Wow, how incredibly selfish of me," Peter said. "I apologize for being worried about you."

"Well then, I accept your apology, so you can leave now."

"Are you drunk?"

"No," she said, taking a sip of the drink, "but I'm working on it."

"You need to stop, Alex," Peter replied. "That's not going to help."

"Oh for Christ's sake, Peter, lighten up. You're not my mother."

"No, I'm not, but I care about you just the same."

Alex shot him an angry look. "Don't presume to think you know anything about how my mother *cared* for me."

"I just meant…"

She waived her hand dismissively at him as she walked back into the living room with her drink and sat down on the couch.

Peter followed her in and joined her on the couch.

"I'm sorry," Alex said as she cradled the glass in her hand and stared out the window. "I'm just in a terrible mood."

"It's okay, I understand," he said softly.

"Do you?" Alex asked.

"Yes," he replied, "and no. I mean I've lost patients before, but I can't imagine it is comparable to what you are going through."

"Not really," she admitted.

Alex wondered how could she explain to him that the pain that she was trying to chase away had less to do with the case and more to do with her feeling of being alone?

"I'm sorry," he said. "I wish I could say something that would make it go away."

She turned to look at him. She knew he was only trying to help her. Even if he didn't understand everything that was going on, there was no need for her to be a bitch to him.

"That's sweet, Peter," Alex said. "It really is and I appreciate it, but it's late and you should go home."

"Are you sure you are going to be okay?"

"Yeah," she said with a pained smile on her face. "I'll be fine."

Bates looked at her, trying desperately to gauge the sincerity of the response. He didn't want to leave her this way, but he had learned the hard way that she was a force to be reckoned with when she was angry.

"Okay," he said with grudging acceptance, "if you say so."

"I say so," she replied as she stood up. "I'll be fine."

Bates got up and slowly headed toward the door, pausing in the entryway to grab his jacket.

"Promise me you'll call if you need anything?" he said as he put the coat back on.

"You're so sweet," she said as she leaned in to kiss him goodbye.

What had started as a quick kiss lingered a moment longer as she felt the warmth of his lips on hers.

She closed her eyes; aching to capture the moment. She felt his hand clasp the back of her head as the gentle goodbye kiss turned passionate. She wrapped her arms around him, holding him tightly, as she felt his lips drift from hers, making their way down her jaw, until she felt them on her neck.

"No," her mouth protested, even as her body willed him to continue.

He backed her up against the wall, his body pressing hard against as he devoured her with his mouth.

Alex moaned loudly, even as the internal battle raged deep inside her.

"Oh, God," she murmured as she felt his hand slide down her back.

She wanted him to stop, wanted to push him away. Her mind was screaming for her to take back control, but she couldn't do it. Something deep inside her pushed away those thoughts and she surrendered to her desire.

Alex reached up, grabbing the lapels of his jacket and pulled it down. Peter pulled away for a moment, allowing her to jerk the coat free. In that moment, their eyes met and each of them saw the wild look of unbridled lust in one another's eyes.

Peter reached down, picking her up in his arms as she wrapped hers around his neck, their lips meeting again. He carried her back into the living room and laid her down on the couch.

Alex stared up at him, watching as he stood in front of her and removed his shirt. She bit down on her lip as she watched the material give way to reveal the taut muscles beneath.

Something had changed in him, she could see it. For the moment, the kind Dr. Bates was gone, replaced by someone who struggled to contain the smoldering desire that was coursing through his veins. It was a look that she had never seen before. A desire for her, and her alone, that sent a chill through her body.

Peter reached over, turning off the living room light, and descended upon her.

The room was bathed in the fiery glow of the flames as they flickered danced across the logs in the fireplace.

Alex closed her eyes and as he opened up her robe. She moaned as she felt the warmth of his skin against hers, and this time she didn't resist.

CHAPTER THIRTY-FOUR

"Is everything all right?" Hannah asked, her voice tinged with concern.

Tatiana raised her head up from the binoculars, allowing her mind to process the scene that had just unfolded in front of her.

"Yes, my love," she smiled. "Everything is just fine."

"Jeez, you scared me for a moment," Hannah said.

"I'm sorry, I didn't mean to. I was just lost in thought. What did you say your cop's name was?"

"Alex," Hannah replied. "Alex Taylor. She came to Penobscot for the chief's job just over a year ago."

"Interesting," Tatiana said. "Do you have plans for her?"

"I hadn't thought about it, to be honest. I mean, she is a cop."

"She's a cop, but she's not immortal."

"Yeah," Hannah replied, "but we have made it a point to steer clear of any threats."

"No, you're right, we have" Tatiana agreed. "I was just wondering how different a game it might be, if we were to go out of our comfort zone."

"Do you think that's smart?"

Tatiana looked over at Hannah. She reached up and gently brushed an errant hair from the girl's cheek.

"What I'm thinking right now has nothing to do with anything but you," Tatiana smiled.

"Oh really?" Hanna asked coyly. "And what exactly is it you were thinking about?"

"How I need to get you to a motel quickly."

"Oh, I like the sound of that," Hannah replied. "What are we waiting for?"

Tatiana smiled as she reached down and turned on the car's headlights, taking one last look at the now darkened house across the lake, before she pulled away.

One day soon she'd have to arrange another encounter with the young blonde woman, and this time she would make certain she didn't get away.

BOOK PROGRESSION

I have had several inquiries asking how my books should be read. While each of these novels has their own storyline, there are still underlying plot lines and character introductions that are best read in a chronological order.

Therefore, in order for you to get the most from your reading experience, the books should be read in the following progression:

PERFECT PAWN

QUEEN'S GAMBIT

SMALL TOWN SECRETS

BISHOP'S GATE

Cold Case: The Katherine White Murder - Case #13-098

LITTLE BOY LOST

KNIGHT FALL

BROOKLYN BOUNCE

Cold Case: The Rosary Bead Murders – Case #14 - 102

GLASS CASTLE

ABOUT THE AUTHORS

Andrew Nelson spent twenty-two years in law enforcement, including twenty years with the New York City Police Department. During his tenure with the NYPD he served as a detective in the elite Intelligence Division, conducting investigations and providing dignitary protection to many world leaders. He achieved the rank of sergeant before retiring in 2005.

He is the author of both the James Maguire and Alex Taylor mystery series, and the NYPD Cold Case novella series. He has also written several non-fiction books including: *Where Was God? An NYPD first responder's search for answers following the terror attack of September 11th 2001*, and two which chronicle the insignia of the New York City Police Department's Emergency Service Unit

Nancy A. Nelson spent a lifetime in the unforgiving arena of motherhood where she learned a myriad number of skills that would prepare her to deal with the ever-increasing needs of an author husband. She has been a bookkeeper, owner of an embroidery design company, and now an editor / publisher.

Little Boy Lost is her first novel collaboration.

For more information please visit us at:

www.andrewgnelson.org

ANDREW G.
NELSON

www.ingramcontent.com/pod-product-compliance
Lightning Source LLC
Chambersburg PA
CBHW070303260626
47160CB00003B/690